A KNIGHT AT SEA

First published in Great Britain by Black Apollo Press, 2010

Copyright © Bob Biderman 2010

A CIP catalogue record of this book is available at the British Library.

ISBN: 9781900355131

A Knight at Sea

R. J. RASKIN

BLACK
APOLLO
PRESS

Chapter 1

I killed a man. Maybe I'll tell you about it sometime. Maybe not.
It doesn't matter much at any rate because this story isn't about
me. It's about Ray. And it's about another man whose true name
I didn't know until much later. It's also about a woman who
wanted to change her name. Names mattered then. They
matter now, too, though in a different way. But I guess that's
what this story is really about. Names. Names and the not so
simple art of murder.

It all began some years ago. The twelfth of April, 1955 if you
want precision in your life. I can take it or leave it myself. But
the date does stick in my mind. I was a physician in those days
still floundering in the aftermath of a failed marriage. The years
right behind the war had left me little time to think. And I
preferred it that way. To think would have been to ponder the
ravages of my life. So I didn't think. Instead, I returned to
Chicago and plunged into the cesspool of the filthy rich courtesy
of Paula's father whose practice and whose daughter I inherited
all in one go. But the practice was about the same as the woman
who became my wife. She was as bright and beautiful as a
platinum wrist watch that can't tell time. She had everything she
ever wanted. And for a while she had wanted me.

It took all those years for me to discover that something
wasn't right. Maybe I had hoped too hard that the world would
be made anew. Maybe it was my conscience catching up with me.
I don't know. All I can say is that one day I chucked it in. I
packed up and left. I disappeared. No note, no forwarding
address; I just vanished from the scene. By then Paula and I
had been separated for several months. We had no kids. I
should have felt a free man. Somehow, though, I felt anything
but free.

I travelled aimlessly for a couple of weeks. I started by taking
the bus to St. Louis. Why St. Louis? Why not? Why anywhere?
From St. Louis I caught the train to Washington DC. In

Washington I spent a day caught up in a mob of Sunday patriots tiredly making the rounds of marble monuments while trudging through acres of pigeon surprise. From there I worked my way up the coast to New York City.

It rained in New York while I was there; it never stopped. I was in Horne and Hardart, the great Manhattan automat where you stick your quarter in a windowed safe deposit box and out comes a stale piece of pie, when I saw a notice in the Times. I cut it out and stuck it in the pocket of my trousers where a gentleman might keep his watch if there were either pocket watches or gentlemen who wore them anymore. Then I folded my paper and walked out into the rain, ducking under soggy awnings and dodging lethal umbrellas carried by the single-minded folk who own those streets (or think they do at any rate), unfurled upwards to catch the wet, then lowered as a prod to speed their way.

The notice I had seen in the Times was an offer of passage on the ocean liner, Mauretania, to a surgeon of "fine reputation" in exchange for services "of a professional nature." It was as if they had my name and had used that cumbersome device to get to me only because there was no other way. So I suffered the downpour and the mean streets, charting a course across town to the offices of the Cunard Line just to let them know that contact had been made and to formalise this call of fate by putting down my name.

When I got there I was immediately interviewed by a nervous young man (a Mr Ramy, I recall - his name reminded me of "clammy" and so did his hands) who seemed delighted I had come. He asked if I could be available for the crossing within two days. I said yes, maybe I could. Then he asked me for my references.

"We must be very careful," he explained, rubbing his clammy hands. "We cater to a rather special class of passenger, you understand."

"I do understand," I replied. "In Chicago I wouldn't accept any jerk whose blood was blue. There's lots of blue bloods now. I made sure they had the purple kind."

"So you treated the members of - how shall I say? - high society?"

I raised my brow in the patronising way I was taught to do in medical school when someone asked for your advice. "High society? My standards were so stiff that even their dogs had to have a pedigree."

That may have been too much for him. "You're not a vet, are you?" he asked, suspiciously.

I assured him I only treated the human brand of canine.

In the end, he seemed satisfied, especially since one of my references was an old school chum who had followed his practice all the way to the White House as the President's personal MD. (I had given him a call when I was in Washington and we had met for a quick drink, so he was certain to remember me.)

But the way I figured it, Ramy hadn't much choice anyway. The simple fact of the matter was that the ship's surgeon had taken ill and no replacement could be found at such a short notice unless he was ready to scour the back alleys for some quack who sawed the wrong person in half and was on his way to Dar-es-Salaam.

"Your official status will be that of a passenger," Ramy told me while his left eye twitched away. "Your only obligation will be to remain 'on call' lest an emergency arise." He leaned forward. I wondered if his face would stop when the twitches reached nine hundred and ninety-nine. "Emergencies, however, are quite normal on a ship with more than a thousand passengers whose average age is well beyond the pale." He tried to smile.

I came back later that afternoon when the paperwork had been completed and put my John Henry on some forms he had me sign. I was given a ticket and a letter of introduction.

I left Mr. Ramy still rubbing his hands and went off scarcely conscious of what I had done. I had forty-eight hours to collect the necessary documents and to purchase the few things I thought I might require. Then I was shipping myself off to heaven-knew-where. England, I supposed, though, to tell the truth, I really didn't care.

*****

The Times and the Tribune of April twelfth both said it would rain. They were right, though as far as I was concerned it was like predicting ice in your freezer or oil in the crankcase of your car. Through the rear window of the taxi driving toward the West Side piers I could see the rows of concrete coffins - "skyscrapers", New Yorkers say - jabbing through the heavy clouds. The drops of rain gave them a bent at least. Seen through the watery spray, those tombs for unknown bureaucrats seemed as tipsy as I felt. Anyone who could find romance in all that cement and steel needed their head examined, I thought. But I was due for a lobotomy myself.

The taxi hurled toward the docks. The cabby, I remember, wouldn't stop complaining. He kept telling me about his wife who stole his whiskey and cigars. I pictured her on the fire escape in her housecoat holding a smoking stogie while she poured three fingers of Old Crow, though I doubted that's what he meant. I had a few fingers that morning, myself, so I could picture it pretty well.

My instructions were to board the Mauretania at nine and to present myself to the Purser. My cabin would be issued and the Chief Medical Officer would contact me after we set sail. It was all very causal I thought. But if the ship was well stocked and the liquor good, why should I complain?

Unfortunately, I wasn't the only one to receive those instructions, or so it seemed. The street along the pier was jammed with taxis unloading passengers, friends of passengers, and friends of friends, as well as sea trunks, tea chests and crates of such enormous size they were guaranteed to drive a docker crazy.

I grabbed my suitcase and got out, paid the fare and tipped the cabby a buck. He made a face and drove away. "If you want anything in this world you gotta tip big." That's what Ray told me. Or maybe I read it in one of his books. I can't remember anymore. What I can remember though, what I'll always remember, is the first time I saw Ray.

He was standing on the pavement looking up at the gigantic

ship. It was like one of those skyscrapers turned on its end with a bit chiselled off for a snout. The stewards climbing up the gangway, loaded down with trunks, looked like Lilliputians in Gulliverland. Gazing up at the steel hull, black as coal and slick with rain, I thought of a whale, an enormous whale, ten times the size of Moby Dick and ten times that again, held captive at its concrete mooring with ropes as thick as an elephant's leg, who was about to swallow a thousand Jonahs and maybe even a few hundred more.

Then I heard his voice. Strange, the things that stick in your mind. I can still hear him, even now, talking to the rain.

"'You will find the Mauretania at the quay. Till her Captain turns the lever 'neath his hand. And the monstrous nine-decked city goes to sea.'"

It was a gentlemanly voice. British, I thought, though he later proved me only partly right. I saw him tap his pipe against the palm of his hand.

"Damn thing's out again," he said, noticing me. He seemed almost embarrassed to have been overheard. He stuffed the pipe into the pocket of his mackintosh and then took out a handkerchief and wiped his specs. "By the way, that's a quote from Kipling, not me. It's from 'Song of the Machines'. Do you know it?"

He could have been a schoolmaster, I thought as I glanced at him. He had that look: pale, a little flaccid but with high forehead and penetrating eyes. He was about my height and twice my age. I could tell from the shape of his jowls that he probably liked to drink. But beyond that there was a look of melancholy, maybe a weariness of the spiritual sort. I found myself attracted to him at once.

"Haven't read Kipling since I was a boy," I said.

"At least you read him," he said. "Most Americans think he made fruit pies." He smiled thinly and wiped his glasses again. "Can't see a damn thing out here," he said. "Shouldn't we be boarding? You are a passenger, aren't you?"

"Half and half," I said. "Give or take a little on either side."

"First class? If you're shelling out money to travel on this tub, you might as well go first class."

I rubbed my chin. I never thought to ask. I stuck my hand into my jacket pocket and pulled out my ticket. "First class," I confirmed.

"Good," he said. "Whoever bought your ticket obviously has taste." He picked up his case and started walking. I followed, alongside.

"The gangway for us nobs is the one in the middle," he said pointing to the moveable ramp which led to the deck by the central funnel. He walked quickly for an old fart, I thought to myself. "By the way, what's your name?" He gave me a quick glance without slowing his pace.

"Marlow," I said.

Suddenly he stopped short causing a woman just behind him to nearly collide. He tipped his hat to her. "I beg your pardon, M'am," he said with a sincerity rarely heard nowadays. Then, turning to me, he narrowed his eyes. "You don't spell it with an 'e' at the end, do you?" he asked.

"No," I replied.

"First initial isn't 'P', I hope."

"'J' for John," I said.

His look of relief, the reason for which I only found out later, made him seem even more curious to me. "John's a hell of a name!" he said.

"What do they call you?" I asked him.

"Some things I don't want to hear; others that I do. You can call me 'Ray'," he said, picking his case back up and walking away. From the dock I watched him merge into the inebriated crowd of well-wishers throwing champagne soaked confetti at the seafaring elite who were soon to drench themselves in five days worth of caviar.

Chapter 2

The passageways were stinking of wet fur - sable, mink, ermine and chinchilla. If someone could have put them back together, twenty to a coat, those high-class rodents would have taken over the ship.

I found the Purser's office. So did fifty other people. And they all wanted to get inside the door at the same time. I left them to sort out a pecking order for themselves and went off to see if I could scrounge up a drink.

It wasn't easy. You needed a team of psychic Sherpas to find your way around in that cavernous maze. I asked a young man, not much more than a boy, really, who looked like he was about to call for Philip Morris. He tipped his little pill-box hat (no kidding) and told me that the bars didn't open till sailing time. I asked him how I went about finding my room and he checked my name on a clip-board that he carried by his side.

"Dr Marlow? You're in number 103."

I flipped him two-bits and he threw me a well-practised smile.

"Thanks, Dr Marlow," he said.

"Think nothing of it, kid," I replied. "If you need your appendix taken out in the next five days, you know where to find me."

I went up to the deck where I had been assigned - at least I thought I did. Cabin 203 was one level above Cabin 103. I couldn't turn around because there was a line of people behind me. I couldn't go forward either.

The entrance to Cabin 203 was blocked by a sea chest of such enormous size that if it could float, its owner could have gotten in and sailed across the North Atlantic at a fraction of the price. But on second glance, I realised that it must have been what the wealthy called "antique". It was lacquered a bright orange and trimmed in black. On the face was an etching of a dragon and a knight. It was probably worth a few Madisons, I guessed.

A harried woman with an accent smelling distinctly of fine perfume and tweed was watching the struggling porters trying to do the impossible job of fitting something huge through something little.

"Maybe we'll 'ave to stow it down below, M'am," a burly porter said.

The woman was really flustered now. "Oh, no!" she said. She turned to me. I was waiting patiently to get by. "I have all my things in there!"

"Then you must have quite a lot," I said.

"Not really. It's just you never know what you might need."

"On a five day trip?" I gave my little case a pat. "I got all I need in here."

The burly porter had gentle eyes but his face was a brilliant shade of red. The veins protruded from his neck mapping out a flow of hot, brute strength as he heaved and groaned. But I'll be damned! Somehow he got it through!

"Be careful!" shouted a voice from inside 203. "We don't want you to damage it!"

"My husband," said the woman, still outside. She said it apologetically.

"You have my sympathies," I said. And then I continued down the hall to the staircase that led below. I found Cabin 103, opened the door and walked through.

The room wasn't bad if you liked floating hotels. I'd slept in worse. There was a single bed, a writing table, a comfortable green upholstered chair, a dresser of polished hardwood, a carpet that smelled as if it had been freshly shampooed, a mirror that showed too much of your mug and a dainty, white telephone without a dial. Behind the bed there was a tapestry of trees and birds, in case anyone got sick of water, I suppose. On the dresser was a vase filed with fresh flowers.

I took the flowers and dumped them. Then I threw my suitcase on the bed. I opened it and got out the only thing I really valued. I took the bottle, found a glass and poured myself a long one. Then I sat down in the comfortable chair to take the weight off my legs. I had just about put the glass to my lips when there was a knock at the door.

"Beat it!" I shouted with the enthusiasm of someone about ready to get thoroughly pissed.

The door opened. I saw the pipe, then the man. It was hard to recognise him at first, all brushed and polished like that.

"Hi, Marlow," he said. "Thought I'd see how you were getting on."

"I'll be getting on swell in about five minutes," I said, pointing to the bottle. "Pour yourself a drink, if you're not on the wagon."

He got no further than the doorway. "I am on the wagon, Marlow - till five PM. Thought you might like me to show you around the tin can before it's all packed with sardines."

I looked down at my drink.

"Come on," he said. "They'll be plenty of time for that once we're at sea."

*****

Ray wasn't a bad guide as those things go. He had a real eye for detail. He also had a decent sense of priority.

"There's only three things that matter about this floating bunch of bedrooms," he said. "Your cabin, for obvious reasons, the dining room table they seat you at and the bar. All the rest is passageways from one to the other. The smoking room's OK, so maybe that makes four. The only time you'll probably go out on deck is when we're docked or when you have an upset stomach. The rest of the time it's just a recipe for pneumonia. They'll try to get you involved in the games, because that's their job, so you can't really blame them. But if you give them a few bucks to keep their nose out of your business, they'll usually comply. If they don't, just threaten to throw them over the rail. They won't believe you, but it's usually enough to keep them away." He said all this while escorting me to the central lift.

"I'll keep that in mind," I said, following him inside the cage. I'd only been on board for twenty minutes and there were already a few chinchillas I wouldn't have minded throwing overboard.

15

We sank a couple of levels and emerged again at the restaurant deck where Ray had a few words in private with the maître d'. The restaurant was an enormous hall with a multitude of evenly spaced tables already laid with expensive china on starched white cloth. Chandeliers dangled like crystal daggers from above. I wondered what happened to them during a storm.

Ray came back and nudged me to go. "I fixed it with the maitre d'," he said.

"Fixed what?" I asked.

"I got us seated at a good table," he said, leading me back to the moveable box.

"What's a good table?" I asked again. "Someplace not under a chandelier, I hope."

"The chandeliers are fake," he said. "All the parts are rigid and it's bolted to the deck above. It would take a collision with an iceberg to bring them down."

"Ever hear of the Titanic?" I asked.

Ignoring my remark, he went on. "A good table is one without Los Angeles phoneys, New York braggarts or anyone who tends to giggle like a damn fool after two sips of their martini."

"That seems pretty hard to qualify," I said as we headed back to air.

He chewed down on his pipe and gave me a searching look as if to wonder whether he had made a mistake in befriending me so quickly. "I had him seat us in front, near the Captain's table. Rich people are usually terrible bores, but as a class, new rich are far less interesting that old. New rich are still obsessed with money. The old take it for granted and sometimes talk about other things."

"The old rich I knew in Chicago were obsessed with money, too," I said. "Not how to make it, just how to keep it close. They didn't like it straying away."

"They know about power, though," said Ray. "And power - the way people use it, cling to it and, eventually, are destroyed by it - is a fascinating thing to observe."

I chuckled. "Then why have you taken up with me?"

"Chance meeting, I suppose," he said, sucking at his unlit pipe. "You looked like someone who's been through the mill. You seem reasonably intelligent. You like to drink. And your name is Marlow - without an 'e' at the end."

"I suppose that means something," I said.

"I don't know whether it means anything or not," he snapped.

The lift stopped at the Main Deck and we got out. "Good place to observe," Ray said, walking over to the rail.

"What?" I asked.

"All the fun and games below. Take a gander," he said, pointing to a tight circle of photographers surrounding a mink - laden woman and her porter who was struggling with her trunks. A man in formal dress was vainly trying to break through the knot.

"That's Gloria Morgan, the movie star. The guy in the penguin suit is her manager."

"No kidding," I replied. Then I looked at him, wondering how he could make out her face so far away. "How do you know?"

"I glanced through the passenger list. Saw her name. I've met her briefly once or twice."

"You worked in Hollywood?" I asked.

"For a while. It's like working in a swamp. The longer you're there, the more chance you have of being eaten by leaches."

"Sounds like you loved the place," I said.

"Hollywood is where love was invented," he said, still staring down at Gloria Morgan. "They manufacture the stuff, package it and sell it for ten cents a gross. Even at that price I couldn't afford to buy."

"If you can't afford that," I said, "then you can't afford anything."

He looked back at me and I could tell I struck a nerve. "The real thing," he said, "is free. Except there comes a time when it dies and then part of you dies, too - the part that matters."

I didn't reply. I knew what he meant, though. "That dame has to put up with a lot," I commented, watching the flash bulbs ignite like fire crackers in a Chinatown parade.

"It's part of the business, Marlow. You should know that. She probably paid those guys to be there."

"Great way to start the morning," I said. "A thousand guys with B.O. punching light bulbs in your face."

"You think washing floors is any better?" He turned and looked east, toward the city. "Gloria Morgan's no spring chicken anymore, but I bet there's five million women out there who would give away their wedding rings to be in her shoes now."

"I'll take number five million and one who wouldn't," I said.

He let out a tiny hiccup of a laugh. "Me too, Marlow. Me too." Then he glanced down at his watch and motioned for me to follow him. "Come on," he said, walking quickly toward the aft.

The deck was becoming crowded now with giddy people shouting down to a faceless mob, throwing paper streamers along with the odd glove and shoe. "The pleasures of an early morning drunk," I said to myself as I struggled to keep up with Ray.

"You mind telling me where we're going?" I asked when I finally caught up with him. "Not that I mind, I'd just like to cable ahead for a room."

"The Veranda Lounge," he said through the corner of his mouth, as if he didn't want anyone else to hear. "I found out there's going to be a press conference for the Ambassador. Maybe we can get in. Let me do the talking."

The Veranda Lounge was located several decks above. As the ship was birthed head in, the windows of the lounge looked out onto the Hudson estuary. The press conference had started by the time we arrived. The door was being guarded by an overweight official of the line who had already turned some passengers away telling them it was closed till the ship set sail. He was wearing a blue rain slicker over his uniform so it was hard to guess his rank. His hat was wrapped in plastic to protect it from the rain. But he forgot to wrap his face.

Ray walked up as sweet as you please. "Started already?" he asked the fattish guard.

"Are you a member of the press, sir?" the guard replied, wiping away some dribbles from his hat with a practised forearm.

Ray took out his wallet and showed the man a card. "I'm doing an article for Atlantic Magazine," he said. He pointed to me. "Dr Marlow's my partner in crime."

The official lifted his belly in a rolling motion, like the sea, looked up at Ray and grinned. "Mr Chandler! I'm sorry, I didn't recognise you. Of course, go right in!" Then, looking at me, he said, "I've been instructed only to allow in members of the press, though."

Ray took out a crisp ten spot from his wallet. "I think you can make an exception this one time."

The fat man chuckled. "How about an autographed copy of your new book instead?"

"My new book is still in my head. But stop by my cabin. I'll give you an old one and scribble my name. How's that?"

The guard looked at me with his watery eyes. "If anyone asks I'll say he's a stringer for AP. There's a million of them around who claim to be anyway." And with that he swung the door open with his corpulent arm and we sauntered through.

The scene inside was this: The Ambassador, who turned out wasn't an ambassador anymore but only called that in deference to his past, was standing on a raised platform set before a curtained window. He looked like an Irish cop dressed up as a banker. On either side were the members of his staff. They were seated in chairs and each of them carried a portfolio and maybe a hanky to wipe his nose in case it started to leak. The press were gathered behind a table. They looked ready to pounce.

Ray and I took up our positions with the press mob. He brought out a little notebook and started to jot something down. My job, I guess, was to look pretty and lend an ear.

"You really a writer?" I whispered to Ray.

"That's what they tell me," he said. "You really a doctor?"

"How'd you know I was a quack?" I whispered again.

"Any pill pusher who's got the guts to refer to himself as a quack can't be all bad," he said. "I guessed you were a doctor because the passenger list had you down as John Marlow, MD. I

19

suppose MD doesn't stand for 'must die'."

"If that were the case then everyone would have MD after their name, not only the people who pretend they cure disease," I replied.

"You must be some quack!" said Ray.

Then one of the gentlemen journalists gave me an elbow in the ribs. "Shut up!" he hissed. "I want to quote the Ambassador, not you!"

"What are you getting all steamed up about?" I said, rubbing my side. "I thought you guys make those quotes up, anyway!"

"First we got to know what he says," the reporter shot back. "If we don't like it then we make it up. Not before!"

The Ambassador had just completed a long-winded denial of any ulterior purpose for travelling to Europe other than for a long overdue holiday. The pack of reporters were now braying to be heard.

"Yes. The gentleman from the Times..." The Ambassador pointed to a rumpled, chain-smoking reporter who looked like anything but a gentleman.

"Mr Ambassador, could you comment on Senator Stevenson's call for a joint declaration condemning the use of force in the Formosa Strait?"

"Are we off the record or on?"

"Why don't you give us both the on and off."

The Ambassador grinned like a real pro. "Right you are, gentlemen. First on: 'Adlai E. Stevenson will be the next president of the United States. I'm backing him right down the line. If he says we duck out of a confrontation with the Chinks, it's OK by me."

The scribes scribbled away. Ray chuckled and wrote something down too.

"Now off: 'Stevenson has about the same chance of beating Ike as I have of becoming the prima ballerina in the Bolshoi Ballet. His China policy is one reason why. And if any of you hacks quote me on it, I'll deny every word.'"

Lots of guffaws with that one. The Ambassador was some card!

Then a bean pole stood up and brushed back the hair from his eyes. "Mr Ambassador, I'm from the Post..."

"Washington or New York?"

"Washington, of course. Are you aware that a Russian trade delegation is in Argentina making overtures to General Peron?"

"I wouldn't be surprised," the Ambassador replied. "Is that a point of information or is there some sort of question implied?"

"My question is this - Argentina is begging for investment credits. If we don't give it to them, what are they supposed to do?"

"They're supposed to keep their hands off other people's railways. Nationalising a system that our British allies built and maintained isn't going to win them any friends. Any more questions, gentlemen?"

The Ambassador pointed to a man I couldn't see. "Israel claims there's been five more border attacks by Egypt this past week. Egypt has been reported to have asked America for arms. With Nasser in power over there, do you think we should give it to them?"

"I think we have to be very careful about what we say or do over there, boys. The main thing is to keep the Russians out. If we arm this fellow, Nasser, he's likely to use the weapons against British Tommies as well as the Israelis and Eden wouldn't like that very much. But if we don't, he's likely to get them someplace else."

"So what's the answer, sir?"

"To build the Baghdad Pact and form an iron ring so tight the Russians couldn't bulldoze their way in. But, off the record, boys, I think this might be one place where the Brits might be a little troublesome. They've got old loyalties in that part of the world..."

"What about Israel? Where does that leave her?"

"Israel's our ace in the hole, boys." The Ambassador winked. "That's what'll keep the Arabs on their toes."

"So you defend Israel's right to exist?"

The Ambassador chuckled. "Listen, if Israel didn't exist we'd have to invent her!"

"One more question, Ambassador, sir. The so-called, non-aligned nations are meeting in Indonesia. Word has it that Nasser is going to make an important announcement there today."

"Well, when you find out what he says, I hope you wire it on to me."

There was some laughter as the newsies scribbled on their pads.

"Say, Ambassador!" shouted a reporter from the back. "Did you know that Gloria Morgan is sailing on this ship?"

A few titters could be heard. The Ambassador straightened up and the smile faded from his lips. "No I didn't," he said.

Then someone shouted, "You planning on producing any more films with her?"

The Ambassador winked. "My film days are over boys."

"Looking for bigger game, huh?" someone else called out.

"White House in 1960?" shouted another.

The Ambassador held up his hand for some quiet. "Not me, boys. I'm getting old."

"Which son then?" someone yelled. The room erupted into laughter.

"Which one do you want?" the Ambassador shot back. "I got one in the Senate and two more on the way!"

Laughter again.

Then one of the Ambassador's pet monkeys chimed in. "All right, gentlemen, times up. The Ambassador has a few things to do before the ship sets sail."

There were some groans, but not too many. It was clear that this wasn't going to be a hot news day. Most of the reporters took the opportunity to scurry off in hope of meeting Miss Gloria Morgan. The rest stayed around to shoot the breeze and maybe pretend they were sailing out to sea instead of stopping off at a grubby bar on the way back to their office. Personally, I think I would have chosen the grubby bar if I had it to do over.

Ray made a few more notes in his miniature binder and then slipped it back into the pocket of his vest. His eyes had that certain mischievous smile I soon came to know too well.

"Well, Marlow, what do you think?" he asked as we made our way onto the terrace of what would have been called the sun deck if there had actually been a little sun.

"About what?"

"About the Ambassador. I imagine that if the Roman Catholics ever had a chance of buying this country for the Pope, he's the man who'd swing the deal."

"The Pope couldn't do any worse with it than all the Luthers and Calvins who came before," I replied.

Ray grunted. "You're not an R.C., I hope."

"No," I said. "But on the other hand if Christ came down to earth tomorrow he'd probably be at a loss to choose which organised religion has done the most to blight mankind."

"Forget I brought the subject up, Marlow." He took out his trade-mark and stuffed it with some tobacco from a leather pouch. "If you want to bore someone to the brink of death, you can always try religion."

"Or politics," I said.

He lit his pipe with a large silver Ronson and watched the thick streams of smoke as they were carried away by the wind. "Look out there," he said, pointing with the end of his smoke-stack.

I looked and saw several tug boats hovering by the bow.

"It takes a lot of power to swing an 80,000 ton liner around so she's facing the right way."

"I wouldn't mind a little tug myself, now and then," I said.

Ray let out another stream of smoke. "You're gonna like this trip, Marlow. It's gonna be a real adventure."

"What do you mean?" I asked. I never could stand people talking in riddles like that.

"I don't know what I mean," he said, still looking out to sea. "I just feel it in my bones."

Chapter 3

I didn't feel a thing as we pulled out to sea. Maybe it's because I'd dried up the bottle of Old Crow when I got back to my cabin after Ray finished explaining the intricacies of untying Moby Dick and setting her free. I was just going to lie down a few minutes to settle my head. I guess I must have fallen asleep, because when I got up to answer the banging at the door I realised the carpet underneath my feet had legs and they didn't belong to me.

The kid who was knocking had the same pill-box hat and painted smile he had on before.

"Dr Marlow?" he asked. I guess maybe he didn't remember me.

Yeah? You want your appendix out already?"

"No. There's nothing wrong with my appendix, Dr Marlow. But you're wanted down in sick bay. Could you follow me?"

"Could you give me a minute to brush my tongue?" I asked him. "And I got ten days worth of fur I'd like to shave. Come on inside." I held the door so he could make his entry.

"I'll wait out here, Dr Marlow." Maybe the kid was under orders not to clutter up the rooms.

"Suit yourself," I said. "But if I were you I'd take the weight off my feet. It's liable to be a very long shave. I've never tried doing it on a see-saw before. Maybe I'll cut off my nose. Then I'll have to sew it back on, because I always like to look nice and trim for lunch."

"But Dr Marlow, it's already night!" This time the smile was real.

"No kidding?" I went inside and pulled the drapes and stuck my mug against the glass. Either the porthole had been painted black or the kid was right.

"How long have we been out to sea?" I asked, looking back at him.

"Since two PM, sir."

"What time is it now?"

"A little after eight."

I rubbed my head. I couldn't remember it being that big before.

I went into the bathroom, brushed my teeth and made a quick attempt at shaving. I rinsed my mouth with a swig of brandy from my pocket flask and patted the left-overs onto my cheeks. Then I put on a fresh shirt and trousers. I figured a patient deserved at least that much from his doctor.

The kid was still at the door when I had finished up. "How old are you?" I asked, as he led me down the passageway to the lift.

"Sixteen," he said. If he was sixteen my Aunt Sadie was twenty. And she was in an old-age home.

"How come you're not in school?"

"I been to school, sir," he said, as we went down. "I didn't like it very much."

"You're not supposed to like school," I said, "you're just supposed to go. It's like the measles. You get over it, but it's a hell of a lot easier to take when you're young."

"I had the measles, sir. When I was ten. I had school, too. I didn't learn anything as much as I learn here and I didn't earn no money."

Since I couldn't argue with that kind of logic, I just let it pass.

We got off at one of the lower decks. Then the kid led me to a door marked "Surgery." This time he held it open for me.

It wasn't what I expected. I'd seen clinics half that size in cities fifty times as big as this raft of floating millionaires. Money speaks, I guess. Sometimes it hollers. This money shouted that it was paying a damn lot for the privilege of getting a tube stuck up your butt.

"Dr Marlow! We've been wondering about you!" A tall man in a loose fitting uniform showed me his teeth. "My name's Hart. I'm the C.M.O." He held out his hand.

"What's a C.M.O?" I asked, giving it a shake. "Or shouldn't I?"

"Chief Medical Officer, if you're insisting on formalities.

When you're this far down inside the belly of Beelzebub, you're allowed to be a little more relaxed." He showed his teeth again. The second bicuspid had been fitted with a cap of solid gold.

"That's fine by me," I said, glancing around. "Quite a dump you have here. I know a couple of city hospitals that wouldn't mind laying their hands on some of this stuff."

"It's mostly for show," said Hart. "Keeps the customers from getting too nervous, you know. Some of them start panicking if they miss their daily X-ray. But it's not a bad operating theatre. We're equipped for most emergencies. All we need is our surgeon."

"Well that's me, I guess - chopper-off of warts and bunions. Don't suppose it goes much further than that on most trips," I said hopefully.

"You never know," said Hart. "Last week someone's gall bladder gave out. The week before it was a kidney stone. Sometimes we go for weeks with just the broken arm or leg and then we get a plague of ruptured cysts or a spate of plumbing that's been blocked."

"If you're just a few days out of port, I guess a simple catheter-isation will do the trick," I said.

"Sometimes," said Hart, staring at the redness in my eyes. "Sometimes not. I suppose you'll be the judge. Of course we'd rather not slice someone up if we can help it."

"Bad for business, I suppose. Especially if the slicing gets a bit messy. I wouldn't want to carve a turkey in a stormy sea," I said.

"We're nicely stabilised," said Hart. "You needn't worry."

"Sure. I'll just nail my boots to the hospital floor and glue on the scalpel," I replied.

I guess Hart decided it was better to laugh than cry since he was stuck with me. "Come on," he said, "I'll show you the dispen-sary."

The pharmacist was a young man with a bad complexion who looked to me like he sampled half the stuff in the cabinet just for fun. His name was Carter and he didn't like to smile. With a face like his, I didn't blame him.

"Carter's doing our inventory now," C.M.O. Hart explained.

26

"We keep all our drugs under lock and key. Anything stronger than aspirin has to be accounted for. There's even a form for spillage. And it needs to be initialed by me."

"That's pretty tight security," I said. "I guess you don't want any hop-heads taking us off course, is that it?"

"There's strict customs regulations about drugs, Marlow. We're not allowed to be lax." He didn't show his teeth this time.

Hart gave me a tour of the examining room and spouted off a few more tid-bits. He introduced me to the nurses - Tweedle-Dum and Tweedle-Dee. They were both blonde, blue-eyed and boring. I knew I'd never tell them apart.

"Sick call is every morning from eight to nine for the staff. Passengers just drop in whenever they please," said Hart.

"As long as they don't drop off," I said. "I think I've seen it all. My stomach's starting to grumble so I'm going up to get some grub. Just shout if you need me."

"Don't worry, we will. One thing about a ship, Marlow, you can't go very far." If his ivories were piano keys, I might have tried playing "Show Me The Way To Go Home," by now.

*****

They had already begun eating when I was ushered to my table by one of the stewards.

"I recommend the smoked salmon and capers, Marlow," said Ray as I sat down. "The herrings are a bit salty today. Let me introduce you around."

They said their "howdyados" between bites. There were six others at the table besides Ray and me. Monica Wheetly was a go-getter who had just been finished off by Radcliff or Smith or one of those other schools for wealthy girls. She had a body that made a toothpick look like a redwood tree and light brown hair that fell onto her shoulders, reluctantly, and eyes that tried to gobble everything in its way.

Seated next to her was Señor Mendez, a minor Argentinian trade attaché. He looked like he could have used a few more potatoes in his belly too. He sat up straight and always used the proper fork, but like his country, he was a mixture of the old world and the new - in his case a second generation Spanish Irishman. His temperament depended on the time of day or subject at hand, unless the subject was Argentina. If the subject was Argentina, his Irish was guaranteed to flash.

Then there was Solly Meyers, a white-haired gentleman who was travelling to Israel by way of London. He told us he had been in the clothing trade but, as it turned out, his business was involved with more than cloth. He looked like someone you'd cast as grandpa in your next play, if grandpa was supposed to hold a Gatling gun.

Next to him was Roger Lane. He was in show-biz, though it wasn't clear at first exactly how. Lane had an opinion on everything, from the weather to the world of bumble bees. His wife, Amanda, sat at his side. She was the Englishwoman whose chest I had seen outside Cabin 203 earlier that day. Her role in life was pulling hubby's foot from mouth, though she didn't seem to mind. Of course, she might have been in show-biz herself.

Then came Philip Rinexus, a journalist - if one would dare to use that noble word for his real trade. Maybe I should just say he worked for a Hollywood movie magazine. But if you had anything to do with films, you'd have done well to stay away from him unless you wanted next week's gossip before it hit the rubbish dump.

Then there was Ray. And me. I wanted to eat. Ray wanted to cook up a stew.

"The Croute-au-Pot's not bad," Ray went on, "and I'd go for the escargots. You can have escalope de veau or Tongue Florentine..."

"I never eat what's been in someone else's mouth, even if it is Italian," I said.

"In that case try the leg of lamb with red currant jelly and mint sauce."

"The duck á l'orange isn't bad either, Mr Marlow," said Miss Wheetly, trying to look sophisticated by batting her eyes.

I ordered roast chicken and mashed potatoes. Food is food. Forget the fancy stuff.

28

The Argentine poked at his sirloin steak and said, "They have the nerve to call this beef!"

"What should they call it, Mr Mendez?" asked Solly Meyers, the white-haired grandpa to his left. He pointed his fork at the Argentine's plate. "It looks to me like that once was part of a cow..."

The Argentine threw a couple of daggers with his eyes and said, "Where I come from we feed this to our dogs!"

"Where he comes from some people eat their dogs," muttered Roger Lane, taking a nibble of his foot.

"Dogs are quite a delicacy in some parts of the world," said his wife.

Rinexus, the purveyor of half-baked truths, leaned forward and between bites of Glanatine of Turkey mixed with candied ham he said, "In Peru - I kid you not - they take a dog and tie it up to a wooden stake and force grain down its throat through a plastic funnel until it's so fat it looks like a goddamn balloon and then they cut off its head and its feet and roast it over a spit. I kid you not!"

"Are you sure the funnel is plastic?" asked Roger Lane.

"Maybe it's tin. I dunno," said Rinexus giving him a funny look.

"That's absolutely disgusting!" said the girl's school grad, wiping her mouth with the tip of her napkin and staring down at her unfinished food.

"What's disgusting?" asked Grandpa Meyers. "Have you ever been inside a slaughter house? There's nothing polite about the way they kill a cow."

"Cows are usually milked and fucked by bulls to bear meat producing cattle, Mr Meyers," said Roger Lane. "They're rarely slaughtered except when the dairy industry wants to drive the milk prices up."

"I think he was speaking metaphorically, dear," said his wife.

"Where's the metaphor?" asked Roger Lane.

"Probably chewing on your sock," I said.

"My point, gentlemen," the Argentinian began and then bowing his head slightly, "and ladies, is that a luxury ship should have luxury beef and luxury beef is produced on the pampas of the Argentine. It is the difference between Gordon's finest and bathtub gin.

"Have you ever tasted bathtub gin, Mr Mendez?" asked Mr Meyers with a little twinkle in his eye that looked like maybe it had a story, too. "If you can tell the difference between it and the real stuff, I'd be very much surprised. It's nothing but denatured alcohol and flavoring."

"Except that one of them can make you go blind," said Roger Lane.

"You can go blind wanking, too," said Rinexus, stuffing his mouth with rolled ox tongue laced with horseradish.

"That's an old wives' tale," I said. There are a few things we doctors do know about.

Rinexus pointed a fork full of macaroni al sugo at me. "Told by old wives who couldn't get enough of it!" He began to laugh so hard he choked. Amanda Lane gave him a motherly slap on the back - rather hard.

"You bribed the waiter to give us this table?" I asked Ray underneath my breath.

Ray smiled mysteriously and winked.

We were a couple of tables over from where the Captain held court and where the passengers who really mattered had been placed. The Ambassador was there with his eyes, ears and muscle trio. Another lady, I figured to be his wife, sat next to him. She was a dowager type - by that I mean you wouldn't ask her to go roller-skating in the park - but she was clearly having a good time, if a good time meant loading yourself with sparklers and enough gold and platinum to give Brinks a heart attack.

On the other side of the table, the side facing Ray and me, was Gloria Morgan. She could do a lot more with less than the Ambassador's wife. But actresses are paid to do that, aren't they?

I saw her get up from her chair. When a woman like that gets up from her chair, fancy gentlemen make a show of getting up too. That means if she has a weak bladder and goes a couple of times pretending to powder her nose, someone like her could really disrupt a meal.

30

But this time she must have been really finished because one of the buzzards actually kissed her hand. Another had jumped up to light a smoke she had taken out of a silver case, while a third had grabbed a wrap from the back of her chair and tossed it over her shoulder. What the Ambassador's wife thought about all this, I can only guess, but if I was laying odds for Reno Schwartz - an old school chum who went on to become one of the top income producing gynaecologists in our class - I wouldn't have given more than twenty to one that it was about exchanging recipes for Angel Food cakes.

She walked our way - it was the only way she could if she wanted to get out. When she was about to pass our table, she stopped. She wasn't more than a foot away when I looked up and saw her face. It was like someone you'd seen all your life walking down from the silver screen without the benefit of filters. It never occurred to me before that those people age. But looking at her up close like that I realised this lady was pushing sixty without pushing very hard.

Rinexus straightened up his tie and grinned. "Hello Gloria," he said. Maybe that's a little weak. It was actually more of a bellow.

Gloria Morgan stared at him coldly and said, "Oh, Mr Rinexus. Fancy meeting you here." And then she turned ten degrees and smiled.

"Why, Mr Chandler! How good to see you again! I had no idea you were on board!"

Ray shoved back his chair and stood up. "It's quite an unexpected honor," he said.

She still had something, that dame. Sixty or not, if you saw her walking down the street, you wouldn't turn away.

"But such a charming surprise!" she said.

"Surprises all around, I guess," Ray said, nodding back to the Captain's table.

"Oh, I knew about him, Mr Chandler. But what was I to do? I'm opening in London next week and I just hate to fly!"

What an actress that lady was! That "But what was I to do!" line was played right from the gut. I mean, I was on the verge

31

of tears and it ain't so easy to get a toughy like me to cry. Then, sweet as you please, she changes gear and smiles like a kid who's just been caught stealing bubble gum.

"We must have a drink, Mr Chandler. It would be lovely to talk about old times!"

"There's no time like the present," says Ray.

"But, Mr Chandler - your dinner!"

He put a hand down on his spare tire and gave it a pat. "You've saved me from another added pound, my dear. I'll be forever in you debt!" What an old phoney was that guy, Ray!

The laughter trilled from her lips like a princess in a fairy tale after she had kissed a frog. "Well then, come on. We'll order some champagne!"

And off they went together leaving us bumpkins at the table with our traps open wide enough to catch a flying stowaway.

Chapter 4

Rinexus had put down his fork. His face had turned the color of an over-ripe salami. "I thought I knew that guy!" he said. "That's Raymond Chandler!"

"Who's he?" asked the college girl as if the question were a quiz on an exam.

"The writer..." Rinexus began.

"The writer?" Monica Wheetly's hand went to her mouth. "And he was sitting next to me!" She paused. "What does he write?"

"Detective books. Those ten cent crime throwaways that are all the rage. He worked in Hollywood a while. That's where I know him from..."

"You mean he was a movie star?" I could see that Monica felt she may have hit the jackpot now.

"He was a Hollywood hack - a scriptwriter. Did a couple of things with Wyler and Hitchcock, I think. Like a lot of those two-bit scribblers, he made his bundle and then accused Hollywood of taking him for a ride. I read an article of his in The Atlantic once. He said Hollywood's idea of production value was spending a million dollars dressing up a story that any good writer would throw away."

"Sounds like he hit it right on the button," said Roger Lane.

"Fine and dandy," answered Rinexus. "If you want to be an artist, go find yourself a garret and live on bread and cheese. Hollywood's an industry and it feeds a lot of mouths. And it didn't get that way by smart-ass writers who thought they could whistle up a better tune. That ain't what sells pictures. The way to sell pictures is by knowing what the public wants and giving it to them."

"And what does the public want, Mr Rinexus?" asked Roger Lane.

"A nice pair of legs, big tits and eighteen changes of costume," said Rinexus, pursing his lips as if he were considering his order

33

for dessert. "I'd say that's what they want, wouldn't you?"

"Maybe we have a different conception of the public," said Lane, tightening his napkin round his fist. "Maybe yours wants its periodic dose of voyeuristic sex. There are other publics that want something else from their entertainment industry."

"The word you should underline is 'industry'," said Solly Meyers. "An industry concerns itself with products that are bought and sold. A dress you design on paper might be very nice to look at, but if it's too expensive to produce or if your customer wants it white instead of red, with chocolate bows or stars and stripes, and you go ahead and make the one you want, you better plan to learn a different trade."

Roger Lane pulled the napkin tighter so his knuckles turned a nasty shade of grey. "The fashion industry has never asked their customers if they want white or red or bows or stripes, Mr Meyers. They tell them what the style is each season. Women buy what they are told to buy, not necessarily what they want."

"The customers, however, are not the women who buy dresses in a boutique," said the Argentine eater of fine beef. "The customers who buy the fashions from the manufacturers are the shops that sell them. Not the women who wear the clothes."

Rinexus let out a deep and satisfying burp. It was a good way of getting our attention. "Listen, if the broads don't think the guys will like the dresses, the shops can't sell them, can they? Dresses are only packaging material to sell something else. And that thing - I won't beat around the bush, ladies, so close your ears if you don't want to hear - is pure and simply sex. Am I right?" he asked.

"What men can like the clothes that women wear these days?" asked the Argentine. "They're ghastly! They're better suited as sacks to put potatoes in!"

"That's because women are often treated like potatoes, Mr Mendez," said Monica Wheetly looking at Amanda Lane. I could be wrong, but I think I saw the foot-taker-outer throw her back a secret smile.

"And so are films," said Roger Lane.

Monica Wheetly was warming to the subject. "That sounds

34

like one of the topics we might have discussed last year in philosophy class: 'How are films similar to potatoes?'" She giggled and then reached for her glass of water and took an embarrassed gulp.

"Ask him," said Roger Lane, pointing over at the Ambassador who seemed to enjoy shooting the breeze with the Captain while his wife puttered with her dessert.

"Why him?" asked Miss Wheetly, growing red around the ears. "Is he in movies, too?"

"Anyone with money to burn has been involved with Hollywood, my dear," said Mr Meyers. "Smarter men than him have been tempted to buy dreams."

Roger Lane shook his head. "Why buy a dream when you can manufacture your own with the starlet of your choice?"

"Except he fell flat on his keester with that one," said Rinexus with something of a gloat.

"But he understood why films are not potatoes," said Roger Lane. "Potatoes are sold for money and money alone. Films are sold for money and something else..."

"And what is that something else, Mr Lane?" asked the college kid.

"Power. The power to define the things that people dream and the fantasies that rule their lives. No potato could ever do that."

"Bullshit!" said Rinexus in his own delightful way. "There are laws for good entertainment. People know what they want and what they don't. That's why they kicked the commies out."

I heard a sound like a knuckle being cracked. I looked up to see Amanda Lane draw her fingers over her husband's paw. Maybe he had wanted to chew on something and she thought he had enough.

The Argentine let out the kind of laugh you hear in gentlemanly clubs when they speak about inferiors. "You North Americans see communists under every bed."

"Communists are bad for business," said Solly Meyers. "America is built on business. Therefore, Communists are bad for America."

35

"That's a tautology, Mr Meyers," said Monica Wheetly, very smartly.

"Oh, is that what it is," said Roger Lane. "I always wondered."

Amanda Lane's fingers were firmly knotted round his hand.

"And that dressed up toy soldier who runs things in your neck of the woods? What the hell is he if not a Communist?" asked Rinexus looking over at the Argentine like a picador about to goad a bull.

The bull let out a snort. "President Peron is à man of the people, señor!" he said sharply. "He is not a Communist!"

"He sure talks like one, my friend," said Rinexus, picking his teeth with the starched edge of his napkin.

"I am not your friend!" said the Argentine, straightening himself even more stiffly in his chair. "And you wouldn't know a Communist if he took a book of Lenin and hit you on the cerebellum!"

"I rest my case," said Rinexus throwing up his hands as if he was a barrister and we were the jury. "Who else but a Communist would talk about Lenin at the dinner table?"

The Argentine drew back his chair and stood up, pretty gracefully I might say for a man whose carotid artery was doing a hefty tap dance on the side of his head. He smiled at the ladies. "Please excuse me," he said, "I have a meeting and it is getting late."

When he left, Monica Wheetly turned to Rinexus and said, "I think you were being awful to him, Mr Rinexus and I don't mind telling you so!" It took a lot of guts for the kid to get that out. And it deserved another gulp of water.

"Aw, those dime store phoneys really bother my bananas!" said Rinexus. "Besides, anyone who can't take a joke shouldn't go around ribbing people all the time."

"Did he rib you, Mr Rinexus," asked Amanda Lane. "Maybe I didn't hear..."

"What's that bit about Americans seeing commies under every bed then?"

"Perhaps it was a social comment by an outside observer. Like an anthropologist studying ancient Rome might have observed that they rather enjoyed throwing Christians to the lions," said Roger Lane.

Rinexus stared at him. Lane returned the look in spades. "Don't I know you from somewhere?" asked Rinexus.

"I don't think you had the pleasure until today," said Lane.

"You look familiar," Rinexus persisted. "You said you were in films?"

"I said I was in the entertainment industry..."

Lane was cut off by his wife. "Roger, I thought you promised to take me on a walk around the deck tonight." She gave his hand a squeeze.

"Oh, very well," he said.

"Please excuse us," said Amanda Lane, apologetically. "You see, I suffer rather easily from mal de mer..."

I thought Rinexus had a bellyache from all the horseradish he had eaten judging by the look on his face. But after they had left he said, "I swear I know that guy from someplace!"

"You seem to know a lot of people, Mr Rinexus," Grandpa Meyers said.

"Anyone who matters," said Rinexus, "and too many who don't."

"Then you probably don't have many friends," said Monica Wheetly who had just begun to find her stride.

"Listen, sweetheart," said Rinexus, "in this life it's who you know and what they can do for you. If I can fix you up, then I'm your friend. If you can do the same for me, then you're mine. On that basis I got more friends than Carter's Little Liver Pills."

"Well, I feel very sorry for you," said Monica Wheetly, staring right into his big, fat eyes.

"Lady, you can feel sorry for me when I can't afford an ocean cruise like this one anymore. I'm sure your momma and papa could tell you why."

"My mother and father have nothing to do with this conversation!" said Monica Wheetly, extremely cross.

"Oh, but they do, you poor, little rich girl!" said Rinexus, struggling to his feet, wiping his mouth and then throwing the napkin onto the remains of this plate. "They most certainly do!"

And with that he walked out.

"Nice chicken," I said, tossing in my towel. "Not too greasy. The potatoes had a few lumps in them, but they were better than the dried up flakes we used to have in the army..."

"That man is absolutely horrid!" said Monica Wheetly, brushing away a tear from her eye.

"Don't let him upset you," said Grandpa Meyers. "Let's take a walk out on deck. Look up at the moon. Breathe in the air. You'll feel better when you're outside."

She smiled. "That sounds very nice, Mr Meyers." Then, turning to me, she said, "Would you care to join us, Mr Marlow?"

"Me?" I said. "I think I'll head over to the bar..."

Chapter 5

The cocktail bar was at the tail end of the Boat Deck and looked out upon the momentary furrow the ship was hoeing through the sea. The bar, itself, was carved out in a rounded shape: a half moon of solid oak with a wipeable lacquered top and an edging high enough to dam the flood if the worst should take place. The little rounded tables were a good martini's throw away, on a semi-circular terrace that you reached by going up three stairs. If you got there in one piece, without spilling half your drink, it was good sign you arrived and you might as well stay.

I ordered a double shot of Jack Daniels from the bartender and gave it the old heave-ho before he turned around again.

"Another sir?" he asked, raising his eyebrows without moving any other muscle in his face.

"Wouldn't mind," I said.

He poured again. I picked up the glass and let it slither down the hatch.

He had the bottle ready. "One more time, sir?"

"Keep it coming," I said. "I'll tell you when to stop."

"Hey, Marlow!" I recognized the voice. I turned around. Sure enough, it was Ray. "Why don't you join us for a drink?" he said.

Gloria Morgan was seated with him. She smiled at me. When someone like her smiles at you, it's like getting an engraved invitation from the Queen. But I was never much for royalty, even on a choppy sea.

I raised my glass toward them. "I'm just having one more for the road," I said, "before I turn myself in."

"Well, have it up here with us, why don't you," said Ray. A guy like him doesn't give up too easy. He wants to have his way.

"Please do join us, Dr Marlow," said Gloria Morgan. "Mr Chandler's told me so much about you!"

"Already?" I said, trying to manage the three stairs and keep the whisky in my glass. "I just met the guy today."

Ray got up and grabbed a neighboring chair. "Marlow," he said, by way of introduction, "this is Gloria Morgan."

She stuck out her hand and held it there. Her pinkie was wiggling slightly. I couldn't decide whether I was supposed to kiss it, feel the pulse or take off one of the rings. As a compromise, I gave it a shake.

"What type of a doctor are you, Marlow?" she asked as I sat down.

"The type that doesn't like the sight of blood," I replied, chalking up my third Jack Daniels of the evening.

"Marlow, here, works for the AMA," Ray explained. "He's on their publicity team. His job is to give the profession a new and cleaner image."

"I've known a lot of doctors in my day," said Gloria Morgan. "In my experience they're either pumping you full of drugs or trying to think of a reason why you haven't very long to live."

"What we really want is your money, Miss Morgan. The rest is just a bunch of fancy rationalisation," I said. "Can I get you folks a drink?"

Gloria Morgan smiled like a certain lady in a Shakespearean play. "What refreshing honesty you have Dr Marlow. I'd like a daiquiri if you don't mind. I wonder if they make them frozen like they do in Acapulco?"

Ray ordered Old Forester. I stayed pat. Why draw into an inside straight?

"Gloria and I were talking about films, Marlow. She and I worked together once..."

She patted his hand. "A long time ago, dear boy. Let's not give away our age."

"Not that long ago," said Ray, "but long enough."

"Are you involved with films, Dr Marlow? It seems everyone else on this boat is - or has been."

"I go to the pictures occasionally," I said. "When I want to sit in a dark room, eat stale popcorn and wile the hours away."

"A connoisseur is our man Marlow," said Ray.

Then he turned to the ageing starlet and said, "You were

telling me about the company - the one you had set up..."

"Ah, yes," Gloria Morgan let out a sigh. It was directed to the balcony, I guess. "My contract with M.G.M. had run out and I had to make up my mind whether or not to sign with them again. But I wanted to try something new. An actress only has so many years, you know, before she withers in the public mind. So I hired a director and a staff and decided to go my own way."

"Bravo!" said Ray.

"It was marvellous! For the first time in my career, I could actually choose the picture that I wanted to be in."

"Certainly, Miss Morgan, a star like you could always choose her picture," said I.

She looked at Ray. "Poor child," she said. "He doesn't know anything, does he?"

"Few people do," said Ray.

"Let me explain the cinematic birds and bees to you, Dr Marlow," she said, turning back to me. "When you sign a contract with a studio, they own you, dear boy. They own your person and your image. They own your hairdresser and your couturier. They own your house - in that you depend on them to pay your monthly mortgage - your fancy car, your publicity man and your maid. They even own the words you say."

"You say them very well, at least." That was me. "Couldn't you change studios if you weren't pleased?"

"They own the lawyers, too," she said.

"And the judges," said Ray.

"My, my," I said, polishing off another Jack," they own quite a lot, don't they."

"More than you think," said Ray.

"So how did you do on your own?" I asked. "Or shouldn't I?"

"Very well, thank you," she said. "It was the greatest moment in my life. I was finally able to make the kind of film I really wanted. Except..."

"Except?" Me again. I get nervous when thoughts are left hanging in the air. I'm always afraid they'll fall, like that crystal chandelier, and hit me on the noodle.

"You see, to make a film isn't enough. If you want someone

to see it, you have to sell it back to the studio once more."

"Maybe it's the whiskey," said I, "but that sounds pretty fuzzy to me. I thought the whole point was to get away from them."

"The problem is," said Ray, "the studios own all the theatre chains. You might invest your money to make a film, but you can't show it anyplace without getting the studios to do your distribution."

"So that put you back where you started, huh? Don't mind me, I get a little dense this time of night."

"Not quite," said Gloria Morgan. "At least I had a film."

"But no money," said Ray.

"That was a problem," said Gloria Morgan with a tiny laugh.

"It must have been a problem if you still needed that mortgage, fancy car and couturier," I said.

"That's why I signed with the corporation," she said. "They brought in their own lawyers and accountants and made the deals with the studio that got my film shown around the world."

"Is that what's called a happy ending?" I asked.

"Not quite," she said. The smile wasn't nearly bright as before. "You see, I freed myself from the studio only to find that I was now owned by the corporation." She looked at Ray. Ray nodded his head.

"But your film got shown," I reminded her.

"That's true," she said, "but the corporation made me sell the rights for a pittance. The studios made a fortune on the deal while I was still in debt."

I shrugged. "That sounds better than the kick in the teeth most of us get out of life."

She looked at me as if trying to make up her mind what to respond. Then she let out a laugh. "Perhaps, you're right, Dr Marlow. Perhaps you're right. It's just once you've had the taste of freedom, it stays with you. I'd love to make a film like that again. Not for money. For art." Her eyes toyed with me like a wind-up poodle dog. "You wouldn't deny an old lady that, would you, Doctor?"

"Miss Morgan?" That wasn't me. Or Ray. I looked up. It was one of the Ambassador's gorillas. He didn't look like he had

42

come to have a drink.

She looked up, too. Her voice was sharp. "Yes? What do you want?"

"The Ambassador would like to know whether you could join him in his suite."

"Can't you see that I'm with friends?" she said in a wooden voice.

Did you ever hear a wooden voice and ask yourself whether it came from a wooden head? And then did you wonder whether it wasn't part of a puppet on a string?

"The Ambassador would appreciate it if you could join him now," repeated the gorilla.

"Oh, very well!" I had the feeling then, the string that was being pulled was more like a noose. So did Ray, I think.

"I guess the party's over," he said, as he watched them walk away.

"Not for her," I said.

"I meant for her," said Ray. He took out his pipe and struck a match. "There are contracts for exchanging any commodity under the sun," he said, "but the movie industry is the only one I know that contracts for your flesh and for your soul. You want a drink?"

I looked down at my glass and wondered whether I could stomach another. "I'm done," I said, "I think I'll drag myself below and make my bed."

"Me, too," said Ray. He looked as weary as I felt, maybe even more.

Somehow we managed to get up from our seats and head ourselves toward those three little stairs. Before we got there, though, Ray put his hand on my shoulder.

"Isn't that the Argentine sitting over there?" he asked.

A dark man sat brooding at a table in the corner of the lounge. Several glasses had been emptied and put to one side. Another, full, was on the table, right below his nose. He looked to me as if he were considering whether or not to jump inside.

"You want to say, 'hello?'" asked Ray. Suddenly he seemed wide awake again.

43

"Does that look like a man who wants to be said 'hello' to?" I replied.

"No," said Ray. "But that wasn't the question I asked."

Ray sauntered over to the Argentine's table. "Would you mind if we joined you for a drink, señor?" he said.

The Argentine looked up and stared at Ray. For a moment he said nothing and then, since he probably had gone to a school for cardboard diplomats and realised that saying "no" would be like having a permanent stain on his cravat, he didn't. Say "no", that is. Instead he said, "Please sit down." Reading the expression on his face, a few unspoken words were added which boiled down to - "If you must."

As far as I was concerned, a drink's a drink. Especially if Ray was buying. The little walk we took, all fifteen feet, had given me a thirst. Anyway, the thought of going to my room was beginning to seem pretty bleak.

Ray put in his order - Old Forester, my friend Jack and a Manhattan for the Argentine. When the waiter made his rounds Ray picked up his glass and said, "To the finest Pampas beef." And then the old devil smiled.

The Argentine lifted up his glass and toasted to the same. Then it was up to me. I lifted up my drink and said, "Here's to a liquid diet."

Ray let out a laugh. The Argentine lit up slightly, too. At least enough to call out, "Waiter! Another round, if you would be so kind!" He looked at us. "The same as before, gentlemen?"

"Why not?" I said. "If you're drowning yourself anyway, why change the water?"

"Why indeed?" asked the Argentine. "Why indeed?"

"I take it your important meeting didn't go so well," I said.

He glared at me. He seemed to be smouldering like an afternoon bonfire of wet leaves. "How did you know about my meeting?" he asked.

"At the dinner table - you said you were leaving to go to an important meeting. I figured it was an excuse to get away without ruffling any more feathers."

"Yes," he said. "Of course." And he downed another drink.

I could see Ray was studying the man as if he were a character from one of his stories. Of course, never having read any of Ray's books then, it would have been hard to say which one.

"I don't mean to intrude in your affairs, Mr Mendez," he said, "but I wonder if it isn't true that you are going to Europe in order to plead for loans. I say this only because I understand the plight your country is in."

The Argentine narrowed his eyes and stared at Ray. "My country's plight, as you say, is no secret, señor. We have been starved of funds from American and European banks. Without funds we can have no industry. Without industry we must depend on grain and beef."

"I thought we just toasted Pampas beef," I said.

"And your southern states can toast their cotton, too," said the Argentine. "But wasn't that what your war was all about? The British gave you credit for your cotton - on their terms, of course - and sold you their machines. Your war of liberation was in 1776 but the British still controlled the cotton trade."

"Maybe I read the wrong school books, but I always though you were a colony of Spain," said I.

His smile was thin and full of what Ray might have seen as irony, but I just thought was mean. "A colony of Spain? Linguistically, perhaps. Economically, we were the same as you."

"So - let me get this straight - what you're saying is our Washington is your Peron? Does your guy also have wooden teeth?"

I think I got him there. "Wooden teeth?" he asked, staring so hard he nearly crossed his eyes.

"My little joke," I said.

He looked at Ray. Ray just shrugged.

"Oh, hello..." It was a little voice, like a tweety bird. We all looked up.

There she stood with her glass of ginger ale. Monica Wheetly. Pushing the pair of glasses she hadn't worn to the dinner table back up her nose.

"I don't want to intrude, but we saw you sitting here and we wondered whether we couldn't join you. That is if you don't mind."

We? Maybe another glass of Jack and I'd see two of her.

The Argentine tried to stand out of forced politeness. He gave up midway and fell back into his seat. Ray did a little better. He almost stood up straight and told the "charming young woman" to pull up a chair.

She brought over two chairs. "Mr Meyers just went to the little boy's room," she said with a silly little girl's grin. "He's going to join us too."

"There aren't two of him, are there?" I asked. "If there are, you should have brought over four chairs."

"Oh, hello, Dr Marlow," she said. "I didn't see you in the dark."

"That's because there's only one of me right now," I said.

"We were discussing the plight of Argentina," said Ray, I suppose as a way of orienting her to our group of lushes.

"Does Argentina have a plight?" she asked. "I'm dreadfully sorry. I didn't know." She said it in a tone of voice you might use on someone if their aunt was down with a bad case of flu.

The Argentine was too far gone to comment now. He had slumped down in his chair to brood again.

Monica Wheetly turned her attention to Ray. "Mr Chandler, I understand you're a writer and you have no idea in the world how exciting that is for me because that's what I've always wanted to be!" The words gushed out of her mouth like water from a wide-opened spout.

There was a sudden stillness in the air. For a moment, all I could hear was the sloshing of the swell against the hull in perfect synchrony with the sloshing of Jack Daniels in my hold.

Ray stared at her and didn't say a word.

Monica Wheetly's hand went to her mouth. She blushed and said, "Oh, my!"

Ray bit down on his pipe. One thing about Ray that I noticed from the very start, he could never leave a lady in distress.

"Have you ever read my books?" he asked.

The blood drained from her face. For an instant I thought that she might faint. "Oh...I'm sorry, Mr Chandler. But before today I never heard of you." And realising that's not exactly what she meant to say, her hand went to her mouth again. "Oh, my!"

Ray couldn't help but laugh. "That's all right, my dear," he said. "Most people who I'd like to read my books, haven't. I'll tell you what, stop by my room sometime and I'll lend you a few."

Her eyes lit up like a Kansas sky on the Fourth of July. "Oh, Mr Chandler! Would you really? That would be so kind!"

"You can thank me after you're read them, not before," he said.

"Oh, I know I'll love them, Mr Chandler. I understand you do detective stories and I adore mysteries! I've read all of Agatha Christie I can get my hands on!"

Ray's face darkened like the beginnings of a solar eclipse. "That woman I despise!" he said between his teeth.

"Me?" said Monica Wheetly. She looked like she was just about to cry.

"Not you, child!" said Ray. "That Christie Woman! Agatha! The name itself gives me the creeps!"

"But why?" asked Monica Wheetly, her eyes still clouded over and threatening tears. "What's she ever done to you?"

"I've never had the displeasure of meeting the women, if that's what you mean," said Ray. "But her very popularity has done more to inhibit the art of detective fiction than anything else I can think of."

"I'm sorry, Mr Chandler," she said, starting to regain control of herself again. "I just don't understand what you're trying to say. I suppose she's popular because people enjoy reading her. How does that inhibit art? After all, it's only mysteries she's writing. She's not pretending to be George Sand or Hemingway."

I thought Ray would break the stem of his pipe the way he ground his teeth. "Miss Wheetly, good detective fiction is art. Books like Madame Christie's do us a grave disservice because they don't really come off intellectually as problems and they don't come off artistically as fiction. They're too contrived and too little aware of what goes on in the world. They try to be honest, but honesty itself is an art. The poor writer is dishonest without knowing it and the fairly good one can be dishonest because he doesn't know what to be honest about. Madame Christie, and her cohorts like that Sayers woman, think a complicated murder scheme which baffled the lazy reader, who won't be bothered itemizing the details, will also baffle the police, whose business is with details. Their kind of detective story is an arid formula which can't even satisfy its own implications. They're second grade literature because they're not about the things that could make first-grade literature. If their books start out to be about real people, they very soon do unreal things in order to form the artificial pattern required by the plot. And when they do unreal things, they cease to be real themselves. They become puppets and cardboard lovers and papier-mâché villains and detectives of exquisite and impossible gentility."

Monica Wheetly nodded her head like an attentive student sitting in a chemistry class. "I think I understand what you're saying now, Mr Chandler."

"No, you don't Miss Wheetly. The problem with writers like Christie and Sayers was that they couldn't give their characters heads and let them make their own mysteries. It took a much simpler and more direct mind than theirs to do that."

"Like you, Mr Chandler?" she asked.

"Like Hammett, Miss Wheetly," he said. "Maybe me when I'm at my best."

"Did someone mention Hammett?" Solly Meyers sat down at the table and took a drink of white stuff that I assumed was milk.

"Hammett I like," he said, putting down his glass and wiping off the moustache from his upper lip. "Especially the way that fellow Humphrey Bogart played him in that film about a statue of a bird. He wasn't so nice to the woman at the end, but I suppose in films you don't have to be nice to women anymore. Times are changing. In my day, people would have been more polite."

"I don't believe detectives are meant to be polite, Mr Meyers," said Monica Wheetly looking over at Ray for approval.

"Polite or not, Miss Wheetly, he's meant to be a hero. And to be that he must be a complete man; he must be a common man and yet an unusual man. He must be, to use a rather weathered phrase, a man of honor..." Then Ray stopped and turned to me. "Like our man Marlow, here."

I lifted my glass. "I'll drink to that."

"I don't mean in real life," said Solly Meyers. "In real life detectives are crooks - just like the rest of us. But who goes to movies, I ask you? Women and children, that's who. Life is hard enough without giving them bad dreams."

Monica Wheetly rubbed her chin, like a young sage feeling if she had whiskers "Then what you're writing, Mr Chandler, if I read you correctly is..." She hesitated for a moment. I suppose she was trying out the word. "...romance."

Ray closed his eyes. Maybe he was tired after all. "Miss Wheetly, you haven't even begun to read me yet."

By this time I was beginning to question whether I had ever read anything myself or if I ever would again. Maybe it was me, but the motion of the ship no longer seemed straightforward. Sometimes we seemed to be going up, sometimes down. Sometimes side to side. Colors, too, began to change. From pastel pink to a sickly shade of green.

"Dr Marlow?"

That was my name, all right. I could still recognize it, even though it looked like it had been beaten on the head and left overnight inside a garbage can.

"Dr Marlow?" It was the kid with the Philip Morris hat. "I'm sorry to disturb you, Dr Marlow, but you're wanted."

It's nice to know you're wanted, sometimes. Sometimes it's not.

"I was sent to accompany you, sir."

I tried standing up. "Not where I'm going, kid," I said.

Chapter 6

Even if it is a luxury ship, take my advice: it isn't where you want to be after a heavy meal followed by a baker's dozen worth of drinks, with the ocean swell making it all go back and forth and up and down and sideways.

"You don't look too good Dr Marlow," said the kid as he escorted me across the deck, then down and through a bulkhead door.

"Well," I said, "if you took a can opener and used it on my belly, you'd probably understand."

"I used to get sea sick, myself," said the kid, "before they told me why."

"It's not the why that bothers me," I said, "it's the where and when."

"Oh," he said, "I know what you need, Dr Marlow. It's straight along and to your left. And he pointed to a door.

I went inside and let it flow. I felt a little better when I came out. The world wasn't completely back in shape, but it wasn't so drably olive either.

"It's just a matter of the mind," the kid said, as he led the way again.

"That's what they used to say in medical school," I told him. "'It's just a matter of the mind.' It took me a while before I found out what they really meant was they didn't mind and we didn't matter."

"Did they really say that in medical school?" he asked. I don't think he believed me. I hated to disillusion somebody so young.

"No, they didn't really say that in medical school," I assured him. "We said it ourselves when we started our practice."

"That's very funny, Dr Marlow. You're a very funny man, sir."

I guess that's what I am, all right. A very funny man. I'd only seen the kid a couple of times and he already had me pegged.

We had reached the deck right above mine where the other first class cabins were located. These were the fancier ones;

mostly suites. The kid stopped before a door.

"I thought we were going along to surgery," I said. "Are we stopping here for a rest?"

"It's one of the passengers, sir. She's feeling ill."

"If she's feeling ill," I said, "she doesn't want to see me. The way I look right now, she'll only feel iller. Besides, you have a staff of medics down below. You don't need me. I'm the cut and paste man, remember?"

"I'm sorry, sir," he said knocking on the door. "She insisted I find you."

By this time it was too late to run and hide. The kid had sold me out. I hope he got more than the two bits I put into his grubby little hand that morning.

"Come in," said a voice from inside. It's not that easy to get such depth of emotion in those two little words. Only Sarah Bernhardt could have done better.

I suppose I could have walked away right then and there. If I was smart, that's what I would have done. But if I was really smart I would have stuffed the ad I tore out at Horne and Hardart back in Manhattan.

Instead of what I should have done, I opened up the door and went inside. She was reclining on the bed. She wore a silk negligee with fancy trim that clung to her like a leopard and its spots. Her feet were hidden inside some fluffy pink stuff. Over her shoulders was a piece of fur which may or may not have been alive. She looked at me and said, "Thank you for coming, Dr Marlow. I hope I haven't put you out."

I never understood what they meant by bedroom eyes until I met hers. They not only offered you the key to the boudoir, they pulled back the sheets, warmed the covers and put out the cat besides.

"My stomach aches and my feet hurt," I said. "I had a little too much to drink. I'd like to got to bed. I guess maybe you did put me out."

"I wouldn't have asked you to see me, Dr Marlow, if it wasn't important."

"I'm sure it is important - to you. Famous people think a

liverwurst sandwich is important if they feel hungry for it then. The person who brings it to them might not have the same sense of urgency about it though."

Maybe I was being too rough on her. But I didn't feel that great myself.

"You don't like me much, do you, Dr Marlow?" she said, struggling to sit up.

I moved closer. The bedroom eyes were intensified by dilation of the pupils. This star, I thought, is pretty high.

"I don't not like you, Miss Morgan. I don't know you. I do like your pictures though, if that makes you feel any better."

A trace of smile crossed her lips. "You've seen my films?" she asked. "Which ones?"

"If you're asking for names, you're asking the wrong man," I said. "But I liked the one that was set in LA about the ageing movie queen."

She held out her hand. "Come over here, dear boy. I promise not to bite."

I walked over to the bed, reached down and took her hand. It was soft and very warm. Her flesh yielded in my grasp. I slid my fingers over to her wrist and felt her pulse.

"What are you on?" I asked.

She pulled her hand away. "You're not a very nice man, Dr Marlow!" she said.

"Before, up at the bar, you said I had refreshing honesty. Maybe being honest isn't very nice."

"What is honesty, Dr Marlow?" Her head was back on the pillow now. She was staring up at the panelled ceiling, trying not to cry.

"You tell me," I said.

"An actress knows honesty, Dr Marlow, if she's any good that is. I am a good actress."

"I know you are," I said. I glanced at her maple side table by her bed. There was a bottle full of pills sitting on the edge. The top was off and the cotton stopper pulled out. Next to it was a glass half full of water.

"But sometimes a good actress forgets herself. The roles

begin to get confused. Her parts begin to merge inside her mind."

"That happens to a lot of us," I said, "even if we're not on stage."

"I want a chance to be a good actress again," she said. She turned her face and looked at me. Her mascara had started to run making a trail of crows legs at the corner of her eyes.

"Who's stopping you, Miss Morgan?"

"Who's stopping me?" She laughed. A good actress can do that pretty well - laugh, then cry, then laugh again. "No one's stopping me, Dr Marlow. No one you know, that is."

"Look, Miss Morgan," I said. "I didn't do my training in psychiatry..."

She didn't let me finish before she lashed out. "You're a very insolent man! How dare you speak to me that way!"

I turned around and, as I did, I lifted the bottle of pills from the maple side table into my hand, glanced at the prescription and put them down again. I did it very quickly so I doubt if she could see. Then I walked over to the door. "Thanks for the invite," I said. "Maybe we can meet sometime again."

I went outside into the passageway, closing the door after me. I stood there for a moment. I rubbed my eyes and then walked down the corridor not bothering to see which way the numbers went.

When I got to the end of the passage, I realised I had been going the wrong way. I turned around, and as I did, I thought I saw Gloria Morgan's door close again. But I'm used to distortions of the mind in my line of work. Especially when you have a two ton rhinoceros sitting on your head.

I passed by her door again. I thought I heard voices. Sometimes they carry through the steel. But voices weren't strange to me either. Sometimes I hear entire symphony orchestras, complete with bassoons, trumpets and French horns.

But who knows what goes on behind all those cabin doors? When someone has money and five days on the open sea, it can be a heady combination. There's no end of things they can think up during periods of enforced boredom - especially those people who are used to being entertained. The curse of privilege never ceased to amaze me when I was in Chicago. The things they could think up simply as amusement for their addled lives would chill a fried tomato on a sultry summer's night.

I discovered the stairs to B deck around the bend. I climbed down to the next level and walked along to 103. I went inside, took off my clothes and flopped into my bunk. Even before my head hit the pillow, I was fast asleep.

Chapter 7

I put the pillow over my head to stop the ringing in my ears. That didn't help. How do you tell a telephone to shut up? Here I was, a couple of hundred miles out in the middle of the sea and still tormented by A.G. Bell's device to wake the dead.

I grabbed the receiver and shouted down the line. "Can't it wait?"

"Marlow?"

"Yeah, without an 'e'. What do you want?"

"You missed breakfast, Marlow. It's time for lunch. If you're not careful, you'll miss dinner, too. And there's not much more to do on this goddamn tub except to drink and eat!"

I looked at my watch. It was half past eleven. "Where are you calling from?" I asked. "London? Maybe it's lunch time there. My clock says it's still morning."

"I'm in the lounge trying to get tanked. That Wheetly girl is on my tail. You got to help me Marlow."

"Give her a couple of your books," I said. "That ought to keep her occupied."

"I did - last night. She already finished one. Those college kids read fast!"

"You should have torn the pages and given them to her one by one."

"Why didn't you tell me that last night?"

"I was too busy nurse-maiding your movie star," I said. "Did she miss breakfast too?"

"Yeah. Say, Marlow, you're not ... you didn't ..." His voice sounded a little strained.

"I didn't what? Share her spots? Listen, if I'm going to be devoured by a carnivore I'd rather choose the four-legged kind. I gather she was feeling kind of blue. She couldn't call a shrink, so she called me."

"I know she's been upset. You give her anything?"

"I saw she had some pills. A mild form of barbiturate. She had taken one or two, I think. It's exactly what I would have prescribed for her, but she had them already. Dames like her think everyone is at their beck and call, the world is there to give them sympathy. They have no idea that others might have had a raw shake too."

"Sounds like you've been through the mill," said Ray. "Or am I wrong?"

"I've been through the war. Ain't that enough?"

"Yeah, that can do it. I know what you mean. I was in the trenches too. World War I. You can't see men die like that and ever be the same."

"You can't see children stacked in graves or twenty year old women, bald and toothless, with their wombs cut out, praying just to die, and then go back and wipe the noses of the rich either, Ray."

"Are you talking about the war? Sounds more like you paid a visit to Hell, Marlow."

"Maybe I did. Maybe I'll tell you about it sometime. That Wheetly kid still stalking you?"

"She's waving at me right this minute. Still has that goddamn gingerale stuck in her hand."

"Same one from last night?"

"Looks like it."

"It's bound to lose its fizz."

"She provides her own gas, Marlow. Listen, I need your help. SOS! Mayday! Mayday!"

"Why don't you just tell her to buzz off?"

"I can't do that. I'm just a fat old drunk who can't refuse a pretty girl. I'm putty in their hands. I need you, Marlow, or I wouldn't have called."

"Seems like I heard that somewhere before."

"Maybe you did. Now you're hearing it again. You coming or not?"

I sighed. "Ask her to recite the Gettysburg Address. I'll be there before she's through."

*****

I showered and shaved and slapped on my rum. I put on a clean shirt, zipped up my trousers and tied my shoes. It's amazing what a good night's sleep can do for you.

Unfortunately, I got there too late. Ray was already baited, trapped and nearly skinned by the time I arrived.

He wiggled like a fish caught on a coat hanger as he stood up and waved. "Marlow! Over here! Order me an ancient wood chopper if you don't mind."

"What for you, Miss Wheetly?" They were sitting on the balcony overlooking the bar. Close enough so I didn't have to shout.

She held up her pale glass of gingerale. "I'm fine, thank you, Dr Marlow," she said, sweet as you please.

I ordered an Old Forester for Ray and a Jack. The waiter said he'd bring it up. That was OK by me. I remembered those three little stairs from last night. They could be a killer.

"You shouldn't have started with that one," Ray was telling her when I pulled up a chair. "I wrote it when I was feeling old and useless and maybe a little mean."

"But I thought *Little Sister* was a wonderful book, Mr Chandler!" she gushed. "Your metaphors are simply brilliant! Your language is so alive!" She hesitated for a moment and then said shyly, "I must say, however, I didn't really understand the ending, though."

"It's implicit in my theory of mystery writing, Miss Wheetly, that the mystery and the solution of the mystery are only what I call 'the olive in the martini'. The really good mystery is the one you would read even if you knew someone had torn the last chapter out."

"I guess you could say the same thing about the telephone directory," I said. Maybe I shouldn't have put my two bits in, but I happen to like tidy endings myself.

"My favorite kind of book is one that never ends," she said stirring her soda dreamily with a plastic martini stick. If it had an olive on its point, she could have given it to Ray for his next book.

She looked at Ray and said, with all the bright sincerity she could muster, "I want to write, Mr Chandler. It's what I want to do more than anything in life!"

Ray looked at me. His eyes were pleading for a drink. I motioned to the waiter to hurry up.

"I'd be most grateful for any tiny bit of advice you could give me. Any little scrap at all."

The St. Bernard arrived up the mountain just in the nick of time. He deposited our nectars and Ray took a grateful gulp.

"How old are you, Miss Wheetly?" he asked, his courage somewhat bolstered by the spirits.

"Twenty," she said. "Nearly twenty-one," she added quickly.

"When I was twenty, I wanted to be a writer, too."

"But you are a writer, Mr Chandler," she insisted.

"I am now. I wasn't then. In fact, I had a position in the civil service. Came in third among six hundred candidates and first in the examination in classics."

"You took an examination in classics for a job in civil service?" I asked. "Isn't that like taking a test in rocket design in order to sharpen pencils?"

"This was England, 1907, Marlow. People were educated for boredom there. We still had an Empire to run, you know."

Monica Wheetly seemed confused. "I must say it's hard to picture you as English after reading your book, Mr Chandler. Although looking at you, your pipe and all, and hearing you speak..."

"Oh, I'm a strange breed all right, Miss Wheetly. Like anyone who went to an English public school, I'm too British to be an American. But after forty years in LA, I'm too American to be British."

"Maybe this is where you belong then," I said.

"Where's that, Marlow?" he asked, looking at me curiously.

"Right here, Ray. In the middle of the Atlantic Ocean."

"So you left the civil service to became a writer, Mr Chandler?" asked Monica Wheetly, who could be like a bulldog running after a postman when it came to finding something out.

"I was a clerk at the Admiralty. I could have had a life-long and perfectly safe position with six weeks vacation and ridiculously easy hours. But after six months I packed it in and left. The idea of being expected to tip my hat to the head of the department every morning and every evening of my life struck me as verging on the obscene."

"You're speaking metaphorically, of course," said Monica Wheetly.

"I'm speaking literally. I probably was one of the only clerks ever to leave that sanctuary. Everyone was appalled."

"What did you do then, Mr Chandler?" Monica Wheetly leaned forward. I thought she'd fall in her stale gingerale.

"I holed up in Bloomsbury, of course. That's where I began my literary career."

"How romantic!" Monica Wheetly sighed. "Bloomsbury is on my tour of London, you know. I want to see where people like Virginia Woolf lived." Suddenly her eyes lit up. "I just thought of something, Mr Chandler! Maybe your house will be included in my visit, too!"

"I doubt it, Miss Wheetly," he said. "The room I had deserved to have been firebombed, though my writing then didn't exactly set Bloomsbury ablaze."

"Were you writing mysteries back then, too?" she asked.

"I was writing poetry. My first poem, I recall, was written on a Sunday while I was in the loo. It was entitled, 'The Unknown Love' and I am very fortunate in not possessing a single copy."

"What a terrible shame," said Monica Wheetly. She showed her commiseration by reaching out and touching his hand which Ray immediately pulled back.

"It is not a terrible shame, Miss Wheetly. If that poem was ever found, it would be a distinct embarrassment to me."

She blushed again. That girl could really blush, I thought. She turned red right up to the roots of her hair. "I must tell you, Mr Chandler. I... I write poetry, too." It was a frank admission which must have taken every ounce of courage for her to say.

"I'm sure you do, child," said Ray. "I'm sure you do."

"But when did you start writing mysteries?" she persisted.

"Not until much later. I came to America, lived in LA, went to war, got married, went into business, managed an oil company, got drunk, suffered through the depression and only then did I become a writer."

"That sounds like a long time. How old were you then?"

"I was over forty."

"Over forty?" she said in disbelief.

He nodded his head and took out his pipe.

"That's when you really got started?"

He nodded again, stuffed the bowl with his smelly tobacco and pressed it in with the ball of his thumb.

"But that's such an awfully long time to wait!"

"Not everybody waits that long. That's only what happened to me," he said, lighting up and blowing a cloud of smoke which seemed to settle right above my noggin.

She took in a breath, like a scuba diver getting ready to submerge ten fathoms deep. "Well, if that's how long it takes..."

"It took that long, Miss Wheetly, because I had no subsidy. My wife and I had bills to pay."

Here's where I decided to butt in. "Lucky for you the depression came along. No one could pay their bills back then anyhow. You might as well have become a writer - or a tamer of wild chimpanzees."

"Marlow's right," said Ray. "If you didn't have a job to quit, it took the fear out of trying something new. Lots of people became writers back then. At least you gave yourself a chance."

"But why did you start writing mysteries?" she asked.

"I was looking for a form," said Ray, "something that I felt I could plug into. Back then there was a magazine - Black Mask it was called. I read a few issues on a train - they weren't great, but I was entertained. And I thought to myself that I could probably do as well. I found out they paid writers a penny a word, which wasn't a fortune even then, but you could hope to make a meagre living at it if you could churn out enough copy."

"How did you learn, though. You still haven't told me that, Mr Chandler."

"I learned by taking some of the stories I liked, doing a thorough outline, and then writing them again."

"You mean you plagiarised?" she asked, straightening herself up and looking at him aghast.

"You look so shocked, Miss Wheetly. Settle down or you'll give yourself indigestion. All writers are plagiarisers in one way or another. You'll find out one day that there's absolutely nothing you can say that hasn't been said many times before. The craft is putting it together in a slightly different form and saying it with a little style."

"But those stories - the ones that you rewrote..."

"Don't worry, Miss Wheetly," he said. "I threw them all away. But they gave me the confidence I needed to do more of the same."

She shook her head in dismay. "You were a classics scholar, Mr Chandler, or so you say..."

"And I still love the classics, Miss Wheetly. Indeed, they formed the background for my work. My hero is a classical hero. The language that I use has the same fascination, vigor and freshness to me that Elizabethan language had in Shakespeare's day."

"I do enjoy the language that you use," she said. "It's stylish without being stylised."

"That's because I decided to work in American instead of literary English. Literary English, you see, is basically a class language full of forced pretentiousness."

"Not in the hands of Virginia Woolf," she said.

"Perhaps not," said Ray. "Nor for someone like Somerset Maugham, who, in my estimation, is one of the great story-tellers of our age. Have you read him?"

"Oh, yes!" she said. "I just loved *The Moon and Sixpence*!"

That was about all I could take. Ray might have sent me an SOS to keep this college girl at bay, but I could tell he was starting to enjoy himself. And I could just see a full-blown literary cloud billowing out from Ray's over-heated pipe about to asphyxiate me.

I finished my Jack Daniels and got up to leave.

"Are you going someplace?" asked Ray.

"I thought I'd try a spot of fishing from the boat deck," I said. "Maybe I can catch a flounder."

Chapter 8

Lobster was the fish of the day. Well, the tails at least. They probably were Australian. I got that feeling because they seemed to jump around on my plate like a kangaroo every time I tried to dig in.

"Look at him over there!" said Rinexus, pointing a butter - dripping fork at what I thought was me. "He doesn't even know where to begin!"

"I would if you gave me an axe," I said.

"Why use an axe? You're a doctor, ain't you Marlow? I'm sure you got some pill that would be less bloody and do just as good."

I looked down at the end of the crustacean lying in my dish. "Are you trying to tell me this thing's not dead yet? No wonder it won't stay put!"

Rinexus pointed again, this time over my head. "I'm talking about the Argentine over there, preening like a peacock and trying to impress the ladies with his highfalutin manners. We weren't good enough for him, I suppose!"

I took a look. The Argentine was at the Captain's table, engaged in animated conversation with Gloria Morgan. What they were talking about, I could only guess. It might have had to do with Pampas beef.

"Maybe he belongs there," I said. "After all, if it's credit that he wants, he's better off talking with the guys who have the bankroll than with you or me."

"The doctor's right," said Solly Meyers. "I always did my best business over dinner. It's hard to give a firm 'no' to anything with your mouth full of chopped liver. However, if I were Mr Mendez, I'd rather make a deal with Mephistopheles than with our fine Ambassador over there."

"Mephistopheles who?" asked Rinexus.

Roger Lane made a gesture of impatience by slicing through his omelette with unnecessary force. "I'm sure in your line of work you've made pacts with the devil before, Mr. Rinexus," he said. "He goes by many names."

"I'll make a deal with anyone," Rinexus growled, buttering up some bread. "It just depends on how much he pays." Then looking at Solly Meyers he said, "What kind of dope do you have about the Ambassador that makes you love him so much, Pops? If you know him so well, how come you ain't siting over there instead of with us slobs?"

"I don't know him personally. But I know someone who had some conflicting business interests, that's all," said Solly Meyers. "Business isn't very nice. It's not supposed to be. A good businessman, who's been out-bargained, forgets the past and just goes on. Tomorrow maybe he'll out-bargain you." He made reference to the Ambassador by motioning his head. "But that man over there doesn't forget. And he doesn't forgive. He's not a real businessman."

"That friend of yours once sell him a pair of pants that still had some legs in 'em, Pops?" asked Rinexus with a burst of laughter, like the quiet ripple of a Tommy gun.

"You could say that," said Solly Meyers, concentrating on his special diet of prunes and cottage cheese.

"Mr Mendez is up against the wall," said Roger Lane. "According to the press, his country's almost bankrupt. So for him it's do or die. When you're faced with that, you'll bargain away anything."

Lane said those words like he understood what they meant. His wife threw him a secret smile. Maybe she thought no one could see. But I noticed. It wasn't like the lobster I was eating; it was something tender.

"Well, he looks happy now," said Rinexus, with a sour face that may have been caused by a momentary stomach spasm. He looked down into his food. "Maybe he made his deal after all."

"He was pretty glum last night," I said, forgetting about the lobster and winding up some noodles on my fork instead. "Tried to drown himself in drink."

"He didn't look depressed when I saw him last night," piped in Amanda Lane. "Furious is more the word. I saw him storming out of the Ambassador's suite round about eleven."

"I guess he worked it out of his system," I said.

"It's amazing how fast inner conflicts can be resolved," said Roger Lane.

"Inner conflicts are bad for the digestion," said Rinexus, letting out a burp. "If you're gonna do something, why gripe about it?"

"I'm not talking about people like you," said Roger Lane.

The waiter brought over the dessert cart just in time to divert another dagger being tossed. Instead of following Lane's parry with a thrust, Rinexus opted for pie made out of chocolate. Lane was served an apple tart. His wife received a bowl of fruit. Grandpa got the custard. I had ice cream. The flavor, if you're interested in things like that, was vanilla.

"By the way," said Rinexus, digging into the chocolate stuff, "where's Chandler and that college broad. You don't think they hit it off together, do you?"

"You never know about these May and October romances," I said.

"May?" Rinexus shouted through his pie. "She's more like March - and him, December. But more power to the old goat, if that's what he's up to. I kind of like those little Lolita babes myself!" He wiggled his eyebrows up and down. What a clown! I thought   What a clown!

"Anyway, last night I remembered this great story about Chandler that Billy Wilder told me," Rinexus went on. "Seems Wilder had this option on a book by James M. Cain. *Double Indemnity* it was called - a pot boiler about a man, a woman and an insurance scam. Anyway, the guy he was collaborating with at the time just hated it - thought it was awful and refused to work on it at all. So Wilder's looking for someone to help him write the dialogue - him being German-speaking like a lot of those Krauts they had in Hollywood in '43. Anyway, someone suggests this LA writer who's all the rage 'cause a couple of his books had made the rounds at M.G.M. So Wilder calls him in. And the writer turns out to be Chandler. Now get this - he's lived in LA twenty years and never been to Hollywood before. Wilder talks to him about the *Double Indemnity* book and asks him to collaborate. Chandler says OK and asks Wilder for a copy of a screen play so he can see how it's done. So Wilder gets him a screenplay and Chandler gives it the once-over and then says, 'OK, it'll take me at least a week and I wouldn't do it for less than a thousand dollars.'

"Wilder, of course, thinks the guy's a loony bird, but Chandler has a reputation, so he says, 'Mr Chandler, I'll give you 750.' Chandler gets really outraged now and stomps his foot. 'A thousand or nothing!' he says. 'I won't work for a penny less.' Then Wilder says, 'Calm down, Mr Chandler. I mean $750 a week with a thirteen week minimum!'"

Rinexus laughed so hard, I had trouble seeing how he'd keep his food from coming up.

"Double Indemnity was a pretty good film," said Roger Lane. "I didn't know Chandler did the scripting for that."

Rinexus waved his hand like he was swatting down a fly. "Aw, Wilder says he was hopeless. Sure he wrote decent dialogue, but my dog can do that. He says working with Chandler was a real pain in the butt. He says the guy was so over-sensitive that one day he doesn't show up. Wilder finds out that instead of coming in for work, Chandler went to see Houseman, who was the producer, with a list of grievances written on a sheet of legal-size paper."

"What kind of grievances?" asked Roger Lane.

"He wrote 'em up real formal-like, Wilder said. Things like 'Mr Wilder will at no time swish under Mr Chandler's nose or point in his direction the thin, leather-handled malacca cane which Mr Wilder is in the habit of waving around while Mr Chandler works.'"

"Maybe that would annoy the hell out of me, too," I said.

"The point is, Chandler was a real prima donna. Guys like him don't understand how Hollywood operates, so, sure he can't last. And when they leave, 'cause they don't have what it takes, they try to put in the knock. They make it seem like it's us who's the problem, not them."

"Sounds to me like Mr Chandler had your kind pretty well sized up," said Roger Lane.

"What would you know about it, Lane?" asked Rinexus, vacuuming up the crumbs of chocolate pie with a moistened finger.

"Enough," said Lane, pushing back his chair and getting up. "Come on, Amanda," he said to his wife. "I think it's time for our walk."

"I know I've seen that creep somewhere," said Rinexus, after they had left.

"You said that before," I reminded him. I'm a slow eater or I would have been gone by then, too.

"Well I'm a guy who can't forget a face," he said.

"Yeah," I replied. "It can be a problem. Especially when you know a face you wouldn't mind forgetting."

Chapter 9

She was leaning over the rail. The choppy water splashed against the ship's black skin and sent a finely atomised spray into her hair, turning it from mousy brown to auburn gloss.

I came up to her side. "The clouds are mackerels today," I said.

She turned to me and smiled. It wasn't the same kid, I thought. "They say that means rain, Dr Marlow. If you believe in those kinds of things."

"If a sailor tells you it's going to rain, believe him. If a mackerel tells you, think about it twice."

"What if a mackerel tells a sailor?" she said.

"That's OK, too. I knew a seaman once who could tell the weather from the condition of his bunion. If it was blue, you could bet your last dollar and be sure it would rain. I told a friend of mine about him and they went into business together selling fail safe reports to a newspaper syndicate. They made a fortune."

"Do you ever see them anymore?" It was a sensible question, I suppose.

"No. When people make their fortune you kinda lose track of them."

She tuned her face outward to the sea. "You know, my parents really aren't all that rich."

"I wasn't asking," I said.

"He's just a minor capitalist. He owns a very small steel mill."

"I didn't know there was such a thing as a very small steel mill," I said.

"Oh, yes," she said. "There are some very big ones and some very small ones."

"And your dad has one of the very small ones."

"Well, two, actually. But he only has a part share in the second."

She turned her head back again and looked at me. I was

always a sucker for cornflower blue eyes.

"It's not my fault that he's rich," she said.

"I didn't say it was." I guess I thought it, though.

"I didn't have to tell you," she said.

"You wouldn't be on this boat if you were poor," I replied.

She laughed. It wasn't the same self-conscious giggle I had heard from her before. "Well, I never met a poor doctor, either."

I held out my hand. "Sister, you met one now."

She took my hand an gave it a shake. "You took a vow of poverty or something?" she asked.

"More like the story of Robin Hood," I said. "Only in my case, I steal from the rich and give it back to them as well."

"That doesn't make any sense," she said.

"There isn't much in my life that does," I replied.

She put her hand in mine and let me hold it for a moment. "I think I like you, Dr Marlow," she said.

I let it drop. "Don't go asking for trouble in your life, Miss Wheetly," I said. "There's plenty of it around as it is."

"I thought trouble was your business, Dr Marlow."

"Maybe. But the trouble I have is no one's business but my own. Where's Ray, Miss Wheetly?"

"Please call me Monica," she said, looking into my eyes.

"OK, Monica. Where's Ray?"

"Ray's in his cabin."

"He missed lunch," I said.

"We had a sandwich in the bar. He's such a fascinating man!"

I looked up toward the sun. It was ready for its plunge into the western sky, coloring the water like an impossible painter with an imagination that was far too vivid for any gallery.

"Did you know that his wife had recently died?" she asked.

"No. I haven't known him long. Just two days," I said.

"They were very close," she said. "Her name was Cissy. That's a lovely name, don't you think?"

"It doesn't sound to me like the name Ray's wife would have."

"He showed me her photgraph. It was taken when she was very young. She was a beautiful woman. He said her eyes were very much the color of mine."

"Cornflower blue?" I asked.

"That's what he said. She was a pianist. For the last few years she was confined to her bed. Ray nursed her every day."

"Doesn't sound like he got much writing done," I said.

"I think it's a lovely image though." Her eyes followed the sun's path through the water. "He's such a dear, sweet man."

"Most of us drunks are," I said.

"But he's an artist!" she said, looking at me reproachfully.

"That's his problem, Miss Wheetly. Not mine."

*****

I left Monica Wheetly standing out on deck. I went in for my afternoon drink. The bar was empty. Sometimes it's OK to drink alone. Sometimes it's not. I decided to give Ray a phone.

"Hello, Marlow," he said when I got the operator to track him down, "I was trying to get some work done."

"Sorry, Ray," I said. "The bar was empty, I was wondering if you might want to join me for a drink."

"Why don't you drop by here," he said.

"I thought you were trying to write," I replied.

"Damn pen's jammed again," he said. "No one here has any ink."

"Maybe you could try another pen," I suggested. "I'm sure Miss Wheetly would be more than happy to lend you one."

"I can't help it, Marlow. I know I shouldn't lead her on..."

"Who's leading who?" I asked.

"You mean, 'who's leading whom', but never mind. It doesn't really matter, does it?"

"That's just what I was going to say."

"So come on down," he said.

"Where do you live?" I asked.

"Cabin 131. Same deck as yours but on the port side of the ship. I wanted to be POSH - Port Outward, Starboard Home - but I could never get it straight whether 'outward' was away from England or America. Do you know?"

"Outward is away from anywhere I am at the time. I'll see you soon, Ray."

It took me about five minutes longer to get down to Cabin 131 than you might expect, seeing we were so close. I had stopped off at my room to get some cigarettes. Coming back out I saw the burly porter with the gentle eyes who had managed to stuff Amanda Lane's sea chest through the door when we had first come aboard. He was taking a quick smoke and didn't see me till I was almost next to him. When he did, he quickly snuffed it out against the heel of his boot.

"You don't have to worry about me," I advised him. "After watching you handle that sea chest, I'd say you deserve to smoke wherever you want."

I took out my pack and offered him one to make up for the cigarette he had just snuffed. He took it, gratefully, and lit up.

"Funny thing about that chest," he said. "I was just in there helping her move it around. It ain't so heavy now."

"She probably unpacked," I said.

"That's just the point," he said. "It's one of them closet chests. You know the kind, with drawers and everything. I was helping her stand it upright. It weren't easy to open 'cause the catch was bent in the move. As far as I could tell, it was still filled with all her things.

"Did you eat any spinach for dinner last night?" I asked.

"Yeah," he said, giving me a funny look. "How'd you know?"

"Well, that explains it then. Don't you remember Popeye?"

He slapped his leg and let out a laugh. "Well, blow me down! Maybe that little guy knew something after all!"

It's always nice to make someone's day. I should try it more often, I guess. Maybe next time I have to cut somebody open, I'll say, "'Scuse me while I open up a can of spinach. Har! Har!"

I walked across the corridor that led to the port side of the ship and banged on the door of 131.

"Come in, Marlow! The door's open!" he shouted out. I came in. He was sitting at his desk, tapping away at a portable Underwood.

"I thought you used a pen," I said.

"I told you it ran out of ink, remember? Pour yourself one,

71

Marlow," he said, without looking up. "I'll be with you in a second."

I did pour myself one. His room was just like mine, except a mirror image. I sat down in the easy chair and watched him type.

"You writing a book?" I asked.

"A letter."

"Long letter. Most I ever get out is 'Feeling lousy, send more beer.'"

He turned around and glared at me. "Well, you're American, Marlow. What the hell did you expect? I'll do the writing, you do the talking. OK?"

"OK by me," I said. "What are we talking about, by the way?"

"Division of labour," he said. "The puppet cannot be allowed to manipulate the puppeteer. It's against the rules of nature."

"I see," I said, taking another drink. "You want I should pour you one?"

"In a minute," he said. He knocked off another line and then ripped the page out of the typewriter and read it over to himself.

"Who you writing to?" I asked. "Your publisher or your bank?"

"A fellow author."

"Another mystery writer? There a lot of you guys around?"

"Yeah," he said. "Too many. The guy I'm writing to accused me of looking down on the mystery novel. He thinks I'm a frustrated novelist."

"Are you?" I asked. "Not that it would mean much to me if you were..."

"You want to hear what I said?"

I shrugged. "Not particularly."

"I'll read it to you anyway." He cleared his throat and then let fly. "'It's possible that had I been a little younger when I started to write fiction, had I been a better observer and a better remem-berer, I might have made a reputation as a straight novelist. It never occurred to me to try. I thought I was extremely lucky to get as far as I did in our field, and believe me when I say lucky I am not talking to the birds. Talent is never enough. The history of literature is strewn with the corpses of writers who through no fault of their own missed out on the timing or were just a little too far ahead of their generation. An old and wise friend of mine once said the world never hears of its greatest men; the men it calls great are just enough ahead of the average to stand out, but not far enough ahead to be remote.'"

He put down the paper. "Well, what do you think?" he asked.

"I think you wanted to be a novelist and didn't have the guts to try," I said.

He pointed his finger at me. "That's my whisky you're drinking, Marlow! Need I remind you?"

"You want me to put it back?" I asked.

"I didn't finish," he said, picking the letter back up and searching for the place where he left off. "I went on to say: 'I believe there is a peculiar kind of satisfaction in taking a type of literature which the pundits regard as below the salt and making of it something which the fair-minded among them are forced to treat with a little respect. You must never admit to yourself that the kind of writing you and I do is by definition inferior. It is as good as the man who writes it and the record proves it will outlast 99.44 percent of the touted best sellers.'"

He put down the paper again and looked at me. I think he expected a response.

"Well," I said, "you convinced me."

"Convinced you of what?"

"Whatever you were trying to convince me of."

"Come on, Marlow!" He was beginning to show his dander. I know these old codgers. I was thinking of prescribing a laxative. Constipation is usually the main cause of their distress.

"Why don't you read it to Miss Wheetly?" I asked. "I'm sure she'd understand."

"I don't want to get into that kind of discussion with her, Marlow," he said, coming over and pouring himself a drink. "She's far too young."

"You don't want her to know what a cynical old goat you are, is that it, Ray?"

Suddenly he stiffened up. "I didn't give you permission to talk to me that way," he said.

"Listen," I said, putting down my glass and walking to the door, "I called you up because I thought you might like to join me for a drink. I don't mind a chat, but I don't want to listen to you moan!"

I opened up the door.

"Wait a second, Marlow," he said. It was his tone of voice that made me turn around. Maybe it's because I never heard an old guy cry. Sure, I've heard them cry in pain. But this was a different kind. It was a cry that came straight from the heart.

I looked at him and it suddenly occurred to me that I had hurt him more than I had meant. Not that I had meant to hurt the guy at all. I just can't stand to hear people moan. Not after all that I had seen. I felt people like Ray just don't have the right. They were dealt some damn good hands when you look at all the poker games around. But maybe I was wrong. I've been wrong before.

"Look, Ray," I said. "Maybe I was too hard."

He took out his pipe and, with his free hand, searched for some tobacco in the pocket of his robe. "You were wrong about me not having any guts," he said. "It's not easy to live by your wits no matter what you choose to do. No one in this world owed me a dime and I never owed it to them. I was lucky. I had a wife who understood. Some people don't. They're the ones who have it hard."

"Maybe I had you wrong. Maybe I was talking to myself."

"But you were right about not wanting to listen to me moan. Sometimes I can be a God damned fool!"

"We all can, Ray," I said.

"I'll tell you something, Marlow," he said, lighting up his pipe, "and then we'll let it drop. Two months ago I thought my life was over. My wife, my precious Cissy, had just died. I had written all that I had wanted to write. And what I had written was all dedicated to her. I decided nothing more was left. So I shot myself."

"You're not too good a shot, I guess."

74

"That's right, Marlow. I missed."

He lit his pipe and stared at me. He disappeared behind a haze of smoke.

"I'll catch you later for a drink," I said. And then I left.

I walked back down the corridor to my room. I went inside and poured myself a drink. If you have to drink alone, you might as well do it in good company. I stared into the mirror and lifted up my glass. "Cheers," I said. "Here's mud in you eye!" My image stared back at me. The phone began to ring. I went over and stuffed it in the drawer.

Chapter 10

I wandered down to the restaurant when dinner-time came round. Ray was right about something, I thought. There was nothing much to do on this tub except to drink and eat.

They were there already, the whole crew of them. Like me, they hadn't waited for a second call.

Rinexus was mad. I could tell that from his face which looked like cucumber - the kind that was pickled. He was waving a piece of paper at Ray as if it were a fan.

"You know anything about this, Chandler?" he said, with a hiss that would have done a leaky steam pipe proud.

Ray took the paper, read it and then handed it to me. It looked like one of those notes a kidnapper might send. The letters were pasted onto a white sheet of paper and had been cut from magazines. It said: "Beware! Someone on this ship is going to die!"

"What is it?" asked Monica Wheetly, trying to look over my shoulder without falling off her chair. I handed it on to her. She read it and said, "Oh, good! A parlour game!"

"May I see?" asked Solly Meyers. She handed it on to him. He shook his head. "It's like a child playing with a loaded gun," he said. "No one should write things like that unless they mean it!"

"Maybe they do," said Roger Lane, reading the paper that had been handed on to him and then passing it to his wife.

Amanda, put her fingers to her face. "Oh, this is dreadful!" she said.

Rinexus held out his meaty hand. "Give it back to me," he demanded.

"How did you come by that quaint collage?" asked Ray. He had taken out his pipe and was fingering it.

"You tell me," said Rinexus. "You're the detective writer - at least that's what your press releases say."

"You've got it wrong," said Ray, who had stopped playing with his pipe and had picked up the menu instead. "If you ever read my books, you'd know how I detest these sort of games."

"Then who'd put something like this under my cabin door?" Rinexus persisted.

Ray put down his menu and gave him one of his iceberg stares. "If you're asking me to guess, Mr Rinexus, I'd say you put it there yourself."

"Me?" He seemed astounded at the idea, even though it probably made sense. "Why the hell would I send an idiotic note like that to myself?"

"Because you probably are on expense account and you promised your scandal sheet a juicy story from the trip."

"And you think I'd stoop that low?" asked Rinexus, starting to steam again.

"Oh, I think you'd stoop much lower than that," said Ray. "In itself the note's not much. A good scandal needs a victim. I have every confidence you'll soon provide one for us."

"I'm sure Mr Rinexus wouldn't do such a thing!" said Amanda Lane, looking truly horrified.

"Well, if he didn't do it, which one of us did?" asked Monica Wheetly. She was definitely getting into the spirit.

"Maybe none of us," said Roger Lane.

"Someone did," said Rinexus, waving his flag again.

"Yes," said Roger Lane. "But that someone doesn't have to be sitting here." He motioned to the Captain's table. The Captain was missing this evening. In his absence, the Ambassador was holding court. Gloria Morgan was there, seated next to the Ambassador's wife. She seemed tired. Maybe she was feeling her age. On the other side of the table, the Argentine had a worried look. He smiled every now and then, but his smile seemed very pale.

"Perhaps you should show your note to someone in authority," said Amanda Lane.

"And make a dummy out of myself?" asked Rinexus. He let out a laugh. "If you want to show it around, be my guest. Just don't get me involved."

"Mr Rinexus is perfectly correct," said Solly Meyers. "Forget about the note. Someone is either being very foolish or else they are being very stupid. In either case, the best thing to do is to ignore it."

"But we have to do something!" Monica Wheetly protested. "If it's a game, I'd like to play. If it's not, we can't just sit here and let it happen."

"Let what happen?" asked Ray. "The note said, 'Someone on this ship is going to die.' In fact, we're all going to die. The only question is where and when. And the note isn't very specific about that."

"Which means it's all nonsense," said Solly Meyers.

"So it is a game!" Monica Wheetly clapped her hands.

"You want to play a game?" asked Rinexus. He wadded up the note and threw it in the center of the table. "Go ahead and play!" Then he got up, out of his chair. "But leave me out of it!" he shouted as he stomped off.

"That guy must be pretty angry," I said, "if he doesn't want to eat his dinner."

Ray rubbed his chin and then took out his pipe again. He thought a moment and then he said, "Maybe this is more interesting than we think."

*****

I didn't meet Ray for an after-dinner drink. I don't know where he went. I had a few at the Veranda Bar and then tried the game of finding my way back.

The mackerel had been right, I guess. The night was brewing up a storm. It started slow, like a Stravinski dance. Just a few drops at first and then a few more. Then a little harder. Within moments, the sheets of rain came down in gusts, pelting against the porthole window in an angry torrent sweeping the silence away as if it were a messenger of a ferocious god from one of Ray's classic would-be novels.

I tried riding out the storm in bed. It wasn't easy. Someone very big was intent on rocking the boat. I tried to hold it down. But that's always a mistake. Whenever a patient of mine asked, my advice was always, "Let it flow."

I did.

It felt better. I took a shower. Then I shaved. I was just putting on my clothes when I heard a knock at the door.

"Come in!" I called out. There was no answer. "Come in!" I shouted out again.

I went over to the door and opened up. It was Ray. He was sopping wet. He looked like the dog that was thrown in the lake. Water dripped from the top of his nose to the tip of his tail.

"What's up?" I asked.

He walked in. He didn't say a word.

I went into the bathroom again and got a towel. I came back out and threw it to him. He took off his specs and wiped his face.

"I'm surprised you could see with all that water on your windscreens," I said.

"Did she call you?" he asked.

"Who?" I replied. Ray was shivering like the last leaf of Autumn clinging to its branch.

I poured out some bourbon and brought it over to him. He drank it down. "Thanks," he said.

He reached into his pocket and brought out his pipe. He stared down at it and said, "Damn thing's wet!"

"It'll dry out," I assured him.

He stuffed in some tobacco from his pouch. Then he looked up at me. "Gloria Morgan phoned me about an hour ago," he said.

"She ask you to take her for a swim?"

"She said she needed help. She sounded groggy, like she had been asleep."

I poured a drink for myself. "You went to her room?" I asked.

Ray lit his pipe. It steamed for a minute and then went out. "I knocked," he said, "but there wasn't any answer. I shouted out. I thought maybe she went back to sleep. Then that Argentine, Mendez, opened up his door. His cabin's right down the hall from hers. He said he saw her just a while before. She had a cigarette stuck in her mouth. Asked him for a light. Her eyes were glazed - like she was in a trance. He says he lit her up and she walked on."

"So you went on a hunt?" I asked.

He nodded. "I saw that Lane woman - what's her name?"

"Amanda," I said.

"She thought she'd seen Gloria out on deck."

"In that storm?" I asked.

"Maybe with a man But it was hard to see in all that rain. She went with me to search."

"You didn't find her, I suppose."

Ray shook his head. That wasn't all that shook.

"You should get into some dry clothes, Ray. I've heard your cough. It ain't that nice to get pneumonia."

"She's in trouble, Marlow," he said. And then he dissolved into a series of ugly coughs. When he got himself back together he said, "You have to help me find her."

"Go back to your cabin and change your clothes," I said. "I'll meet you down at her room."

"You've been there before, haven't you?" he said, looking into my eyes. His were red and watery.

"Yeah," I said. "And so have you."

Chapter 11

Gloria Morgan's door was unlocked. I pushed it open and walked in. Her bed was mussed. Someone hadn't slept very well, or else that someone had a fight with demons while she was asleep. The leopard's spots lay crumpled on a chair. The bunny shoes were upside down. The wardrobe was wide open. Some empty hangers had been strewn across the floor. If she went out, she had dressed for the occasion.

I looked over at the bedside table. The prescription container was still there. The cotton was pulled out. I picked up the bottle. It was empty. So was the glass of water by its side. I bent down and examined the floor. I found one pill that had dropped. I searched again but I couldn't find any more.

"You have any trouble getting in?" I looked up. It was Ray.

"Her door was closed - it wasn't locked," I said. I pointed to the empty bottle. "That thing was full when I was here the other night. If she popped all of them, your lady friend's in trouble."

"How long would she have?" asked Ray.

"Depends on how many she swallowed if she swallowed them. And if she swallowed them it depends on how many she kept down."

"You check the bathroom yet?" he asked.

"Not yet," I said. He led the way. I followed.

It was an elaborate bath with expensive panelling on the walls. Some people down below in closet rooms wouldn't have minded sleeping in this space, I thought. "The toilet's clean," I said, lifting up the lid.

"So I would expect," said Ray.

"She could have flushed them down the drain," I said.

"Why would she do that?" he asked.

"Don't ask me," I replied. "Gloria Morgan's your friend, not mine."

"We better call the Captain," said Ray, going over to the phone.

"Let's phone the CMO first," I suggested.

"Who's the CMO?" asked Ray.

"The Chief Medical Officer. His name's Hart. If she were sick or someone found her, he'd know about it."

I took the telephone from Ray's hands and asked the operator at the switchboard to put me through to surgery. Hart came on the line. I told him what I knew.

"You're in her room now?" he asked.

"Yeah," I said. "With Mr Chandler - Ray."

"I'll come right up. Stay there."

"I wasn't planning on running away," I said.

There wasn't anyplace to run. Gloria Morgan probably knew that too. Even on a ship as big a this, there's not much room to hide.

*****

CMO Hart took a quick look around and then said, "You got those pills? I'd like to see..."

I pointed to the bottle on the table. He took it and inspected the label. He gave the bottle a sniff. "None left?" he asked.

"I found one on the floor." I handed Hart the little white pill. He snapped off a tiny piece and ground it between his finger and his thumb. He tasted it and made a face.

"Funny thing," said Hart. "We just lost a bottle of this stuff today."

"Lost?" I said. "I thought you told me all your drugs are under lock and key."

"It was missing from the inventory. When I asked Carter, my pharmacist - I think you met him, right?"

I nodded. "Yeah. He's got a face to stop a clock."

"That's Carter," said Hart, shaking his head. "Boy, what I have to put up with!"

"You were saying," Ray prompted while lighting up his pipe. "You asked Carter and..."

"He said he dropped it. He made me out a spillage form."

"What happened to the pills?" asked Ray.

"This was a liquid suspension for injections. Same barbiturate though."

"And your man Carter says it was dropped. Today?" Ray asked.

"Last night," said Hart. He scratched his head. "You shouldn't make too much of it. After all, we're working on a ship. Things like this happen all the time."

"Did Miss Morgan call into sickbay yesterday or today?" I asked.

"Not that I know of," said Hart. "We can check with the nurses though." He looked around the room again. "You sure she's missing? I mean, it's not unusual for passengers like her to..."

"To what?" asked Ray. "I really wish you'd complete your sentences."

"Well, to camp out in another room," said Hart giving him a knowing wink.

"The problem is that she'd be camping pretty high," I said, pointing to the empty pill bottle.

Hart shrugged. "Who's to say how many pills she took?"

"The bottle was nearly full last night," I said.

"How do you know that?" he asked.

"I was called down here by your little messenger who wears the pill box hat. He said Miss Morgan wanted to see me."

"Professionally or otherwise?" asked Hart, narrowing his eyes till they became nothing more than slits.

"That wasn't clear to me either," I said. "She was pretty down at the mouth. But so was I."

"You should have contacted me, Marlow," said Hart. He made it sound like a reprimand. Maybe that's what it was.

"Why? You want to know of every passenger who feels blue?"

"Yes. When they're blue enough to want to see a doctor," he said. "Was she drugged?"

"It's hard to say. Her eyes were dilated but she was alert. I felt her pulse. It was strong. I checked the prescription on the bottle. It seemed OK. Nothing out of the ordinary."

"Except she's gone and the pill bottle is empty," said Hart. He made a sound like a balloon letting out its air. "I guess we'll have to call the Captain. But there's not much we can do except wait for her to turn up."

"Or not," said I.

"He can start organizing a search," said Ray.

"In this weather? At night?" asked Hart. "Not much chance of that."

"She might have passed out on deck," said Ray. "She might be sleeping in a lifeboat."

"She might be in a ventilation shaft," said Hart. "There's a million and one places she can be if she's not at the bottom of the ocean or in someone else's bunk."

"One thing's for certain," said Ray, chewing down on the stem of his pipe. "We're not going to find her in here with our fingers up our snouts!"

*****

The Captain was notified and a search was begun. Late at night, in the torrential rain, the tarpaulins were removed from the life boats and men with torches climbed inside, inspecting every nook and cranny for a sleeping Movie Queen. Others checked behind the shafts and towing lines and winches - anyplace a body could lie quietly, unobserved.

I went with Ray to check the Boat Deck where Amanda Lane said she had seen Gloria Morgan in the company of a mysterious stranger an hour or so before our search began. The gale force wind was whipping the canvass that had been lashed over the cargo hold, rending it from its ties so that the terrible flapping, the relentless sound of its beat, made it seem like the tattered sail of a forgotten ship condemned to the merciless sea.

It was all I could do to cling to a lanyard and hope I wouldn't be blown away. I turned to look for Ray and damned if he wasn't standing there flush to the wind, trying to light his pipe in the rain!

"Marlow!" he shouted into the gale. "Look here!"

His thin grey hair was matted to his face, plastered down by the terrible wind. He pointed with the stem of his pipe toward the rail. Even with the ship's lights blazing down from above, it was hard to see anything through the storm.

I moved toward the edge, gripping onto the lanyard, till I got close enough to notice what he was shouting about. It was so tiny, so delicate, clinging to the rail like an orchid in a hurricane.

"Marlow, can you get it?" he yelled.

His words were swept out to sea. I didn't want to follow them.

"It's knotted to the rail," I shouted back. "It ain't going anywhere!"

"You have to get it, Marlow! It's important!" His soaking body shivered.

"You want me to risk my life for that?" I shouted back to him.

"Your life's not worth a plugged nickel, Marlow and you know it! You get that goddamned thing or I'll never use you as a hero again!"

"I don't know what the hell you're talking about, Ray!" I yelled.

But, somehow, I reached out and grabbed the thing. I don't know why or how.

Chapter 12

He was drenched. So was I. But I was thirty years younger. When someone like Ray, whose tank is usually topped with high grade alcohol, gets a chill, it could easily lead to bronchial disease. I know. I'm a doctor.

Now me, I take good care of myself. I always brush my teeth after meals and make sure I wear warm shoes. Maybe I drink a little too much, but I also take high potency vitamin pills. Too much alcohol kills vitamins, you see. So I just put some back. And when I kill those off, I put back some more. That way I never get so much as a cold.

I made him take a hot shower and lie down in bed. Then I went back to my cabin and changed my clothes as well. Two nights out at sea and I was already nearing the bottom of my case. Luckily there was a bar aboard.

Ray was sitting up in bed when I got back to 131. He was as white as one of those starched sheets down in the dining hall.

"What's wrong?" I asked. "You want a drink?"

"She's dead, Marlow," he said. His voice was weak.

"We don't know that for sure yet, Ray," I said.

I don't think he heard me. Anyway, he didn't act as if he did. "She's dead," he said again. "I couldn't save her."

I saw the liquor bottle atop the table near the sink. I saw a glass. I went and poured myself a drink. I drank it down and wiped the glass. Then I poured another and brought it back to him.

"Here," I said. "This one's for you."

He shook his head. "I'm on the wagon for a while," he said.

"Since when?"

"Since now."

I shrugged and drank his down as well.

He held the tattered scarf I'd retrieved in his hand. He had put it to his face and rubbed it up against the grizzle of his chin. "It's silk," he said, looking at me with child-like eyes, even though his were raw and red. "Pure silk."

"We're travelling first class," I reminded him.

"It's hers," he said.

"How do you know?" I asked. "Did you buy it for her?"

"I've never seen it before, but it's hers all right." He sounded pretty definite about it. "She's dead," he said again.

"Maybe not. They're still looking. She might be in somebody's room."

"What about the note?" said Ray.

"That's someone's little joke," I replied.

"Whose?" he asked.

"Maybe even Gloria Morgan's," I said.

"That's the way you ask for help," said Ray. "I know."

"Maybe she wasn't asking for help. Maybe it was someone else."

He glared at me with all the fire he could muster in the coldness of his frame. "She's dead, Marlow! Can't you get it through your thick head? The woman's dead! And we're to blame!"

"You're only to blame when you accept responsibility," I said. "I accept responsibility for no one anymore."

He sat up in bed. "You're a coward, Marlow. A crummy, insignificant coward." He said it not in anger, but regret.

I laughed. It was the only response there was to this defeated man, lying prostrate on his bed. "Maybe I am, Ray," I said, "but does it really make much difference anymore?"

A tear trickled down from his eye - the left one, I think. It was a real tear. It wasn't fake. But at that point, I couldn't have cared less.

"Leave me alone, Marlow," he said. "Go away."

"Sure," I said. I walked to the door. I turned around. He was silently staring at the wall. "See you, Ray," I said. "Have a good night. I'll give you a call."

Chapter 13

There's nothing like someone's death to give a ship a buzz; even if the death's suspected. If you want to give it a real zing, then have the victim be a movie star.

The storm had quieted over the night. The slop buckets had been taken back in to wash. The violent rocks and rolls had ceased. People filed down to the restaurant to replace what had erupted from their stomachs the evening before.

I got there late. They were gobbling away by the time I had come. All except Ray, that is. His seat was vacant. Well, maybe not. Like the ghost that filled the empty chair at the Captain's table, Ray was there in spirit. He always was.

"Did you hear?" asked Monica Wheetly, wide-eyed and bushy-tailed, like a chipmunk gathering its nuts, "Gloria Morgan is missing!"

If she expected a response, she was disappointed. I picked up my menu and said, "Is that all there is to eat?"

"Twenty-five versions of cooking an egg ain't enough for you?" asked Rinexus.

"I was hoping for flapjacks and jam," I said.

"This is your first breakfast with us, isn't it Dr Marlow?" asked Solly Meyers. "They do have lox. But they call it smoked salmon. Unfortunately, it isn't the same."

"It rarely is," I said.

"Is Mr Chandler all right?" asked Amanda Lane, looking concerned in a maternal way. "I know he got very wet and a man of his age needs to take precautions."

"Mr Chandler is resting in bed," I said. "Mr Chandler is pondering whether there is life after death or after Old Forester. It amounts to the same thing."

The waiter came by and I ordered poached eggs on toast. I hate poached eggs, but that's what the morning felt like to me.

"They look pretty glum over there," said Roger Lane, motioning to the north side of town.

"Do you really think she's dead?" asked Monica Wheetly in a hushed voice. She was determined to get the conversation rolling one way or another.

Rinexus waved his arms. "Dead? That broad? She's got more lives than a Cheshire cat!"

"There was that note," said Amanda Lane, somewhat hesitantly.

"Can't you people see when you're being set up for a publicity stunt?" Rinexus let out a winded laugh, like a bag-pipe without quite enough air.

"Perhaps I'm being a little naive," said Roger Lane, "but what's the stunt? How can falling off the side of a ship in the middle of a storm be strictly for publicity?"

"Who says she fell off the ship?" said Rinexus.

"Where is she then?" asked Monica Wheetly, as if she truly expected Rinexus to give some special secret away.

"Probably shacking up with the bo'sun if I know her," he said with the lecherous look of a reporter for a movie magazine.

"Do you know her?" I asked, looking Rinexus in the face. It didn't make my eggs taste any better.

"What's that supposed to mean?" he tried to growl. It came out as more of a snort. But it was still morning, after all.

I shrugged. "It means whatever you want it to mean."

"I meant I know her type," said Rinexus.

"Then what were you doing in her room the other night?" asked Roger Lane. He smiled. "I don't mean to pry, but I happened to be passing by her door. Her cabin's right down from mine."

"What time was that?" I asked.

"A little past midnight, wasn't it?" said Roger Lane, looking at Rinexus for confirmation.

Rinexus ground his teeth. "So? I was asking for an interview."

"Reporters keep late hours, I suppose," said Solly Meyers, eating his lox on a piece of toast and looking as if something was terribly wrong. "Just like movie stars."

"Any luck?" asked Roger Lane, still with a grin.

"None of your beeswax," said Rinexus.

"I guess you got your story then," I said.

"What story?" he asked, flinging his arms in the air again. Maybe he was used to flying kites. "'Has - Been Actress Jumps In Ocean?'"

"Gloria Morgan still makes news," said Roger Lane. "Did you see all the press flocking around her before we sailed?"

"Ah, those guys got nothing better to do than go down to the dock and see a ship off. They'd interview a tuna if it got them out of the office long enough to get a drink."

"But she was a star!" said Monica Wheetly. "Or is..."

"Stars come and go, kid," Rinexus said to her. "Look up in the sky tonight and see how many you remember."

"On the other hand," said Solly Meyers, still contemplating his fishy toast, "you thought enough of her to make a midnight rendez-vous."

"You gotta keep busy, don't you," said Rinexus digging into the eggs benedict the waiter had just put before him. "Idle hands makes Jack a dull boy - or something like that."

"I think the phrase is 'Devil's plaything', Mr Rinexus," said Amanda Lane.

"Whatever," said Rinexus, wiping some egg off his face with his personal towel. "I didn't kill her and she ain't dead."

"But nobody accused you of killing her, Mr Rinexus," said Monica Wheetly.

"You would if you could," said Rinexus. "I'm smart and I'm tough. I'm a hard nosed survivor in a word that don't give a shit about people if they ain't got a nickel or a lousy dime."

"That's exactly why no one would accuse you of killing Miss Morgan, if, indeed, she's dead," said Solly Meyers. "People who have to tell everyone how tough they are, usually aren't."

"At least I'm not a marshmallow, pops," he said, sticking a toothpick in his mouth and getting up from the table. "Maybe I'll order a suit from you some day if you learn to keep your nose clean. I know it's a big job with a shnozz like yours!"

"What a nasty person he is!" said Monica Wheetly watching Rinexus walking away.

"No more nasty than anyone else in his line of work," I said. "Every profession brings its own demands. It probably took him years and years to perfect being a donkey's ass."

I noticed that Rinexus had made a detour by the Captain's table on his way out. There he had stopped to say a few words into the ear of the Argentine who was sitting next to one of the Ambassador's monkeymen. The Argentine stared at him and then nodded and Rinexus went on his merry way.

Monica Wheetly looked down at her plate. "I do hope she's OK," she said. I assumed she was speaking about Gloria Morgan. Though she might have been referring to the kipper in her dish that she had barely touched. If it was the kipper that concerned her, I could definitely assure her that it was dead. Gloria Morgan was a fish of an altogether different kettle.

"I hope so, too," said Amanda Lane, looking at the college girl with some sympathy. "But I suspect the worst. That was a terrible storm last night. No one should have been out on deck, especially..." Her voice trailed off. This time it was the husband who put his hand on hers.

"Especially what?" I asked.

She hesitated. "I was going to say that she didn't look that well."

"You could tell that from a distance?" I asked. "It usually takes some careful observation for me to diagnose that sort of thing."

"It was the way she walked," said Amanda Lane.

"How did she walk?" I asked. "This is a ship, you know. It was the middle of a storm. I have trouble putting one foot before the next. She was lucky she could walk at all."

"That's just the point," said Amanda Lane with some justifiable frustration. "It was very hard to keep one's balance. Anyone foolish enough to go out on deck in conditions like that could easily have fallen overboard."

"But you went out on deck," I reminded her. "So did Ray. So did I, in fact."

"Why are you badgering my wife, Dr Marlow?" asked Roger Lane, angrily. I suppose he was right. What the hell did I care, anyway?

"Dr Marlow is a rational man, dearest," Amanda Lane said to her husband. "Any man of science wishes to find out reasons for the unexplained. Am I not right, Dr Marlow?" She smiled kindly at me.

"I don't know who ever told you that MDs were either rational or men of science. If anything they're more like priests," I said.

"Not the Jewish ones," said Solly Meyers. "They're more like rabbis."

"But isn't anyone here interested in finding out the truth?" asked Monica Wheetly, in a voice filled to the brim with youthful anxiety. Maybe it was another question in her philosophy class.

"Of course we are, dear," said Amanda Lane. "But sometimes the truth isn't that simple. Is it, Dr Marlow?"

"Any truth I know is in a bottle," I said. "I don't know whether that's simple or not."

"Of course," said Roger Lane, "doctors are used to prescribing drugs for anything. If the world is about to go up in flames, why not prescribe a pill?"

"Sounds good to me," I said. "What would you prescribe?"

"A little sanity, I suppose," said Lane getting up from his chair.

"You can find that in a bottle, too," I replied.

*****

The wind was still gusting outside, but it wasn't a howl. Compared to last night, it wasn't even a breeze. But it was blowing enough to muss up Monica Wheetly's hair. She took a scarf out of her pocket to tie down her mop.

"Good thing you don't go in for permanent waves," I said.

She turned. She looked surprised. "Oh, Dr Marlow, you startled me!"

"You think I was a shark?" I asked.

She knotted the scarf underneath her chin. "I lost one of these the other day," she said. "The wind swept it out of my hand just as I was tying it on."

"Good thing you buy your scarves in pairs," I said.

"Yes." She smiled weakly and looked out at the blackening waves. "How horrible to think of someone being swept overboard and falling into that..." She motioned toward the endless sea. Then she looked back at me. "What happens to them, do you suppose?"

"I suppose they drown, Miss Wheetly," I said.

"But do they try to swim or do they just sink to the bottom like a stone?"

"If they try to swim in weather like last night, they don't swim very far. They'd be flushed straight under by the waves. They'd swallow a gallon of water and then they'd try to breathe. When they did that their lungs would burst."

"Oh my God!" she said. Her eyes looked like a set of giant 'O's. "Would their lungs really burst, Dr Marlow?"

"Try filling a balloon with salt water and see what happens," I said.

She shook her head. "No. I believe you." She looked out to sea again. "It's so dreadful! I can hardly comprehend anyone being swallowed up in that murky brine."

"It's no worse than any other way to go," I said.

"Oh, yes," she insisted. "It's far worse. It's so cold, so lonely..."

"Death isn't so hot, even on a warm beach in Acapulco," I said.

"So you think she fell in, too, do you, Dr Marlow?" She could be so sweet sometimes.

"I didn't say that."

"But that's what you think, isn't it?"

"What I think doesn't really matter, Miss Wheetly," I said.

"But if she didn't fall in, then what happened to her?"

"Maybe she decided to shovel some coal in the boiler room and fell asleep," I suggested.

"You don't think that," she smiled.

"No, I don't think that."

"People don't just disappear, though, Dr Marlow," she insisted.

"Sometimes people do disappear" I said.

"Just like that?" she asked.

"Yes," I said. "Just like that."

93

Chapter 14

Ray didn't make it down for lunch. Rinexus didn't too. Neither did the big boys at the Captain's table. The Ambassador's wife was sitting there lonely and regal. Like an elderly Queen who had long ago lost her throne.

The chit-chat was about the search which still went on. A team had been set up, under the direction of the First Officer, to lead the investigation. The Lanes had been interviewed, they said. So had all the others on their deck. According to Amanda Lane, they seemed under pressure to issue a report. Maybe the company was nipping at their heels. Losing a famous movie star at sea is not that good for business, I suspect.

"I'm worried about Ray," Monica Wheetly whispered in my ear. I had come down late and now everyone was gone. Everyone, that is, except her. I don't know what she was whispering for. There was nobody around to hear.

"I'm sure he'd appreciate the thought," I said.

"Have you seen him since last night?" she asked.

I shook my head.

"I tried calling his room," she said. "There was no reply."

"Maybe he doesn't want to be disturbed," I suggested.

"Aren't you concerned?" she asked.

"About what?"

"That perhaps he's missing too!"

"Miss Wheetly," I replied, "Ray's the kind of guy who's done pretty well taking care of his affairs for over sixty years. Right now, I suspect he's feeling sorry for himself. I wouldn't want to intrude."

She stiffened her pose in a girlish and self-righteous way. "Didn't you take an oath or something when you became a doctor?"

I looked up from my coffee. "Real life doesn't work the same as the girl scouts, Miss Wheetly," I replied. "You might help an old man across a street, but if he doesn't want to be on the other side you're not doing him any favors."

"I'm not talking about crossing streets, Dr Marlow," she shot back. "I'm talking about an elderly man whose health might be endangered."

"That's why there's a sick bay on this ship," I said, finishing up my coffee and getting up to go. "If he wanted them, he'd call."

*****

Don't ask me why I went down there. Analysing stupidity isn't exactly my game. Maybe I just wanted to make sure the Wheetly kid wasn't right. Not that bit about the oath. Oaths are set up by bureaucrats to keep the rest of us in line. I wasn't interested in the question of morals, not after all I'd seen. But she had posed a question of a different kind. Not about reason or philosophy - I'm not interested in that crap, or any other half-baked excuse to put my head out on the chopping block again. It was something unexplained. Maybe I went down simply to make sure that he was there. That it wasn't as Miss Wheetly said - "Perhaps he's missing too..."

The only problem was I didn't come alone.

"So, Dr Marlow, you're not that insensitive after all!"

I turned around and saw her smiling face. I felt a pain in my stomach at the same time.

"I left my toothbrush in here the other night," I said. "I need it back."

"I know you, Dr Marlow. You're not as bad as you make yourself out to be."

"Badness is in the mind of the beholder," I said. "If I steal your wallet, it might be bad for you. Then, again, it might be good for me."

She grinned. I think she thought I was kidding. She knocked on the door. There was no response. She knocked again.

I was about to say that maybe we should take the hint and leave when a voice from inside bellowed out, "Who is it!"

Her eyes lit up. "It's me, Ray!" she called out. "And Dr

95

Marlow. Can we come in?"

There was silence. I was ready to turn around and go when, suddenly, the door jerked open. And there was Ray. His face was flushed. His eyes were blazing. His pipe was pouring out steam like an engine chugging up a heafty run.

"Come in! Come in!" He nearly dragged us inside. "I was just about to call you on the phone!"

The place was a mess. Papers scattered everywhere. Some were cut out, some pasted together. There were diagrams and drawings which might have meant something to him, but appeared to be a bunch of squiggly lines.

"Find yourself a chair!" he said. "Sit down! Marlow, pour yourself a drink! Monica, there's no gingerale, but we can order some."

I just had water. It's OK to drink alone. But to drink with two others who ain't can only lead to misery.

"We don't really want to intrude, Ray," said Monica Wheetly, "but Dr Marlow and I were becoming a little concerned."

Ray puffed at his pipe and gave me one of his stares.

I shrugged.

He looked back at her and said, "You needn't have concerned yourself about my well being. Dr Marlow here will tell you that I get stronger as I advance in years. Even bullets can't harm me anymore."

I glanced at all the papers again. "Looks interesting, Ray. You designing another ark?"

He started gathering up the mess. "Marlow," he said, "I decided something last night. I decided that I've been put in an intolerable position. A position so heinous that it rankles me to even think about the implications."

"Sounds like a pretty bad position," I said.

"What position are you in?" asked Monica Wheetly. "If you don't mind me intruding. I mean if this is personal, between the two of you, just tell me. I'd be happy to leave."

She said it, but we both knew she wouldn't.

"That's all right, Monica," he replied, "you can stay. We might need your help."

She grinned just like a pussycat that's been given an unexpected stroke.

He shook his pipe at me. "Do you realise, Marlow? I'm being forced to solve a puzzle like one of those that Christie woman would set up?"

"Someone holding a gun to your head, Ray?" I asked.

"Of course no one's holding a gun to my head!" he snapped. "But I know damn well that someone's trying to manipulate me!"

"That's terrible!" said Monica Wheetly. "What are you going to do about it?"

"There's nothing I can do about it!" he shouted. "I've already been manipulated! The puzzle's been set up. The crime has been committed. I can't ignore it. It's happened. And I'm here."

Then he grinned. A little slyly, I thought. "So let's get to work!"

I guess that's what it took to put a sparkle in his eye. The guy looked ten years younger and twice as spry.

"You mean we're going to solve the case of the disappearing movie star!" asked Monica Wheetly. "And you want me to help?" She said it as if she were being offered joint partnership in a detective agency.

"Well," I said, standing up to go. "I'll leave you to it then..."

He pointed at me with the stem of his pipe. "Marlow! Sit down!"

It takes a lot to startle me. Frankly, I was startled.

I think he realised he went too far. He looked a little shocked himself. "Please - as a favor."

"Ray," I said, "I'm in no mood to play your games."

"No games," he said, "I promise. Pour yourself a drink. As many as you want. I won't ask you for a thing."

"Then what do you want me here for?" I asked.

He smiled. "I just like having you around."

Please stay, Dr Marlow," said Monica Wheetly. "At least you could hear what he has to say."

"Besides," said Ray, "I may need medical advice." His eyes lit up even more.

The alternative was staring out at sea at midnight in the dark,

I thought to myself. So I poured myself a drink - whisky this time, the water tasted off - and sat back down. And Ray began his show.

"The situation, ladies and gentlemen, is this: we have a missing woman. Not an ordinary woman, mind you, but a movie star. She may have taken too many pills. She may have fallen off the ship. She may even have been murdered..."

"Oh, my!" said Monica Wheetly, plugging up her fly trap with her extra hand. "I forgot about that!"

Ray gave her the schoolmasterly look. "I emphasise the word 'may', my dear, because that's what someone wishes us to believe."

"You mean the note," I said.

"Precisely!"

"But the note didn't say anything about murder!" said Monica Wheetly. "It just said someone might die!"

"Think about it, my dear," said Ray. "Why would someone write a note like that?"

"To scare us?" she asked. Then, remembering back to yesterday, she said, "I thought it was a game!"

"A note like that is written only because someone wants us to believe a murder will be committed. It's a warning. Why else would we suspect Miss Morgan's death - if she is dead - had any sinister overtones, if not for the note! And if she isn't dead, then someone wants us to suspect it none the less."

Monica Wheetly wasn't satisfied. She rarely was. "But why? If someone knew that Miss Morgan was going to be..." she hesitated and then said, "...bumped off, why wouldn't they tell her or the authorities? Why put a note under Mr Rinexus's door? I mean if I wanted to warn someone of something I certainly wouldn't give the note to him!"

"Aha!" said Ray, gesticulating with his pipe and accidentally spewing ashes on his bed. He looked at me. "Tell her Marlow!"

"I think I'll wait till the fire department arrives," I said, pointing to the smoking mattress caused by the burning embers.

Ray took a pitcher of water from the table and nonchalantly dumped it on his quilt.

Monica Wheetly, who clearly hadn't seen the pyrotechnics,

stared in amazement. She was probably too polite to ask Ray why he had just tossed a pitcher of water onto his bed.

"Don't worry, my dear, the maid will clean it up," he assured her.

"Yes," said Monica Wheetly. "I'm sure she will."

Monica Wheetly was probably used to maids who cleaned up her messes. I didn't know who cleaned up Ray's. Not then, at least.

"Anyway," Ray continued, "if Marlow refuses to impart his wisdom today - take another drink, Marlow; maybe it will loosen you up - I'll answer you myself. The note was written to make us believe a murder was committed because it's in the interest of the writer of the note to have us believe a murder has been committed. It was passed on to Rinexus because he is someone who spreads gossip the way a farmer spreads manure before he plants his crops. In this case someone wanted to plant an idea. Rinexus was used to spread the manure, but he's not the farmer."

"Does that mean Miss Morgan isn't dead?" asked Monica Wheetly.

"She may be dead. She may not be dead. That is entirely irrelevant."

"Not to Miss Morgan," I said.

"Ah, Marlow!" he said, turning to me. "I was hoping you'd join us!"

"But Dr Marlow is right," said Monica Wheetly. "I don't care about the note. I care about Miss Morgan."

I hated to take the wind out of her sails, but I didn't particularly care about Miss Morgan. It just sounded like a good wisecrack at the time.

"We all care about Miss Morgan, my dear," said Ray, with undisguised paternal airs. "We're trying to make sense of the situation. You see, we've been set up. The question is why. The answer is logic."

"I think I understand," said Monica Wheetly. "What you're saying is that we have to analyse the problem and then logically come to a conclusion and then we'll solve the case."

"Precisely," said Ray. He turned to me. "Don't you think she'd make a good detective, Marlow?"

"As long as you didn't mind your bed going up in flames," I said.

"Marlow's just trying to be funny, my dear," said Ray, turning back to Monica Wheetly. "He hasn't quite learned how to speak to young ladies yet."

"Oh, I don't mind," said Monica Wheetly. "I know he doesn't really mean it."

I poured myself another drink. I wasn't trying to convince her of anything.

"Show him how much you've learned, my dear," said Ray. "Now what are we trying to find out?"

"Whether Miss Morgan is dead, of course. And if she is dead, whether she was murdered or just fell off the boat."

Ray shook his head and let out a sigh.

"No?" She looked at me. I looked back at her. "But that's what I want to find out," she said.

"What we are trying to find out," said Ray, "if you would have listened carefully, is why someone wants us to believe that Miss Morgan is dead. If we discover their motive - or motives - then everything else will follow."

"But how do we find that out?" asked Monica Wheetly.

"We need more information," said Ray.

"What kind of information?" She looked Ray squarely in the eye.

"I don't know yet," he said.

She looked at me.

I said, "Neither do I."

Chapter 15

Dinner that night was pretty dull. Not the menu - though I was beginning to tire of the circular journey from plate to mouth to stomach to loo and then to plate again. People like Rinexus, of course, could keep it going forever. Even, I suppose, in death. He'd probably bribe some greedy worms to make the necessary connections.

The dullness was in the air. The excitement of the idea that they were Johnnies on the spot, first to hear of what was meant as world news - "Movie Star Missing From Luxury Ship ... Presumed Dead ... Stay Tuned For Further Announcements" - had started to go sour along with stomachs courtesy of North Atlantic weather.

Ray said it was midway blues that happened every trip. It didn't need a zonked-up mermaid sinking to the deep. But I was miserable enough on land. Now I was beginning to feel like an ancient mariner depressed on the briny sea.

The exception was the Wheetly girl. And Ray. The old guy had bounced back like an India rubber ball with a shot of Vitamin B. They were all smiles while the rest of us were glum. But sparkling on like that in the face of people who would just as well mope didn't do much for your popularity.

"I wonder what they got to sing about?" said Rinexus after they went off. "That guy is up to something. And I bet it's to do with a missing broad."

"More likely it has to do with one he's found," said Roger Lane.

"Or one that found him," I said.

"You chum around with Chandler, don't you?" Rinexus said, looking straight at me. "What's up Marlow?"

"If I knew that, I wouldn't be on this ship," I replied. And then, pushing back my chair, I said, politely, "Excuse me folks, it's time for my injection."

"Are you ill, Dr Marlow?" asked Amanda Lane, with the look

of concern that she could do so well.

"Not really, Mrs Lane," I said. "At least my embalmer doesn't seem to think so."

*****

They were in the bar. Drinking gingerale. Ray, too. I looked at him in disgust.

"Sit down, Marlow!" he ordered. "And stop looking at me that way! You're a doctor. You should reinforce my attempts at going straight."

"If you want to drink sugar bubbles, go right ahead," said I. "Just don't smile at me."

"Why would I smile at you, Marlow?" he asked. "You're not funny to me right now."

"Was I ever?" I asked.

"There were times..." he began. He didn't finish. So I don't know what he was going to say.

Besides, Monica Wheetly cut in. "Dr Marlow," she said, excitedly, "we're having a strategy session. We're really going to solve the case!"

"No one ever solved anything over a glass of gingerale, Miss Wheetly," I said. "Unless what they're trying to solve is the reason for a toothache."

She looked a little disconcerted, as if I had come into her church wearing only lipstick and carrying a purse. But Ray spoke up for me. He said, "Maybe you're right, Marlow. But at the moment we're just doing a little supposing and it's not very taxing on the mind."

"Supposing this ship is going to England and supposing we're on it, too. Even that kind of supposing is too taxing for me," I said.

"That's the wrong kind of supposing, Dr Marlow. That kind of supposing doesn't lead anywhere," said Monica Wheetly.

"Supposing you're not trying to get anywhere?" I said.

"Then what are you doing on this ship?" she asked, looking at me curiously.

I looked at Ray. He was almost smirking. Maybe he found his protégé. Maybe he was hooked on gingerale. Maybe Monica Wheetly had already replaced me as his drinking partner.

"What are you doing on this ship, Marlow?" he asked, repeating her question with the emphasis on the "are".

"Don't you know?" I said.

He shook his head. "Tell us."

"How can a puppet tell a puppeteer?" I said. "Didn't you say it was an unnatural act?"

His smirk drained from his face as if I had taken the plug out of his lips. "Let's not get too personal, Marlow," he said.

I shrugged. "You're the one who asked me to sit down," I said. I took a drink. Everything was suddenly beginning to taste like soda pop.

"I really don't understand the two of you," Monica Wheetly said. "Sometimes you sound like the best of friends. Other times you sound like you despise each other."

She had it wrong. I never despised him. In fact I really liked the guy. I can't stand too much bullshit though. But neither could Ray.

"There's some things women can't understand, my dear," said Ray. "Friendship between men depends on the careful balance of unspoken loyalties. Marlow, here, is angry that I've mixed my drinks. He's trying to decide whether it's a permanent change, whether I've joined the Christian Temperance Union - something like that. He's too much a man to ask me direct. So, at the moment, he's giving me the benefit of his doubt."

"Is that right, Dr Marlow?" she asked.

"I just don't like seeing a good man drown himself in gingerale, that's all," I said.

"But, Dr Marlow," she said, "you should be delighted that he's taking care of his body!"

"Look at him," I said. "His body's shot. If he were a car, he'd have been towed to the wrecker's months ago."

Ray stuck his pipe into his mouth and then he pointed to his greying head. "My mind's as sharp as ever, Marlow. I'll tell you that!"

"I won't argue with you, Ray," I said. "You've still got a few years left." I lifted up my glass. "You might as well enjoy them."

"Dr Marlow, I don't know why the AMA would ever hire you!" Monica Wheetly said, outraged.

"Maybe they've learned the secret, too," I said.

"Secret? What secret's that?" she asked.

"That life's a bunch of crap," I said.

Ray glowered at me. "Marlow!", he growled, "There's a lady present at our table! You shouldn't have said that!"

"Did I offend you, Miss Wheetly?" I asked.

"Yes," she said. She looked offended, too.

"I didn't mean to offend you, Miss Wheetly," I went on. "I just say what's on my mind."

"You can think what you damn please," said Ray. "You're not obliged to always utter it aloud."

"Is that an unnatural act as well?" I asked.

"It's impolite," he said. That Ray! Such a gentleman! Well, it takes all kinds, I always say.

"Frankly," said Monica Wheetly, "I don't know what Ray sees in you!" She looked at me like I was something her mother would have thrown to the neighborhood cat.

"She says what's on her mind, too," I pointed out to Ray.

"That's the privilege of being a woman," said Ray. Maybe he was right. Maybe they didn't have too many of the other privileges that had been passed around.

Monica Wheetly stood up to go. She didn't look so happy anymore. "I don't think you two really want me here," she said.

"Sit down, my dear!" said Ray. He looked at me. "Marlow will behave. Won't you, Marlow?"

She stared down. "Will you, Dr Marlow?"

"Will I what?" I asked.

"Behave?"

"I am," I said. "I'm behaving just as I was taught."

"Who taught you to behave like that?" she asked me.

I smiled and looked at Ray.

"He'd say something about his life experience, Monica, dear, if he wasn't so repressed," said Ray, lighting up his pipe. "Please,

104

sit back down. I'll vouch for him."

She sat down, uneasily, still looking at me. "Is it true?" she asked. "Did something happen to you that made you act this way?"

To tell the truth, I don't know why I was acting that way any more than she did. The mood came over me. That's about all I can say. Maybe a psychoanalyst could tell me. But I don't believe in them any more than they believe in me. Freud was a smart guy. But if he stopped smoking those damn cigars, maybe they wouldn't have operated on his jaw. On the other hand, if he stopped smoking those cigars, would he have been Freud?

"Don't press him, Monica," he said. "Let him be." And then, turning to me Ray continued. "Listen, Marlow," he said, "You're bored. I can tell that from your eyes. It's easy to get bored on ship - especially when you're tired of the food. Bored men do stupid things. What you need is something to perk your interest. Even if you believe that life is crap."

"There's a lady present," I reminded him.

"I'm only quoting you," he said. "Anyway," he puffed slyly on his pipe, "who's moaning now?"

He had a point. I'd give him that. "What are you suggesting, Ray?"

"I'm suggesting that you help us with a puzzle. Think of it as a mental exercise. Something to pass the time while you're awake."

"Like munching on some nuts while you're drinking beer. Is that what you're trying to say?"

"Precisely," he agreed. "An intellectual game that can be played without using any intellect."

"But it's not a game!" Monica Wheetly shouted out. "It's a life!" Then, realising she had raised her voice too loud, she looked around. No one heard. No one cared, excepting her. Turning back to us, she lowered her voice again, and said, "How can you be so callous? A woman - a friend of yours - might be dead!"

"If she's dead, there's nothing we can do for her now," said Ray, quite soberly for a former drunk. "If she's not, she won't be found by venting our emotions."

"I'll drink to that," I said, ending my romance with a glass of Jack.

Monica Wheetly sighed. "I suppose you're right," she said. "It's just that we keep going round in circles. We talk about doing something, but we never seem to start."

"Don't worry, my dear," said Ray, "we're about to start right now."

"We are?" she said. "That's fine! Then where do we begin?"

"Right here," said Ray, in a distinctly lowered tone of voice.

"Mr Chandler?" It was a louder voice from up above. I didn't like the sound. I looked around and saw one of the monkey men looking blankly down.

"Yes?" said Ray. "What can I do for you?"

"The Ambassador requests that you join him this evening for a drink. Would you kindly follow me?"

"Impossible," said Ray. "I'm drinking here with friends."

The monkey man was clearly unused to that kind of blunt retort. Thinking, I suppose, that Ray had misheard, he began again, with different words. "The Ambassador asked me to say it's quite urgent that he sees you now."

"Tell the Ambassador that I'm not in the habit of obeying commands of petty bureaucrats. In fact, tell the Ambassador that he can go to hell."

The monkey man couldn't believe his ears. Maybe that's why they turned red. "I'll relay your message to the Ambassador," he said.

Monica Wheetly looked at Ray as if his bottom was exposed. As for me, I was starting to enjoy myself again.

106

Chapter 16

I'll tell you how we got there before I tell you where. We got there by invitation of the Ambassador's fine wife. She came into the bar wearing a ton of minks and jewels and said, "I'm so sorry to intrude, Mr Chandler, But I just had to meet you. I've so long been a fan of yours!"

Ray stood up like a shot, unhooked his pipe and spilled his gingerale. Being as he was such a gentleman, I thought he'd lay down his jacket so she could cross the puddle he had made.

"We'd so very much like you and your friends to join us for a drink," she said. "And I do apologise for Mr Dougal. He sometimes tends to be a little too forthright in his approach, don't you agree? It's just that we only now realised you were aboard and there's so little time. The crossing is so short, isn't it? And there was that dreadful tragedy with that Morgan woman! I don't think people should be allowed on deck during a storm, do you?"

Ray was swept away in a dowagerly wave of verbal Chanelle. He was quick to succumb.

"See you later," I waved, as they got up to go.

"Not on your life," Ray hissed at me.

"On what then? My life is the only thing I have left," I said.

"As a favor to me, Marlow. For old time's sake."

For old time's sake? How could I refuse such a request as that?

"Please do join us, Dr Marlow. I really insist!" said the rich old bat.

Ray had introduced me that way. He said, "allow me to introduce, John P. Marlow, MD." I don't know where he got the "P". And I'd rather he forgot the "MD".

"You must come," said Monica Wheetly. Though her voice sounded pretty unconvincing.

Maybe that's why I ended up tagging along. If nothing else, I could annoy her.

*****

The main room of the Ambassador's suite was lavish as any hotel - at least any I had seen. The decor was white on white on ebony, set off by enough gold on gold to finance a small sized city. There was a cosy arrangement of luxury-type sofas and sinkable easy chairs built around a circular coffee table big enough to land anything that could fly. There was a wall-hanging of pink pelicans standing on exotic flowers and a marble bar which was filled to overflow. The place smelled rich and I'd smelled that kind before. I hoped the pelicans enjoyed their stay. I wondered if the steamship line had counted all their feathers.

The Ambassador was in deep conversation with one of the monkeys when we came in. Another ape was writing something on a pad. The third, the biggest gorilla of them all, greeted us with a pre-recorded line: "The Ambassador is grateful you could come." I wondered if he could say that and wiggle his ears at the same time. Probably not. His face was like a rock. If I were his trainer I would have thrown the guy a fish. Maybe that would have cheered him up.

"Mr Chandler! You have no idea what an honor this is!" The Ambassador stuck out his paw.

"I don't shake hands," said Ray. "I've got a skin disease."

Maybe the test of an Ambassador is that he wasn't phased. Like the test of a doctor is when he can shrug it off after cutting someone up and finding the pieces can't be fit back together the same way.

Ray introduced Monica Wheetly, who actually curtsied as if she was practising to meet the Queen. And then yours truly. The Ambassador didn't try the hand trick again with me.

The formalities were over and it was time to get our drinks. We said what we wanted and Chance wrote it down. Chance was the chimpanzee - the gofer. His job was to get. He did it well.

It turned out the gorilla had a name, too. If the Ambassador called out "Dougal!" he would jump. Otherwise, he sat there and looked mean. O'Connor was the monkey who could write. He kept going in and out with his pad of paper and his pen. He'd whisper something in the Ambassador's ear - an ordeal no more difficult than speaking into a cauliflower - and the Ambassador would mumble something back. Then O'Connor would go in and out again. If the monkeys had other names than Dougal, O'Connor and Chance, I never heard. But their last names were easy enough to remember. It sounded like the infield of an Irish baseball team.

Drinks in hand - Ray had tonic without gin - the Ambassador got down to it right away.

"Mr Chandler," he said, "I wonder if I could speak with you privately for a moment." The apes prepared to move into an adjoining room.

"We are speaking privately," said Ray.

"I meant the two of us - alone," said the Ambassador.

We were seated around the landing field. Ray and I were on the sofa. Monica Wheetly was sitting uncomfortably on an adjoining chair. The Ambassador sat on the other side so he could see us all. The monkeys were in the background looking very busy with nothing much to do. And the dowager who had invited us had completely disappeared.

"Do you mind if I smoke?" asked Ray, taking out his pipe.

"Not at all," said the Ambassador, with a pretentious smile. "Why don't you and I move into the adjoining room while Dougal entertains our guests with a song."

A singing monkey act, I thought! Maybe this wasn't going to be so bad after all!

Ray filled his pipe. "Perhaps we could stay here," he said. "Dr Marlow and Miss Wheetly are privy to my thoughts concerning the disappearance of Miss Morgan."

"What makes you think I want to speak about her?" asked the Ambassador, standing up to lead the way.

"Why else would you call me here?" Ray said while he calmly filled his pipe. "Certainly not to collect my autograph. You probably never heard of me before this trip. It's not hard to guess why you'd want to speak with me since your man must have reported I was having a tête-à-tête with Miss Morgan when he came to fetch her for you. She most likely told you who I was

- that we were friends from long ago. You know that she and I had our little chat. Now you want to find out what she said. That's OK with me. But there's something you should understand before we talk. Dr Marlow, Miss Wheetly and I are investigating Miss Morgan's disappearance."

The Ambassador nodded to O'Connor who picked up the cue and vanished into the other room. Then, turning back to Ray, he said, "Mr Chandler, there's something I received the other day that I wish to show you."

Ray lit his pipe and, for a moment, disappeared behind the smoke. "Yes," he said, when he came back, "you want to show me a note."

There was a brief look of surprise on the Ambassador's face which he quickly covered up with a laugh. "O'Connor!" he shouted out, "You didn't tell me he was Sherlock Holmes!"

O'Connor came back holding a sheet of paper - a telex, or so it seemed. "We just have a list of books and his employment record at Paramount and MGM. Nothing here about an alias like that. Seems he writes under his own name."

"O'Connor here is very bright. I couldn't do without him," said the Ambassador with an apologetic smile. "He only reads the sporting magazines for pleasure, though."

"Too bad," said Ray. "There's a lot of wonderful Irish literature he's missing."

"You hear that, O'Connor!" shouted the Ambassador. He looked back again at Ray. "Give him some names," he said.

"He might try J. M. Synge. Have him read 'The Playboy of the Western World'. I'm afraid that Joyce would be completely lost on him."

"Right!" said the Ambassador. "You got that O'Connor?"

O'Connor wrote it down. "Yes, sir," he said.

"Anything else?" asked the Ambassador, turning back to Ray.

"Yes," said Ray, biting down hard on the stem of his pipe. "Please don't refer to me as 'Sherlock Holmes'!"

"I thought that would be a compliment," said the Ambassador, "seeing that you're a detective writer..."

"His scientific premises are very unreliable," Ray snapped,

"and as stories they are pretty thin milk."

Too bad, I thought. I kind of liked that Watson guy, myself.

"Well, we won't quibble over that," said the Ambassador. He took a piece of paper from the gofer who had gone out again and had come back in. "I'd just be interested in how you knew about the note."

"Could I see it please?" asked Ray, holding out his hand.

The Ambassador gave it to him. He read it and then passed it on to me. Monica Wheetly leaned over to read it, too. It was pasted up bits of letters cut out from magazines as the last one had been. This one read: "Mr Ambassador. I know about you and Gloria Morgan."

"Is that what your note said?" asked the Ambassador as I gave it back to Ray, who handed it back to him.

"The one I saw read, 'Someone on this ship is going to die'. It had been placed under the door of a Mr Rinexus, a rather sleazy writer for a movie magazine."

The Ambassador suddenly looked concerned. "Do you know what this is about, Mr Chandler?"

"I was hoping I could clarify some points," said Ray. "But I'd like to do it openly. I think that would benefit you, too."

The Ambassador whispered something to O'Connor who left us once again. Then the Ambassador sat down. "You're absolutely correct, Mr Chandler. I want this all open and above board. The last thing in the world I'd want are unfounded rumors flying all around."

"I thought that was the benefit of being a politician," I said, butting my nose in again. "With so many rumors always buzzing around you like mosquitoes in a swamp, you can do almost anything, call it a rumor and swat it before it bites."

"Dr Marlow likes to use colorful language," said Ray, lighting up is pipe again. "But I assure you that he's a top notch forensic scientist."

"What's a forensic scientist got to do with this?" said the Ambassador, looking as if there was something he should know, but couldn't yet figure out what it was. "She fell overboard! Certainly, there's no body that you've found!"

"No," said Ray. "Not yet. We're still sifting through our clues."

"What clues?" asked the Ambassador, seeming more and more befuddled. "Clues to what?"

"I'm afraid we're not at liberty to discuss that," I butted in again.

The Ambassador looked at Ray. Ray nodded his head. "Marlow said what I was going to say."

The Ambassador was not pleased. The muscles in his face were tense. "Who's authorised you to make this investigation? Certainly not the Captain!" he said.

"We've authorised ourselves," said Ray. "Gloria Morgan was a friend. We'd like to find out what happened to her."

O'Connor was going out and in the connecting door like a waiter in an over-booked cafe. This time when he came back, he whispered something into the cauliflower. The Ambassador seemed very unamused. At least he looked that way. I really didn't blame him. After all, he had invited us for a friendly chat.

Anyway, just then, the Ambassador stood up. "I'm sorry," he said, abruptly, "I've had an urgent phone call. I've got to go. But Dougal, here, will see to your needs. Feel free to have another drink. Perhaps we might continue our chat a little later..."

Chapter 17

We left the Ambassador to his tricks and walked back to Ray's cabin - which was quickly becoming the headquarters of central command.

"He seems so nervous," Monica Wheetly whispered as we made our way down the narrow corridor. "Look at his hand. See how it shakes?"

"Nerves are strange things," I said to her, "they're the electronics of our guts. Sometimes they need their lubrication."

"You mean some kind of oil?"

"If you can ferment it."

Ray was about four paces ahead of us and quickly speeding away.

"How about a drink?" I called out to him.

"I told you, Marlow, I'm on the wagon!" he snapped. "I'll let you know if and when I want to get back off."

We walked down the stairway to the level below and followed as Ray led us to his cabin.

"I must say," Monica Wheetly blurted out as we came in and closed the door, "I was pretty scared! I'd never met an Ambassador before!"

"Not even at your father's dinner parties?" I asked

"I told you," she said, "he's only a tiny capitalist."

"Does that mean you only met little attachés?" I asked.

"I've never met a government official at all!"

"Not even the neighborhood dog catcher?" I asked. "My, my! You have lead a protected life!"

"You need a drink, Marlow," said Ray. "Go pour yourself one!"

"What a nasty man!" said Monica Wheetly as I submitted to Ray's kindly request. "He has absolutely no manners at all!"

"Sit down, my dear," said Ray. "Right now, manners aren't the most important thing. We all have work to do."

"Work?" I said, drinking down his bourbon and making a

face. "What kind of work?"

"Do we really need him, Ray?" asked Monica, so sweetly.

"Yes!" said Ray. He glowered at me. "Sit down, Marlow! You're in on this, too!"

I sat. Sometimes you have to give a little if you want to be amused.

"The Ambassador is holding something back..." said Ray. But Monica Wheetly stopped him there.

"Why did he show us that note?" she asked.

"Rinexus must have blurted it out to someone," said Ray. "The Ambassador knew we saw a note. He assumed it was the same one. He showed it to us to make us believe he was being completely open and above board. He wanted us to trust him."

"Why?" she asked.

"To find out what we know, dear," said Ray, paternally.

"But we don't know anything," said Monica Wheetly.

"Yes, but he doesn't know that," said Ray. "You see investigation is a game of cat and mouse. You must always make the reader suspect you know more than you actually do."

"Reader?" she asked.

"The person you're interviewing, I meant."

"Can I ask a question, too?" I said, raising up my hand.

"What is it, Marlow?" he said, sharply.

"Is there anything we found out? The boat docks in a couple of days and there's a hell of a lot of liquor left to drink!"

"We found out a great deal!" said Ray. He was sitting down on his bed. His skin was pale and appeared to be in a clammy state. I didn't need all those years of training to know what he was going through.

"Excuse me," said Monica Wheetly.

He turned to her. Ray was the kind of guy who could be charming in the middle of an auto crash. "Yes, my dear. Was there something you wanted to ask?"

"You said we found out a lot."

"We did, indeed."

"Well - what?"

He got up and walked over to the sink. He took a towel and

soaked it in cool water.

"Remember my advice about a good mystery," he said. "In order to work it must be implicit in the characters."

He sat back down and began to sponge his head. Monica Wheetly came over to his side. "Here," she said taking the towel from his hand, "let me do that."

"The only problem is that this is real life," I said.

"Is it?" asked Ray.

"Maybe not," I agreed, getting up to take another drink.

"Of course it is!" said Monica Wheetly, continuing to sponge his head. "And that's the point. Your books are fun and games. This is serious!"

"You're out of bourbon," I said, lifting up the empty to show Ray.

"There's another in the drawer," said Ray, pointing to the dresser. "Take some, but leave some for me."

"I thought you were on the wagon?" I said, pulling open the drawer and taking out the virgin bottle.

"I am! I mean for emergencies!"

"Oh, my!" said Monica Wheetly. "I'd hoped you reformed!"

"It's not a matter of morals," said Ray, "it's a matter of performance. Sometimes I do better without it. Sometimes I do better with."

"I lifted up my glass. "That's the alcoholic's creed."

"It's not funny!" said Monica Wheetly. "I knew an alcoholic once. He was a very, very sick man."

"There are many illnesses," I said. "Not many, though, can help you to forget."

"What do you have to forget, Dr Marlow?" she said in a snide, sophomoric way.

"I killed a man," I said.

"I wouldn't doubt it," she replied. "Probably more than one."

"Just one," I said. "One was enough."

She stared at me and then she looked at Ray. "Is he kidding around again?"

"I'm sure Marlow wouldn't joke about anything to do with death," said Ray.

"Or the Church," I said. "Or Motherhood or Apple Pie..."

"You two are impossible!" she said. She threw the wet towel at my face.

I grinned and showed my teeth. "I like you like that," I said. "Better than when you say, 'Oh, my!' and hide your face."

"I hate you!" she shouted out. And then she began to cry. She put her head on Ray's shoulder and she wept.

"You went too far, this time, Marlow!" he said, angrily, while stroking her soft hair with his hand.

"Just playing my part," I said. I don't know why I said that. It just seemed the right thing to say.

"There, there, child," he said, soothingly, still stroking her hair. "Marlow's bark is much worse than his bite."

"You want me to go?" I asked.

"I want you to stay," said Ray. "But I want you to behave!"

Suddenly I felt confused. Maybe it was the drink. Maybe it had gone to my head. "I don't understand," I said. "I thought you wanted me to act this way."

"I need your help," said Ray. He said it strangely. It was almost like a plea. "We both do," he said.

I felt a little weak in the legs. I needed something to eat.

"There's been a crime committed," said Ray. "A terrible crime. A beautiful woman has been hurt. It's our duty to find out what happened. We couldn't save her. That will always be a black mark against us, Marlow. We must atone and to atone, to find salvation, we must solve the crime."

"Why us?" I asked.

"Because," he said, "that's who we are."

"Who are we?" I asked. It wasn't any joke. I was deadly serious. I really wanted to know.

Monica Wheetly sat on the edge of the bed. She looked at us. I could tell from her eyes that she thought we were absolutely nuts. And I couldn't have agreed with her more.

"We're three people," she said, "made out of flesh and blood. We want to know why someone has disappeared. We want to know if someone died. And if that someone died, we want to know if they were murdered."

"Why?" I asked. I scratched my head. "Why do we care?"

"Because it isn't right!" she shouted in frustration. "We want to know why because people just don't disappear on lovely boats for no reason at all. We have to find out."

"Why?" I asked. "I mean it. Really. Why do we want to know! There were millions of people killed in the war. Millions of people burned and slaughtered and cut up into tiny bits of meat. There are millions more without food and homes. Why do we care about a movie star who fell off a boat?"

"Because!" shouted Monica Wheetly at the top of he lungs. "Because it isn't right! Because people just don't disappear in life! Because if people disappear for no reason, what meaning can there be? And if people are allowed to disappear for no reason at all, then maybe it could happen to me!"

Chapter 18

I know when I'm hooked. So does a fish. It wiggles and squirms and the hook goes in deeper. If the fish had any brains, it would know when to give up.

"I'll make you a deal," I said to Ray. "I'll help investigate for a while. As long as it remains a game, OK? If it starts to get serious, I'm out. I'm finished playing God. I've had enough to last my life."

"How about Avenging Angel for a change?" asked Ray.

"I won't have anything to do with something that begins with double A."

Ray brought out his pipe and filled it up. "OK, Marlow," he said, "have it your way. We'll see how far it gets. Then each of us will make our own choice how to proceed."

"Gloria Morgan didn't have much choice, it seems to me," said Monica Wheetly, showing off her academic skills.

"If you want to know something about choice, read the 19th century philosophers," I said. "They had a kick debating whether it was free or not. Of course, none of them spent any time in a Nazi concentration camp."

"Did you?" she asked me in her own delightful way.

"I saw enough," I said.

Ray struck a match and lit his pipe. It wouldn't burn. With a gesture of disgust, he put it to the side. "Don't think I'm enjoying myself," he said. "I'm not! If you want to play word games with each other, go right ahead. I'll read a book or go to bed."

She looked at me and made a face. Then she looked at Ray. "I've never done any detective work before," she said. "How do we proceed?"

"First, you have to understand your characters," said Ray. "You have to find out what makes them tick."

"How do you do that?" she asked. "Dr Marlow's gone to medical school. You'd think he'd know."

"That's far too organic," said Ray. "No school on earth can

teach you how to understand the motives of our fellows in the human race - except, of course, the school of life."

"But basic motivation is quite simple, isn't it?" she said. "Everything really boils down to a particular vice - greed, envy, lust and so on. Am I right?" She stared at Ray with child-like eyes, waiting for his reply.

Ray was sitting on the side of the bed. He leaned forward and said, "Let's suppose you're a politician, my dear, and you had a lust..."

"A lust for what?" asked Monica Wheetly. "I'm not a particularly lustful person, Ray."

"Pretend, my dear. Pretend. Pretend that you're a man. You have a lust for power. It's a lust that grows till it takes over the essence of your being. It becomes your life. You've gotten near the pinnacle, near the highest peak, and there's only one more to attain. It might not be within your power to get there anymore, but you have sons. You've paved the way. You've brought them up to think getting there's a duty and a right. Only one thing's wrong..."

"What's that?" she asked, leaning closer to him, too. I was waiting for their heads to bump.

"A woman. You've fallen into her web. She's become another object of your desires. You've struggled to possess her, but in the process you've given her too much..."

"Too much what?"

"Stop interrupting me with questions every minute!" said Ray, suddenly straightening himself up. "Let me finish! Then you can ask away!"

"I'm sorry," she said, looking like a pup who had a bucket of water emptied on its head, "I'm just trying very hard to follow your thoughts."

"All right," he said. He rubbed his brow and leaned forward again. "You're a Roman Catholic and you're backed up by the Church. It wouldn't do to have a scandal get around. Still, you want her in your power. But, at the same time, you want her kept out of your hair."

Monica Wheetly let out a little sigh. "I think it would be far more romantic if he decided to give up his important position, leave his wife and children and escape with her to some island, far away!"

Ray gave me a helpless look. I shrugged. Then he looked back at her. In fact, he glared.

"If it's that kind of a romance you want, go try another cabin!" he said. He picked up his pipe from the ashtray by the bed and began to clean it forcefully with a ream.

"Oh, I'm truly sorry, Ray!" she pleaded. "It's just that you asked me to use my imagination and pretend I was a man..."

"Why don't you pretend you're a man pretending you're a man?" I suggested.

"You're no help at all!" she snapped at me.

You have to be capable of understanding true motivation," said Ray, after he regained his patience once again. "If you believe a man of power is capable of running off with a woman he desires if it means leaving everything else behind, then you and I barely live on the same planet."

"Maybe we don't ," she said. The corners of her mouth were turned down. "But doesn't detective work relate to facts? And facts are facts. With a little help, I bet I could find some, too!"

He filled his pipe and set it aflame. "Facts are all around you, Monica," he said. "They breed in the air like germs. Without a notion of why people do what they do, a fact is no more than some smoky lace." He pointed to the steam coming from his wooden bowl. "Watch it drift into the air and disappear," he said. "What does it mean?"

"It means you lit your pipe," she said.

I laughed even though I didn't mean to.

She ignored me. "But let's say the politician did want to get rid of the woman - though heaven knows why. I mean, in your story he was supported by the Church. Certainly the Catholic Church looks down more on murder than adultery..."

"I wouldn't bet on that," said Ray. "I know some mafioso who go to church on Sunday with their family and say their prayers for someone they just finished bumping off."

"But that's ridiculous!" she said. Her voice showed her

distress. "How can you compare a gangster with a representative of our country's government?"

"My dear," he said with a twinkle in his eye, "the distinction between the established man of power and the gangster, as you say, is semantic. Both would stoop to anything to gain what he wants. The only difference is that one is sanctified by the state. A word of advice - if you think in stereotypes, Monica, you'll never understand true motivation. If you want to solve a mystery, you have to understand what makes people really do what they do. Not what you think they really do when it satisfies your prejudice."

She looked at Ray and bit her lip. "So you think the Ambassador bumped off Gloria Morgan?"

"I didn't say that!" Ray covered his eyes. "I was just talking about motivation! He's just a suspect of a suspected crime. But right now everybody is! To come to any fair conclusion we need some information!"

"How do we get that?" she asked.

"By snooping around," said Ray. "We find out what we can..."

"You mean listen in at keyholes?" asked Monica Wheetly.

"Just keep your eyes and ears open and remember what you see and hear. That becomes the clay which we mold together..."

"And maybe then we'll have a pot to piss in," I said.

"Do we have to work with him, Ray?" she asked.

"Yes! Marlow is the hero of all my stories. Sometimes I can't stand him, too. But he still works, damn him!"

"This isn't one of your stories, Ray," I reminded him.

"Everything's a story, Marlow!" he said. "Some are better stories than others, that's all! There's a story here someplace. We just haven't discovered it yet."

"But where should we begin?" asked Monica Wheetly.

"We begin at the beginning. That's a good place. We reconstruct the picture in our mind. We interview the people at the scene of the crime."

"But we don't know there was a crime," she said.

His voice was whisper soft. "Oh, yes, there was a crime all right. A terrible crime. In fact, the greatest crime in all my life..."

Chapter 19

Ray had chosen me to see the Argentine. It was ten o'clock at night. I told him he might be asleep.

"So what?" asked Ray. "Just give a knock at his door."

"He might not want to see me," I said. "Why don't you send our little college friend?"

"It's not wise to send a lady to a gentleman's door at night, Marlow. You know that! Monica and I will see Amanda Lane."

I went more out of curiosity than anything else. There wasn't much I figured to find out. But the Argentine was a peculiar guy. He was on a mission. So was I. But his mission was defined. It was clear. He was what we sometimes call "a patriot". Someone who would stake his life for his country and his dreams. That was a little out of fashion now, it's true. But, none the less, I found it sort of touching.

I gave a tap on his door. The Argentine opened up. He was wearing an oriental robe, dark red - maroon, I think. Around his neck was a paisley scarf, the kind that made Ricardo Mantelban so debonair. He had black slippers on his feet. In his mouth was an ivory cigarette holder which held a burning cigarette. He reeked of cologne. Bay rum, maybe. His eyes could have been made of glass the way they stared at me.

"Dr Marlow?" he said, with a vocal question mark. "What brings you here?"

"I thought we might have a little chat," I said.

He glanced at his watch. "It's nine forty-five," he said.

"My watch says ten," I replied. "But I won't quibble."

"I was about to go to sleep," he said. He looked annoyed. Maybe I would have looked annoyed if he came to my door at ten. Christ, I'd be annoyed if he came to my door at all!

"It won't take long," I said.

"What won't?" he asked.

"I'm doing a report," I said. It sounded OK at the time.

"On people's sleeping habits?"

"On people's disappearing habits."

He thought it over. At least, I suppose he did. It took him a minute to say, "Very well. Come in if you must."

I came in and closed the door. I looked around. His room was similar to mine, perhaps a little larger. But being a notch above, the decor was made from ritzier stuff. There was a walnut writing table on the plushly carpeted floor. And a glass display case showing off a miniature bar. The desk was being put to use. There were books and papers and official-looking documents. I could tell that from the way they were wrapped and sealed.

"Sit down, Dr Marlow," he said, pointing to a blue upholstered chair. "I'll fix a drink and you can tell me what's on your mind. What can I get for you?"

"Any whiskey will be fine if you don't have Mr Daniels," I said

He poured two fingers of the amber stuff and put in a few rocks. I didn't ask for ice, but what the hell. He fixed the same thing for himself.

"So what can I do for you, Dr Marlow?" he asked bringing me the drink and then sitting down in a twin chair across from mine.

"You saw Miss Morgan the other night," I said. "The night she disappeared."

"Yes." The Argentine stared at me like a pitcher figuring out which ball to throw. "She knocked at my door."

"What time was that?"

"About the same time you did now," he said, knitting up his brow a half a stitch. "But I told this to the Captain's investigating committee," he said. "Why does this interest you?"

"Let's just say I'm asking for a friend," I replied.

"And what is your friend's interest in this matter?"

"He's a connoisseur of vanishing acts," I said.

That didn't really seem to satisfy him. But he didn't kick me out. I guess he was feeling lonesome that night.

"What did she want from you?" I asked. "A goodnight kiss?"

He made a face. "She wanted a light for her cigarette. She said she hadn't a match."

"So she knocked on your door," I said.

"That's right."

"At ten o'clock at night."

"Yes!" He seemed a little cross. "Look, Dr Marlow, I'm tired and I want to go to sleep. Why don't you get to the point?"

"Why do you think she bothered you so late? Why your door, do you suppose?"

"Because I'm down the hall from her! Because she probably stopped to take a cigarette out from her purse and saw she didn't have a light. She happened to be in front of my door so she knocked. I suppose she wasn't rational enough to realise the time."

He kept looking toward the phone as he spoke. I wondered whether he was expecting anyone to call. "What did she do that was irrational? Unless you think that smoking is an unnatural act. I know some people do."

"I could tell she was on some sort of barbiturate..."

"How could you tell that?" I asked.

He smiled with one side of his face. "You're not the only doctor on this ship, Marlow. I studied medicine as well. Her movements were slow. Her speech was slurred.

"Maybe she was drunk," I said.

He shook his head. "Not with the dilation of her pupils."

"So you lit her up and she went on her merry way. You don't find that strange?"

"Why should I?" he asked. "I thought she probably took a sleeping pill and was going for a walk before turning in. I didn't see her go on deck. I just assumed she'd turn around and go back to her cabin."

"Did you know her very well?" I asked. "Did you ever visit her or did she visit you?"

He stood up. "What are you trying to insinuate?" he asked. The carotid artery I had seen before began another dance.

"I'm not trying to insinuate anything," I said. "It's just that someone saw you with Miss Morgan out on deck. They said you two were getting pretty cosy with each other..."

"Who told you that?" I could see he was about to blow a gasket.

"No one," I said. "I just made that up."

"Look, Marlow," he said, narrowing his eyes. "I don't know what your game is, but I have troubles of my own."

"You speak English pretty well for an Argentine," I said.

"I was educated at Yale!" he snapped. "All right? You want to know the color of my socks?"

"No," I said. "I can see they're green."

"They're blue!"

Just then his telephone rang. He reacted to it like a laboratory dog. "You'll have to go now, Marlow," he said. "I've been waiting for this call."

"Someone calling long distance on a boat?" I asked.

He went over to the side table by the bed and picked up the phone. "Hold on," he said. And then he walked over to the door and opened it.

"It was nice talking with you, Marlow," he said holding open the door. "Perhaps we'll have our drink some other time."

"Maybe we'll invite Miss Morgan, too," I said.

"The lady's dead, Marlow. The Captain has already written his report. She was swept over the side in heavy seas."

"She'll be sorry to hear that," I said.

*****

I went back to my cabin and fixed myself a drink. Jack Daniels. No water. No ice. Just alcohol with a twist of malt.

I lay down in bed and looked up at the underside of the deck above. Something about the Argentine had given me a lump inside my gut. I could almost put my finger on the lump, but not on the reason why.

The guy was sweating about something. Maybe it was the pressure of his job. Maybe he had an ulcer. Maybe he didn't like the idea of ladies who lived down the hall falling in the sea.

My phone rang. I let it ring a couple of times before I picked it up.

"Marlow?" It was Ray. "What did you find out?"

"Not much," I said, "except he went to Yale and he's color

blind."

"Well, that's a start. You know what he took his degree in? I suppose people don't study to be diplomats."

"He said he studied medicine, but I don't know whether he studied it there or in Argentina."

"Medicine? So he's a doctor, too?" Ray sounded interested in that. Maybe he was looking to switch physicians.

"There's enough quacks aboard this sheep to satisfy a fleet of ducks," I said. "He was nervous about something, though. He was waiting for a call. When it came, he wanted me to go."

"OK, Marlow," he said. "You did well. Get some sleep. I'll see you at breakfast."

"If you see me at breakfast, don't wake me, Ray. Just have the steward give my pillow a little fluffing up.

*****

I don't know what time it was but it was still dark. I often wake up at night, but not like that.

The sound was loud enough to wake the dead. I got up and turned on the lights. It took a couple of minutes for my eyes to adjust.

I'm a messy housekeeper. Anyway, that's what my ex-wife used to say. But I don't usually empty my drawers onto the floor. And I don't smash vases in my sleep.

Whoever had come in had left the door ajar. Maybe he left it that way going out. I picked up the pieces of the vase, left my clothes on the floor and went back to bed. In a few more seconds, I was sound asleep again.

Chapter 20

Whoever it was didn't have to bang so loud. Whoever it was didn't have to bang at all.

"Dr Marlow! Are you in?"

I didn't recognise the voice.. "Go away!" I groaned

The banging continued without stop. I crawled out of bed, slipped on my pants and went to the door and undid the lock. A big paluka with muscles on his wrist stood there. Even though he was in uniform, I didn't think he was the Salvation Army.

"If you're the Fuller Brush man," I said, "I could have used you earlier last night. I already swept the floor."

"Dr Marlow," he said, "you're going to have to come with me." It sounded like a command. Maybe I had dreamed myself back into the war.

"What's wrong?" I asked. "Someone stub their toe while emptying my drawer?"

He looked at my bare chest and made a face.

"Sorry," I said, "sometimes I sleep in my clothes. Sometimes I don't."

"I'll wait for you to dress," he said.

I went back in to hunt for my gear strewn around on the floor. "I hope you brought me a corsage," I said, looking back up at him towering by the door. "I expect that from all my dates. It helps neutralise the smell of day-old socks."

*****

We didn't go down as I had expected. We went up instead. We reached the boat deck and then went up some more.

"You're not going to make me walk the plank, are you? I didn't pack my water wings," I told him.

This guy had muscles everywhere but on his face. He didn't crack a grin.

"You want to tell me where we're going?" I asked. "Or don't you know?"

Maybe he was all voiced out from banging on my door.

I followed him the length of the top deck, heading toward the ship's nose.

"It's slippery up here, Dr Marlow, sir," he said, taking down a chain and motioning me forward.

I followed him up the metal stairs to a little penthouse. "Rockefeller live up here?" I asked.

He didn't give a reply - he just ushered me in.

It wasn't as lavish as you might have thought. Comfortable, yes. A great view if you happened to like water. Some fancy charts up on the wall. And enough brass to make a ton of lamps. I recognised just one.

"Hello, Marlow," he said. He showed his golden tooth. There's nothing more obnoxious than the sight of golden teeth before breakfast.

"What's up, Hart?" I asked. "Besides me, that is."

Hart turned to a man who had the face of an English bulldog and enough braids twisted round his sleeve to squeeze the blood out of a day old bun. His eyes had that mixture of tiredness and boredom that you often see in British films or in leaders who have led a bit too long. "This is Dr Marlow, sir," he said.

The Captain tried to size me up by running his tired eyes over what was left of my face. "Sit down, Dr Marlow," he said, pointing to a chair. "Would you care for some coffee or some tea?"

"You wouldn't have a dog with a little extra hair?" I asked.

He grimaced. "Johnson! Fix the man a whisky!" he called out.

Then, turning back to me, he said, "We've been having some complaints about you, Dr Marlow." The guy didn't beat around the bush.

"Have I been snoring too loud at night again?" I asked. "Waking all the burglars up?"

The whisky came, courtesy of Johnson, a man who dragged his feet as if he had a wooden leg.

"Funny you should mention that," said the Captain. "It's what

I wanted to talk with you about."

I downed the whisky. "Good stuff," I said. "Go ahead and talk."

The Captain turned to Hart. "You say he's the surgeon for this trip?"

"Yes, sir," said Hart, scratching the back of his neck and looking like he wanted to apologise.

The Captain shook his head and then looked back at me.

I grinned.

The Captain closed his eyes and then opened them again. Maybe he thought I'd disappear.

"Mr Mendez said you visited him last evening."

"It was just a friendly call," I said. "I wanted the recipe for Pampas beef."

"Last night Mr Mendez had a document stolen from his room," the Captain said. "He suspects the burglary may have something to do with you."

"Look," I said, "I'm not that keen on steaks."

"The Ambassador has suggested you and another of our passengers, a Mr Chandler, I believe, have been making an unwarranted investigation into an accident that took place aboard ship the night before last."

"Did that accident you're speaking about take place the same night Gloria Morgan was dumped into the ocean?"

The Captain made a throaty sound, like a low growl a dog might make before it bites your leg off.

"Dr Marlow, a committee of officers from this ship has made a thorough investigation into the disappearance of Gloria Morgan. I am satisfied that their findings are quite correct."

"Would you mind telling me what they found out?"

"That on the night of 13 April, 1955, while under the influence of barbiturates, Miss Morgan was swept from the boat deck into the stormy sea."

"And are you satisfied with the report, Hart?" I asked, looking over at the CMO.

"I put my name to it. Yes." He didn't flash his ivories at me this time.

"Well, I guess that's that," I said.

"Then there's the matter of the missing document," said the Captain.

"I told you. I went there for a chat. In fact, I've got my own burglary to report if you're collecting stats."

"What do you mean?" asked the Captain.

"Somebody came into my room last night. They emptied out my drawers."

"Was anything taken?" he asked.

"I don't have anything to take except dirty underwear and socks."

The Captain had that look of contempt in his eyes the gentry have when dealing with their footmen. "I must insist, Dr Marlow, that you restrain yourself and mind your own affairs during the remainder of this voyage. I might remind you that you are an employee of this line..."

I shook my head. "That's where you're wrong. To quote your nervous rep back in the States, my official designation is a passenger. I'm trading my services for sailing on this tub. That's all. If you want me to sew your nose back on your face, that's fine. Other than that, I'll do as I see fit. As long as I'm fit to see, that is."

"Dr Marlow, I'm in no mood to argue with you this morning. I've got a ship to run!" The tired eyes were showing signs of life. "But I'm insisting that you leave the investigation of Miss Morgan's death to the proper authorities. A formal inquest will be made when we dock. So don't - to use one of your clever Americanisms - go sticking your neck where it doesn't belong!"

That seemed to me like good advice. I tried to make a habit of not putting my neck on the chopping block anymore than I could help it. I handed in my glass and stood up. "Thanks for the drink." Then, pointing out the window, I said, "Nice view. Don't bump into any floating movie stars."

"Hart!" shouted the Captain. "Please show the gentleman out!"

Hart was only too happy to oblige. As he walked me out the door, I said, "The guy looks like he didn't get a hell of a lot of sleep last night."

"You weren't being very smart antagonising him like that," he said. "But you're lucky. The Captain doesn't have time to concern himself with you, Marlow. He's got other problems right now."

"What's that?" I asked. We had made it down to deck. "More people topple overboard last night?"

"World affairs. There's a crisis brewing up somewhere. Last night the Ambassador and his army took over the communications room."

"You know what it's about?" I asked.

He shrugged. "Something to do with that conference of non-aligned states being held in Indonesia, though what could be so important there is quite beyond me..."

"Politicians talking politics," I said. "Dreaming of new ways to blow each other up."

He stood at the bottom of the metal stairway. He stared at me. "Keep to your own affairs, Marlow. You'll be better off."

"I couldn't agree with you more," I replied.

*****

Once you've been slapped in the face by the cold, wet wind, it's a little hard to back to bed. Breakfast, now that my heater had been stoaked by the Captain's whisky, didn't seem so bad.

On my way down I ran into the kid. He was carrying a tray with enough food to stuff both a horse and a rhino.

"You ever get tired of wearing that hat?" I asked him. "Maybe you could use it as a place to keep your buttons in."

"Oh, the hat's not too bad, sir," he replied. "Sometimes the string hurts my chin, but I have some cream the pharmacist gave me that I put on at night."

The pharmacist is a friend of yours?" I asked.

"His cabin is next to mine," he said. "We play draughts occasionally. We were going to play last night but he cancelled. He was quite upset..."

"Why's that?" I asked. "Did he lose his place in a beauty

contest?"

"No, sir," said the kid. "It seems he lost a great deal of money. It's all slips and slides with him..."

"What do you mean?"

"Well, the day before he had won quite a bit."

"Playing cards?"

"I think it was a personal bet." The kid shifted the tray to his other arm. "That's why I never gamble, sir. I save my money."

"Don't tell me," I said, "you're going to buy yourself a boat of your own."

"I'm saving it to get married, sir."

"At your age? You got lots of time yet before you stick your head inside a noose," I said.

"That's what everybody tells me, sir. But Sarah - she's my girl - she doesn't want to wait. She's in Manchester, working in a mill. If we save for another five years we'll have enough, she thinks."

He shifted the tray again.

"That thing looks pretty heavy," I said.

"It is, sir," he replied. "A bit."

I reached over and lifted the silver cover from one of the plates and took a crepe. "Let me lighten it up for you," I said.

He looked a little shocked, I guess. I winked and then he smiled.

"Who's all this grub for?" I asked, chomping on the crepe. It wasn't bad.

"The lady in Cabin 203, sir."

That was the cabin right over mine. "Amanda Lane?" I said.

"Mrs Lane. Yes, that's the one."

"She's got a healthy appetite," I said.

"She has, indeed," he agreed.

I took a ten spot from my wallet and stuck it in the pocket of his jacket.

"What's that for, sir?" he asked.

"It's not for you," I said. "It's for Sarah. Use it to buy her a bouquet. A girl who'll wait for you five years, isn't one to throw away."

Chapter 21

There was a cheerful gleam of conspiracy in her eyes that reminded me of a candy store and sticky hands. Ray was more sedate. But what would you expect from a professor in the art of crime?

They hardly gave me a second glance as I sat down in my proper place between the Lollipop Kid and the Old Man of the Sea.

"Your wife is ill?" Ray was saying to Roger Lane.

Lane looked up from his scrambled eggs and said, "My wife? Oh, yes. She's a little off. The motion of the ship - you know..." He let a silly smile finish the sentence for him.

"It doesn't seem to have affected her appetite," I said. "I saw a truck load of food being delivered to her door."

"Better to keep your stomach full, they say." Roger Lane pulled back his chair. "Excuse me," he said, "I should be getting back to her."

"He's right, you know," said Rinexus, forking up a pathetic sausage and throwing it into his meat grinder. "You'll feel worse if you stop eating."

"You said you thought you knew him once," said Ray, watching Roger Lane walk away.

"I thought I did," said Rinexus. "I even tried looking up his name in my 'Who's Who in Entertainment' guide."

"What did it have to say about him?" Ray asked.

"There wasn't any listing for a Roger Lane," said Rinexus.

"Does that mean he's not in the entertainment business?" asked Monica Wheetly, trying out her newly acquired investigation skills.

"Not necessarily," said Rinexus. "He might not be important enough to be listed in the book. Your friend, here - Mr Chandler - isn't included. Few writers are. You have to be either rich, famous or powerful - any combination or all three."

"I would wager you're included, Mr Rinexus," said Solly Meyers.

Rinexus threw another sausage to its doom and said, "Of course!" He inspected his plate for hidden victims and, finding none, said, "Can't stay around here shooting the breeze. There's lots to do today." And he, too, pushed back his chair and left.

"The breeze he shoots isn't what I'd like to smell," said Solly Meyers.

"He's just someone who trades on slime, Mr Meyers," said Ray. "And everyone carries the odor of their trade."

"Perhaps I carry the smell of cloth," said Solly Meyers, getting up. "Excuse me, my friends, I have to go."

Ray stood up. "Mr Meyers, I wonder if you would join us for a drink sometime before lunch today?"

Solly Meyers looked at Ray and smiled. "You want to find out about the clothing business? Well, OK. Perhaps we can meet. You tell me where."

"How about my room?" said Ray. "At a quarter to twelve. The number is 131."

"Fine," said Solly Meyers. "I'll see you then."

"He's a lovely man," said Monica Wheetly, watching him go.

"But his odor's not of cloth," said Ray, sitting back down again.

"What do you mean?" she asked, poking her spoon at a marshmallow floating in a cup of brownish fluid.

"He means that people aren't always who they seem," I replied. "For example that man over there." I motioned to the Argentine sitting all alone at the Captain's table eating a bowl of shredded wheat. "He seems calm enough now. But you should have seen him last night."

"Why don't you tell us what happened last night, Marlow," said Ray.

"Nothing much. I had my little tête-à-tête. Went back to my cabin. You phoned me up. And then I went to sleep. A quiet evening. Not much laughs."

"Anything else?" he asked.

"Depends what you mean by 'anything'. I had a dream that a rat came into my cabin and broke a vase."

"The only rats you have to worry about on ships are the one's who desert them, Marlow."

"Thanks," I said, "I'll remember that."

"Would somebody please tell me what's going on?" asked Monica Wheetly. I guess she had finished the marshmallow that was floating in her chocolate stuff and wanted to join in the fun.

Ray gave her a kindly smile. "Why don't we make our summary, my dear?" he said.

"You mean..." She looked at him and made a writing motion with her hand.

"Yes," said Ray, "tell Marlow, here, what we found out about Gloria Morgan's last hours."

Monica Wheetly took out a pen and notebook from her purse. She paged through it till she reached the proper spot and then she cleared her throat. "Gloria Morgan was seen by Mr Mendez at around ten o'clock, the night before last. She had knocked on his door to ask him for a light for her cigarette. Mr Mendez observed that Miss Morgan appeared to be drugged..."

"That sounds similar to what I found out," I said.

She looked up at me. "Yes, Marlow. That's what you told us when Ray phoned you last night. He told it to me and I copied it down. It's all part of the report..."

"You guys keep late hours," I said.

"There was a lot of work to do," Ray snapped. And then looking at Monica Wheetly he said, "You may continue, my dear."

"The only other person to have seen Gloria Morgan on deck was Amanda Lane. She claims that Gloria Morgan seemed to have been leaning against a mysterious man..."

"Excuse me," I butted in, "but how can someone 'seem to be leaning against a mysterious man'? They're either leaning against him or they're not."

She put down her notebook and glared at me. "It was storming outside, Dr Marlow, in case you're forgotten. It was raining cats and dogs. The wind was howling. It wasn't very easy to see that night."

"Well, if it wasn't very easy to see, how did she know it was

135

Gloria Morgan? And if she was able to recognise Miss Morgan, how come she couldn't describe the man she was with?"

Monica Wheetly shot a glance at Professor Ray, and then, feeling her confidence was bolstered by his little smile, she said, "If you knew anything about women, Dr Marlow, you wouldn't have to ask that question."

"If I knew anything about women, Miss Wheetly, I wouldn't be on this ship." I showed her my pearly whites which weren't so white or pearly anymore. "Maybe you could help me understand."

"A woman, Dr Marlow, can recognise another woman by the clothes she wears, the way she styles her hair and the manner of her walk. It's an instinctual thing. All men who wear a hat and mackintosh tend to look the same."

"But Miss Morgan's hair couldn't have had much style in all that rain. If she wasn't wearing a raincoat she would have been pretty wet. And the manner of her walk was more of a lean..."

Monica Wheetly's voice was closer to a hiss. "Then maybe another woman fell overboard that night, Dr Marlow?"

"Maybe no woman fell overboard at all, Miss Wheetly." I looked at Ray. "What about this mystery man?"

But before Ray could reply another man spoke up. The Argentine must have finished his dried up hay and wanted to stretch his legs. Anyway, he was standing over us.

"Dr Marlow," he said, "I feel that I owe you an apology. Last night I thought an important document of mine had been taken from my room. In my distress, I suspected you might have stolen it when I had answered my telephone. However, this morning I found that it had been there all along. I had just misplaced it for a while."

"I'm always losing things myself," I said. "I rarely blame my neighbor for it, though."

"I give you my apologies once more, señor," he said. "I can only say that it would have been very tragic had this document come into the wrong hands. I think you know that there are some people who would stoop to anything in order to see my country's government collapse."

"I hope those people wouldn't stoop to murder," said Monica Wheetly, looking like a cream cake trying to sound tough.

The Argentine smiled like a man with a throbbing headache. "Men who kill for little things are murderers, senorita," he said. "Men who kill for larger things are patriots."

"Perhaps you'd be wise to keep your documents in a safe," said Ray.

"I have taken care that they are secure, señor," said the Argentine. "Thank you for your concern." He bowed his head slightly and walked off.

Monica Wheetly gave a little shudder. "That man gives me the creeps," she said. "He should never have accused someone of stealing something unless he was certain it had been stolen."

"Perhaps it was," said Ray. He looked like he was bouncing something around in his head.

"But he just said that it wasn't!" Monica Wheetly insisted.

"Maybe it was stolen and then put back," Ray suggested.

"Why would someone do that, for heaven's sake?" she asked.

Ray took out his pipe and stuck it in his mouth. "So that someone could steal some information and have it appear that the information wasn't stolen at all." I marvelled at his expertise in talking through his chimney.

"Do you understand what he's saying, Dr Marlow?" she asked me in frustration.

"Not really," I said. "I do know that there's another storm that's brewing, though. And it hasn't much to do with the weather."

"Elucidate, Marlow!" Ray commanded.

"I was invited to have pre-breakfast tea with the Captain this morning," I said.

Monica Wheetly looked very impressed until she glanced at my clothes. "You had tea with the Captain dressed like that?" she asked, raising her eyebrows so high I thought they'd fall right off her head.

"The goon who brought me there didn't give me time to put on my tie," I said.

"Cut the wise cracks, Marlow and tell us what happened," said

Ray.

"He wanted me to stop butting into his affairs," I said.

"How were you butting into his affairs, Dr Marlow?" she asked.

"I think he was referring to movie queens who fall off ships," I said. "Especially when the ship is his."

"But the movie queen, isn't!" she said. Her dander was up. It gave her a glow and she didn't look so bad like that.

"Anyway, Hart walked me back down - you remember, he's the CMO. He told me the Ambassador and his little crew had taken over the radio room last night. It seems to have something to do with Indonesia."

"The conference of non-aligned states," said Ray, lighting up his pipe and blowing out a trail of smoke.

"There's some sort of cover-up going on," I said to Ray. "I wouldn't mind seeing the Captain's report on the Gloria Morgan affair."

Ray grinned a little like the mouse that ate the cat. "I happen to have seen that report, Marlow."

Monica Wheetly looked surprised. "You didn't tell me that!"

"If you did see that report," I said, "your reputation just went up a notch. Who gave it to you?"

"One of the Junior Officers that I know showed it to me on the QT. You met him Marlow, right before we sailed. The fellow who was minding the store at the Ambassador's news conference, remember?"

"You wean the guard who was so fat?" I asked.

"He's not so fat," said Ray. Overweight people tend to stick together, I guess.

"OK," I said, "so a pickle's not a cucumber. Anything I should know about that report?"

"Not much," he said. "Except Amanda Lane backed down on her story about the mystery man. She said it may have been a shadow from the lights."

"You mean she leaned against a phantom in the rain?"

"Perhaps she leaned against a pole," said Monica Wheetly.

"I don't care if she leaned against a Czech," I said.

"Something smells fishy about the starlet who got wet."

"She changed her story back again when she spoke to us," said Ray.

"The woman was confused," said Monica Wheetly. "It was a dark and stormy night. She was upset."

"There were lots of lights blaring down in that storm," I said. "Ray and I went outside."

"But the night distorts things," said Ray.

"So might Amanda Lane," I replied.

"What reason would she have for doing that?" asked Monica Wheetly.

Ray shook his head. "There's something else that's going on," he said.

Monica Wheetly took her pen and readied it to make some notes. "How can we find out what's really going on, Ray?"

"We need to speak to someone who might be able to help."

"Who's that?" she asked.

"The man who I invited to have a drink."

"My mean Mr Meyers? That lovely little man?"

"Yes, that lovely little man," said Ray. "If my suspicions are correct, he isn't Solly Meyers at all but a man called Meyer Lansky."

"I think I heard of him," I said.

"You probably have," said Ray.

"Well, for heaven's sake! Who is he, Ray?" asked Monica Wheetly, playing the role of an ingenue in an Agatha Christie production.

Ray puffed at his pipe, looked at her and said, "He's one of the heads of organised crime in the USA."

Chapter 22

I was beginning to feel like something inside a vacuum cleaner wondering how it got sucked in. It wasn't a question I hadn't asked before.

Ray looked at me like a general about to launch his soldiers. "Marlow," he said, "we need some answers. Why don't you go down to the surgery and see what you can dig up."

"About who and what?" I asked.

"Sniff around," he said. "Who's in charge when the CMO isn't there?"

"You mean the nurses? Tweedle Dee and Tweedle Dum?" I asked. "From the looks of them I might as well be speaking to the Ambassador's gorillas."

"Use your charm," said Ray. "You'll be surprised at what you can get women to tell you."

"With charm like his, we won't only be looking for one missing lady," said Monica Wheetly.

"That's not bad," I said, giving her the benefit of the doubt. "Keep it up and maybe I'll buy you a drink someday."

"Save your money," she said, with a saucy little twist of her head. "Use it to buy yourself a new MD degree."

That wasn't so bad either. But her silly smirk kind of let the wind out.

Ray beamed like a proud papa. "You've go to admit, Marlow, she's getting pretty tough."

"So was Bonnie Parker," I answered back, "and look where she ended up."

"What about us, Ray?" she asked. The kid was batting her eyelashes so fast I thought she'd take off and fly. "Who are we going to interview?"

"You and I are going back to my cabin, Monica," he said. "We've got a lot of research left to sort through."

"That's just dandy," I said. "You're sending me down on some pimpled seaman chase while the two of you go cuddle by the fire."

"When you get to be my age, Marlow, cuddling's about all that you have left. Unfortunately, it can't really go much further. With men like you, girls are still a danger. I'm doing you a favor by keeping you away." Then he got up and started walking toward the door. "Come, Monica," he said, "let's not deter Marlow from his work."

She waited as he left, leaned toward me and whispered, "All we ever do is talk." I felt her lips close to my ear. I turned and brushed up against her cheek. She smiled. Maybe you could buy me that drink after all, Dr Marlow," she said, softly.

"I'll wait until you're ready for something else than gingerale," I replied.

She looked like a debutante who had wanted me to light her candy cane. She got up, gave me one of her ice cube stares, and then she followed Ray.

*****

I knew that I'd never remember their names. Tweedle Dum was chewing gum - I saw the wrapper on the floor, it was Dentine - and polishing her nails a gaudy shade of red. Tweedle Dee had her feet up on the desk. She was reading Vogue with one hand while the other brushed her hair.

"Listen to this, Doris," Tweedle Dee was saying as I came in, "People are wearing nosegays again this Spring. It says here that they come in pastel shades to perk up dark dresses on sunny days."

"Well then you can forget them, Gladys," said Tweedle Dee, painting one more nail and then admiring the view.

"How come?"

"'Cause there ain't no sunny days in England."

"Excuse me," I said. "Is this the bar?"

They both looked up at the same time. One smiled. The other frowned. But don't ask me which.

141

"Hey, you're Dr Marlow, ain't you?" said Tweedle Dee.

Tweedle Dum took an end of her gum and pulled until it became a string. "You should come down more often, doc," she gave me a saucy wink. "You're cute!"

"Cuteness is as cuteness does," I said.

"There anymore like you up above the water line, doc?," asked Tweedle Dee. "You can't believe how incredibly boring it is down here. The only time people come to see us is when they're sick!"

"You think that's bad," I said, "You ought to try first class."

Tweedle Dum pointed her finger at me and let out a prize guffaw. "Listen to him, Doris! He says we ought to try first class!"

"Real rich!" said Tweedle Dee. "Real rich!"

I pulled up a chair and sat on it wrong way round. I leaned forward, balancing the chair on its hind legs. "You ladies got anything to drink?" I asked.

Tweedle Dee giggled. Tweedle Dum gave her a dirty look. "We're not allowed to drink on duty, doc. You must know that," she said.

I shrugged. "OK," I said, taking out my flask. "I guess I'll have to drink all by myself."

Tweedle Dee made a pout out of her lips. "Aw, Gladys, we never have any fun!"

Tweedle Dum looked around, just to make sure the coast was clear I guess. Then she closed her Vogue and put her brush away. She reached down and opened up the bottom drawer of the desk and pulled three beakers out.

Tweedle Dee grinned and screwed the top of her polish back on. "I'll get the mixer," she said. She skipped over to the pharmacy, then turned and wiggled a pretty finger down my way. "Now doc, don't you go nowhere!"

"Where would I go?" I asked. "This party looks like it's just begun." I got up and started pouring out the brew. "Say when." I looked over at the one who stayed.

"Whenever," she replied. This one could talk better with her eyes. And what they had to say didn't bear repeating.

Then the one who left came back in with a bottle full of

142

ethanol. "Great for mixing," she said. "Lousy on its own."

"You kids must have a high old time down here when the weather gets rough," I said, lifting up my beaker and drinking down some of the nasty stuff.

"Oh, yeah," said Tweedle Dee. "Real swell. When Gladys gets finished puking up her guts, its my turn."

"You two sound just like the Queen," I said. "I bet you stay in Buckingham Palace when the ship gets in."

"She's from Brooklyn," said Tweedle Dee pointing to Tweedle Dum.

"She's from the Bronx," said Tweedle Dum pointing to Tweedle Dee.

"I'm from Chicago," I said, holding up my beaker again. "Here's to England."

"Jesus!" said Tweedle Dee. "Do we have to drink to that?"

Marlow got it wrong again, I thought to myself. These two were a barrel of laughs, even if someone did forget the barrel.

"How'd you two cuties get shanghied on this tub?" I asked.

"We wanted to see the world," said Gladys

"We thought it would be more fun than the army," said her echo.

"Now all we see"

"Is the sea."

They both stood up and saluted me. If they were enjoying themselves, who was I to cramp their style?

"We thought it would be glamorous," said Doris, putting it to melody.

"And don't forget amorous." Gladys wrinkled her nose like a Debby Reynolds or maybe that Day girl.

"There are lots of sailors around," I said.

"Oh, them!" Doris made a face.

"I'd rather kiss a porpoise!" said Gladys. Then her eyes glistened like she was tip-toeing off into a dream. "We're both waiting for Cary Grant to come on board."

"Speaking of porpoises," I said, mixing up another drink, "What do you two love birds know about Carter?"

"The less we know about him, the better," said Gladys.

"Popular guy, huh?"

"With some," said Doris. "He called in sick today. I wish he'd do that more often."

"Who dispenses the medicines when he calls in sick?" I asked.

Gladys looked at Doris and said, "Sometimes she does, sometimes I."

Doris shook her head slightly and made a movement with her lips as if she were saying something silently to her twin. Maybe she was trying to correct her grammar. I don't know. Maybe if I were stuck down here for long I'd be talking that way, too.

"I don't want to step on any toes," I said. "Forget I brought the subject up."

"It's all right," said Doris. "It's just that Carter..."

"Doris, you talk too much!" Gladys gave her a look that would have melted rock and turned it into cast iron toads with horns sitting on a pair of steel commodes.

"You're not little Miss Zipper Lips yourself, honey!" said Doris.

I began to wonder what these two said to each other when they really got rolling.

"Can I fix you ladies another drink?" I asked, playing the cheerful bartender role.

"Sure," said Gladys. She was starting to look glum. "She always messes things up!" she said to me. She didn't say who, but I could guess.

"What did I do?" asked Doris. "She can be such a bitch sometimes!" she said, bolting down a beaker full of rubbing stuff.

That kid could really drink. "A few more like that," I said, "and you'll be in England a day before the ship."

Doris let out another one of her boisterous laughs. She could be so sweet.

Gladys had an interesting look on her face. Something like a tiger before it had its meal of the day. She came over and ruffled up my hair. "Let's forget about Carter and get down to business, big boy!" she said. I wondered if she knew Mae West. The line came better out of her with twice the flair and half the muss.

Doris must have figured this was her cue. She started unbuttoning her blouse. Two nurses six decks below and a bottle of rubbing alcohol must be a wicked combination, I decided.

"Does this mean we're finished with our chat?" I asked. Gladys' tongue was in my ear. I guess that's why she couldn't answer. Doris was sitting on my leg. Her hands were starting to undo something I wasn't sure I wanted undone yet.

It was right about that time I heard a shout. It sounded like someone whose tail had gotten tangled inside an industrial flattener of oversized railway engines.

"Marlow! What the hell is going on!"

I looked up and saw the CMO burning a few feet away.

"Hi, Hart." It was my turn to show him a few of my teeth. "Just chatting with your nurses. Hope you don't mind..."

Doris was quickly buttoning up her blouse. Gladys was straightening down the wrinkles of her dress.

"Marlow, you might not be the world's greatest surgeon," he said, "but you've really got a talent for doing the wrong things with the wrong people at the wrong time!"

"Maybe its the three wrongs that make a right," I said.

He thrust his finger in my face. His eyes weren't playing Pagliachi. "Listen, Marlow, I've had about enough of you! I can't speak for the shipping company, but if I were your boss you'd be out on your ass right now!"

"If you were my boss, Hart, you wouldn't have had to throw too hard."

The nurses had retreated into the adjoining room. Probably to get their beauty rest. Actually, I don't know what they were doing there. Maybe throwing up. I know that's what I would have liked to do by then.

Hart took a deep breath, rubbed his forehead, squinted his eyes and then looked. down. "I'm sorry, Marlow," he said. "Maybe I was being a little rough."

"Forget it," I said. "If I were running a boiler room like this and I came down to see my surgeon drunk with a floozy under either arm that were actually my nurses, I might also take offence."

"It's not that," said Hart. He rolled his glassy eyes. "Well, it is

- but that's not why I'm so upset."

"What is it then?" I asked. "Have I horned in on your parade?"

"It's Carter," he said.

"Yeah," I said. "I guess that guy's enough to spoil your day."

"He was found with a knife stuck through his gut."

"How is he?" I asked.

"Not very well," said Hart. "He's dead."

Chapter 23

The door to his cabin was open a crack. I could hear a voice from inside. It was Ray.

"I was born in America," he was saying, "I didn't go to England until I was seven. My father was a swine. My mother was a beautiful woman with soft blue eyes and golden hair. My father left her early on.

"As a very small boy I used to be sent to spend part of the summer at Plattsmouth, Nebraska. I remember the oak trees and the high wooden sidewalks beside the dirt roads and the heat and fireflies and the 'walking sticks' and a lot of strange insects and the gathering of wild grapes in the fall to make wine and the dead cattle and once in a while a dead man floating down the muddy river and the dandy little three hole spring behind the house. I remember the rocking chairs on the edge of the sidewalk in a solid row outside the hotel and the tobacco spit all over the place. I remember a trial run on a mail car with a machine my uncle invented to take on mail without stopping, but somebody beat him out of it and he never got a dime."

"Such strange memories you have, Ray," said another voice. "Beautiful, but in a very special way." It was a voice without a body, like the sound of the wind without the motion of the grass. You have to create your own image for it. The image I had, hearing that voice, was of a different Moncia Wheetly than the one whose father had only a little steel mill and part interest in another one.

I opened the door further and stuck my head inside. "Sorry to intrude," I said, "but I'm looking for a lost bottle of booze. You haven't seen one around by any chance?"

"Come in, Marlow," said Ray, "we were wondering where you'd gotten to."

"Not Plattsmouth, Nebraska, in any case," I replied.

"It was my fault, Dr Marlow," said Monica Wheetly. "I wanted to know what he was like when he was a boy."

Ray made a bumbling attempt at lighting up his pipe. He broke one match and the other one went out. "I told you I don't like talking about that, Monica!" His voice sounded gruff.

"I'm sorry, Ray," she said. She seemed unsure of what to do next so she sent me an SOS with her eyes.

It was a mistake. "Don't look at me, sweetheart," I said. "I'd be pretty embarrassed too if he caught me telling stories about when I was a squirt."

That loosened her up a little, I guess. At least enough for her to say, "Why are men so ashamed of having once been boys? I certainly hope you talk about it in your biography, Ray!"

Ray finally got a match to work. His confidence must have been restored. He took a puff and said, "Thinking about boyhood is a great embarrassment for most men, my dear, because it forces them to consider their numerous betrayals. Besides, everything I'd ever want to say about myself is in my books and letters. I hope to hell that no one ever tries to write about my life!"

"But that would be so tragic," she said. "People are meant to know what motivated a great writer like yourself."

He looked at her and said, "Why? What motivated me is that I wanted to write. I was luckier than most because my stuff got published and eventually I made a decent living at it. If history remembers me I'd just like to be known as an ordinary man with a bad sense of plot and a little touch of magic in my pen."

"But your plots are wonderful!" said Monica Wheetly. "At least in all the books I've read." She thought a bit and then added, "I must admit they get a little confusing toward the end."

"I always knew where I was headed," said Ray. "But getting there was hardly a straightforward task."

"Hello," I said, waiving my hand, "remember me? I'm the sucker you sent to do a little detective work."

"I haven't forgotten you, Marlow," said Ray, clearly glad to be off the subject of his life. "What did you find out about the pharmacist?"

"That he's dead," I said.

Ray exchanged a glance with his blushing friend and then looked back at me. "How did he die?"

"With a knife stuck through his gut."

"Would someone really try to kill you that way?" he asked. "I thought that a knife in the chest would be more likely."

"You've got a mess of ribs up there, Ray. They're easier to saw than knife."

"But how do you kill someone by knifing them in the gut? I heard of people who just walk away with a knife sticking out of their belly."

"It depends on the size of the blade," I said. "If it's long enough to slice through the liver or the kidney."

"How gruesome!" said Monica Wheetly, sticking out her tongue. "Do you really have to talk about it like that?"

"Death isn't very pretty, Miss," I said, tipping my hat if I had a hat to tip.

"Did you see the body?" asked Ray.

"Why would I want to see the body?" I asked in return. "I've seen bodies before. I don't collect them."

He shook his head. "You should have seen the body, Marlow." He gave me a distasteful look "What have they done with it now?"

"Either put it in the freezer or thrown it overboard, I guess."

"They wouldn't have thrown it overboard," said Ray. "They'll need it for the inquest."

"I certainly hope they didn't put it in the freezer with all the meats and cheese and fish!" said Monica Wheetly putting a hand over her stomach.

"Maybe they stuff it with dry ice and throw it in the hold," I said. "How the hell should I know?"

"Well, find out!" said Ray. "What do you think you're getting paid to do?"

"I'm not getting paid to sit and listen to you moan," I said.

Ray ignored the last remark and asked, "Do they know who did it, Marlow?"

"No," I replied. "Hart said the body was found by one of the crew. Carter was always getting into fights. It seems he was an excitable guy."

"What do they think this fight was about?" asked Ray.

"A woman?" Monica Wheetly proposed.

"Not likely," I said. "There aren't many women around for the crew to fight about. If Doris and Gladys were any example, then Carter wasn't exactly the kind of guy women go nuts over."

"Who are Doris and Gladys?" asked Monica Wheetly, showing a spark of interest in the names.

"A couple of cuties who call themselves nurses sometimes. I used to call them Tweedle Dum and Tweedle Dee because I thought they were so boring. But I was wrong."

"That's some admission, Dr Marlow," said Monica Wheetly.

"I'm sure I'll be wrong again sometimes," I told her.

"I wouldn't be surprised," she said.

"We've got to find out more about him," said Ray, rubbing his hand over the stubble of his chin.

"Maybe you could give me a little hint why this guy interests you so much," I said.

Ray stared at me. There seemed to be an emptiness about his look. "Don't you know?" he asked.

"Not really," I said. "I suppose it has to do with the bottle of barbiturates that dropped."

"But you don't know why?" He sounded very disappointed.

"Maybe I don't have the kind of mind that sees every little thing as a potential clue for imagined murder."

"What do you know about arsenic?" Ray suddenly asked me out of the muddy grey sky.

I shrugged. "I don't like eating it for kicks, if that's what you mean. People did at one time, you know."

"What else do you know about it?" he asked.

"It was once used as a erythropoietic," I said.

"What's that?" asked Monica Wheetly.

"Something that increases the production of red blood cells," I said. "Arsenic trioxyde used to be taken in small doses to give people a high. It helped increase your working capacity and gave you a ruddy complexion. It was also used in the treatment of skin disorders in the form of arsenous acid."

"Flowers of arsenic," said Ray. "Such a lovely name for murder."

"Arsenic poisoning used to be nearly always fatal," I said. "That's why it was used in a gaseous form during the war."

"Lewisite," said Ray. "Am I correct?"

"Yes. But the British found an antidote. It was known as Anti-Lewisite. It acted as a chelating agent. That's a chemical that bonds with heavy metals. It was administered intermuscularly in an oil base. We had to learn how to use it when I was in the army."

"Could I asked a question?" said Monica Wheetly. "Why are we talking about arsenic? Is there something I don't know about? Was someone poisoned?"

"It has to do with a case in my book of famous criminals and crimes," said Ray. He got into his story telling pose, brought out some special aromatic tobacco and stuffed his pipe.

"It all started on a ship something like this," he began, "some years before the war. Not the recent one. The one before that." He turned to Moncia Wheetly and said, "We're talking about my childhood, dear, not yours."

Monica Wheetly made herself comfy in her chair and positioned her chin between her hands so she could concentrate. "Go on, Ray," she said, "I'm listening."

I got myself ready too, by pouring myself a drink.

"There was a young woman, charming, well educated, American, going off to Europe for her first trip abroad. On board ship she met a man. He was British, a cotton broker from Liverpool, a gentleman some years older than herself. To make it short, they fell in love and eventually got married. The young bride moved into a fine Liverpool house, gave birth to first a boy and then a girl and, for a few years, seemed to be quite happy." Ray stopped for a moment to light his pipe.

Monica Wheetly sighed. "These are the kind of stories I like - something with a little romance in them."

"I haven't finished yet," said Ray. "It turned out that there were two things the young bride didn't know about her new husband. One was that he was an arsenic user - he took it in small doses as an elixir. And second..." Ray looked at Monica Wheetly and grinned.

"Yes? And second? Go on Ray!" she said, anxiously.

"He had another family somewhere in Liverpool."

"You mean a second wife and kids?" asked Monica Wheetly, looking thoroughly scandalised.

Ray nodded his head and took a puff on his pipe. The air was reeking with briary fumes. "The second wife was a working class woman who he has kept well hidden for social reasons. Their marriage was never sanctified. Whether the younger wife became aware of these two flaws in her husband's character simultaneously, I'm not sure. The point, however, is that it caused her much distress when she did."

"I shouldn't wonder!" Monica Wheetly butted in.

"Unfortunately, the young American woman felt very isolated and alone in Liverpool. All her friends were people she met through her husband and who owed their loyalty to him. She had no one she could really talk with about her problems. Not even her servants, who she began to see as spies."

"How awful!" said Monica Wheetly. She rubbed a trouble-some eye.

"Then, one day, she met a man. He was an acquaintance of her husband's who would occasionally come over to the house. Sometimes when her husband was away on business and she was left alone he would pay a visit. They had a brief affair at a quiet country hotel. And then he disappeared out of her life."

"The rat!" I heard Monica Wheetly say.

"The relationship between man and wife now grew steadily worse. His need for arsenic progressed. And her hatred of him swelled. Then, suddenly, one day he died..."

"Poisoned himself, I should think," said Monica Wheetly.

"And perhaps you would be right," said Ray. "Unfortunately, others in the house thought differently. An inquest was held into his death. And in due course his wife was arrested for the crime of killing her husband by poisoning him with arsenic."

"What?" Monica Wheetly's eyes grew wild. "That can't be,

Ray! How could they accuse her of that crime when there must have been people who knew he took arsenic?"

"Of course there were people who knew. Even his doctor knew that. What she was accused of, my dear, was bolstering the dose. In fact, it could have been the perfect crime. Who would have suspected her of poisoning a man who was poisoning himself?"

"But what was the evidence?" she asked. "How did they know?"

"The evidence, my dear, was flypapers soaking in a bowl..."

"Flypapers? Surely that can't be right!"

He turned to me. "What do you say, Marlow? Was that before your time?"

"'Fraid so," I replied.

"Arsenic was one of the ingredients in flypapers back then," he explained.

"And they thought she was collecting arsenic by soaking the flypapers?" asked Monica Wheetly.

"That's what they thought and the jury thought so, too. She was convicted of the crime and sent to jail."

"What about her children?" asked Monica Wheetly.

"They were taken by the husband's family to raise. She never saw or heard from them again."

"How sad!" I thought I saw a tear roll from her eye.

"Do you think she was guilty, Ray?" I asked.

He shrugged. "Perhaps she was. Who's to know?"

"She knew," said Monica Wheetly. "What did she say?"

"She always professed her innocence," he said. "Many people took up her case. It became a cause célèbre in England and America for a time. Later, in fact, new evidence came forth that cast a different light on the soaking flypaper story."

"What?" she asked. She looked like a pussycat pricking up her ears like that.

A prescription for a facial lotion that her mother found as a book mark in her daughter's bible. It listed the ingredients, one of which was arsenic. You see, she had always claimed that the flypapers were being used for that."

Monica Wheetly clapped her hands. "So she got out on appeal?"

Ray shook his head. "There was no appellate procedure for the British courts back then."

"None at all?" Now she looked so crestfallen you would have thought the kid was about to be thrown into the clink herself.

"The only appeal was to the Crown. Eventually, after many years, she was given a pardon."

"What happened to her then?" asked Moncia Wheetly, anxious to follow the story through to the bitter end.

"She went back to the United States where she became a celebrity for a while," he said. "Like a humpback in a circus side show. Then she disappeared from sight. I don't know what happened to her after that."

"And she never saw her children again..." she sighed. "But do you think she really did kill him?"

"I don't know," he said. "I only know what I would have done."

"Why does this case interest you so much, Ray?" I asked.

"Two reasons, Marlow," he said, getting up and walking over to the sink to quench his thirst. "First, I'm interested in the idea of the added dose. The one that puts you over the top. And second, the woman's name..." He filled his glass with water and drank it down.

"You're not going to tell us her name was Gloria Morgan," I said. "You'll spare us that at least."

"Her married name was Maybrick. But that's not the name that interests me. Her maiden name was Chandler. Same as mine. Her first name was Florence, like my mother's."

Chapter 24

It was a gentle rapping, almost hesitant, as if the rapper had wondered whether he had come to the right door.

"Enter!" Ray shouted. He rubbed his hands together and followed that up with a satisfied look.

The door opened, but not all the way, and Solly Meyers stuck his white head in. There was a little smile on his face, almost impish, as if he had eaten the last cherry from his grandson's birthday cake.

"I couldn't remember if it was 131 or 113," he said. "And then I thought maybe it's 133. I knew it had a 3 in it someplace. Also a one."

"I always work by process of elimination, too," said Ray, standing up and, as usual, seeming awkward about where to put his hands. "Sit down, Mr Meyers. Tell me what you want to drink."

"Hello, Dr Marlow, Miss Wheetly," he said, glancing over at us as he came in. And then, looking back at Ray, he said, "Drink? Water will be fine as long as you don't use the salty tap. I did that once. It tastes worse than Mrs Goldblat's chopped liver!"

Monica Wheetly was looking at him strangely. "Are you really Meyer Lansky, the famous gangster?" she asked, in an awe-struck sort of way.

He gave me a confused look and then gave the same to Ray. "Did I do something wrong?" he asked. He sounded like someone had just finished stepping on his swollen bunion in revenge for something he knew nothing about.

Miss Wheetly got one of Ray's fiercest stares. The kind that might make children want to run away and hide. "I'm sorry, Mr Meyers," he said. "I'm afraid that I'm to blame. You see, I had this little joke. I said, 'What if that gentleman wasn't Solly Meyers at all? What if he were Meyer Lansky?'"

Solly Meyers seemed as if his feelings had just been gently pistol-whipped. "And you thought that was funny?" He sighed and let his appendages fall into a shrug. "I can't understand why anyone would make a joke of that."

Monica Wheetly looked as guilty as hell. "Oh, Mr Meyers," she said, "I'm dreadfully sorry. You don't know how sorry I am!"

He held up a wrinkled hand like an arthritic Jewish cop. "Don't apologise," he said. "What's there to apologise for? You said what you said for whatever reason you said it. I'm an old man. Why people say the things they do no longer concerns me. They say them, that's all. What they say, really isn't important. If it was important, they probably wouldn't say them. At least they probably wouldn't say them to me." He sighed again. The old guy looked downright sad.

None of us really knew what to say to that.

Then he looked up at us with a little twinkle in his eye. "Now if you're asking me whether I know something about Meyer Lansky and some of the people he did business with, well, that's a different story..."

Ray suddenly looked as chipper as a bird who got its worm. "He ran the protection racket in the Manhattan clothing trade, am I correct?"

"A gentleman named Bugsy Segel, who was not such a gentleman, was the man to see if you wanted to insure that your warehouse didn't burn down. Mr Lansky was a confederate of his."

Ray looked as if he were hot on the scent. But where the smell he had picked up was leading him was anybody's guess.

"A day or two ago at dinner you said you had business dealings with the Ambassador at one time..." Ray began.

Mr Meyers shook his head. "Not business dealings, myself. I knew a little about the way he did some business, though. That's all I was trying to say. If a businessman has any competition, he has one or two alternatives. Either he can do better business than his competitors or he can try to shut them down. The Ambassador always chose the later path, I understand. And he was very successful, I might add."

"There was a rumor," said Ray, "that the Ambassador made his fortune in the liquor trade when it was not strictly legit..."

Again Solly Meyers cut in. "He was a bootlegger, Mr Chandler. We might as well call a card by its proper name. And he did it very well. He had good connections in Ireland - or so I hear. He had his own fleet of ships. It was a very profitable business. But he had a terrible temper, I understand. And once, I've been told, Mr Lansky had the misfortune to get in his way."

"What happened?" asked Ray.

Mr Meyers held out his hands, palms up. If a beggar did that you might have given him a nickel or a dime. "What happened? Mr Lansky hijacked one of his trucks. I understand it was a perfectly innocent mistake."

"Tell me, Mr Meyers," said Ray, "how was all that booze brought in? I suppose they didn't unload those ships right at the docks."

"Sometimes they did," said Solly Meyers. "Everyone was in someone else's pay. But more often they transferred their cargo outside the territorial waters and brought the liquor in by speed boat to tiny harbors up the coast."

"And weren't these ships sometimes diverted to Cuba or the Bahamas and offloaded there?"

"It seems to me I heard such stories, too," said Solly Meyers.

Ray scratched his head. If he was just acting dumb he was playing it pretty well. "I've always wondered what happened to all the funds that accumulated during those years. Everything was done by cash, wasn't it?"

Here's where I came in. "You couldn't very well write out a check to your local bootlegger, I don't suppose."

"But all that money," said Ray, seemingly in wonder, "all those piles and piles of greenback dollars. What in the world did they do with them? They couldn't open up an account in their neighborhood bank, could they?" He looked questioningly at Solly Meyers.

"Maybe they went outside their neighborhood," Solly Meyers replied.

"Perhaps they opened up accounts in places like Cuba, do you think?"

"It wouldn't surprise me if they had."

"But then they wouldn't let it sit there. Not piles of money like that. Not for so many years."

"I'm sure they took good care to make it work for them," said Solly Meyers. "Any good businessman would make certain to do that."

"Isn't that what they call 'dry cleaning' funds, Mr Meyers?" asked Monica Wheetly, trying to sound like her tutor in crime but without the pipe.

"I don't think I've heard that term before," said Solly Meyers, shaking his greying head. "But certainly the money had to be spent on projects, shall we say, that used a great deal of cash - the kind that was very hard to trace."

"Like playing the ponies? Projects like that?" I suggested.

Solly Meyers made a gesture with his face which told me my example wasn't up to snuff. "Gangsters might own casinos, Dr Marlow," he said, "but they don't gamble away their hard earned funds."

"Perhaps there's another industry that more hits the mark," said Ray.

"Which one were you thinking of, Mr Chandler?" asked Solly Meyers. If that man played poker, I wouldn't have joined in the game.

"I was thinking of the movie industry," said Ray. "It's awfully difficult to trace the funds that are used to make a film, wouldn't you say?"

"I suppose you're right," said Solly Meyers. "But I really wouldn't know. Clothing is my trade."

"I mean when you think that millions of dollars can be gone through within the course of weeks, it makes you wonder where it all comes from, doesn't it?"

"I've never thought about it myself," said Solly Meyers. "Now that you bring it up..." He shrugged his shoulders again. "But what does it all mean? They make such silly moving pictures these days."

Ray leaned a little forward, like a hawk. "I was just thinking - the Ambassador once made a film, didn't he?"

"So I understand," said Solly Meyers. "Although he doesn't look like the kind of man who would make moving pictures, does he? I usually think of someone with an ivory cigarette holder and a beret."

"But he did make a film," said Ray. "Some years ago. Before the war. And do you know who he cast as his star?"

"The star? You mean the one who played the lead? No, I'm sorry, I can't help you there. Unless, of course, you're asking me a question when it's an answer you already know. You seem to do that sometimes, Mr Chandler."

"It's part of his charm," I said, looking over at Ray.

"You're going to Israel by way of London, Mr Meyers?" said Ray, suddenly changing his tack. "Are you going there for business or just a holiday?"

"For me vacations are business. You happen to meet someone. They're interested in cloth. Maybe you have a few samples in your bag. Maybe something happens. Maybe not. What have you got to lose? I always say."

"I hope you pardon me," said Ray, "I don't mean to be butting in. I'm just curious. That's my trade."

"Curiosity isn't a bad trade," said Solly Meyers. "They say it killed the cat. But maybe the cat had smarter kittens."

"It just seems," Ray went on, "not the best time in the world to be taking a vacation in Israel."

"The time to take a vacation is when your business lets you go," said Solly Meyers.

"But surely you're aware of what happened in the Middle East today," said Ray, looking at Solly Meyers and then over at me.

"You mean the announcement by the new pharaoh they have in Egypt now - what's his name again?"

"Nasser," Ray reminded him.

"Nasser, Schmasser, they're all the same. They all want to kill Jews. So now they're going to do it with Russian weapons instead of those they got from Britain or America. What difference does it make?"

"What difference indeed?" said Ray staring over at the old man. "Perhaps we should ask the Ambassador."

"I wouldn't do that, Mr Chandler," said Mr Meyers with another of his almost smiles. "I think he might have problems of his own right now."

"Yes. I suppose he must be worried about the Baghdad Pact," said Ray. "I went with Marlow to the Ambassador's press conference before the ship set sail. He sounded pretty hot on what he called 'the ring of iron' around Arabia that would keep the Russians out."

"The problem with the Baghdad Pact," said Solly Meyers, "is that Israel was not a part. We're not opposed to keeping Russia out. But Arab unity threatens more than Russia, I'm afraid."

Why the old man looked different now got me wondering. Maybe it was the way he held his head. He didn't look any younger. Maybe a little less elderly.

"Politics really isn't my game," said Ray. "Somewhere along the line I lost my scorecard."

"I'm not much interested in politics either," said Solly Meyers. "I'm interested in survival. I wish I lost my scorecard just as you. But a man called Hitler was keeping score for people like myself."

"And for many others, too," said Ray. "Those were terrible years. I tried enlisting, you know. They said I was too old and fat."

"I was there. You didn't miss much, Ray," I put in.

Solly Meyers stared at me with watery eyes. "You kept the flames of hope alive for old men like myself," he said. "I thank God for all the boys like you. Where did you serve, if I might ask?"

"I was in Germany," I said. "Ten years ago today."

"Just ten years," he shook his head again. "It seems like centuries."

"It didn't back then," I said. "Ten years ago, time was pretty good at standing still."

"Where were you?" he asked. "I had people...you know..." His voice was getting weak.

"It was near Weimar in the East. A place called Buchenwald," I said.

He was quiet for a moment. "So you were there..." he started to say. His voice seemed like a tire going flat.

Then he got up from his chair and put the water that wasn't salted on a nearby chest of drawers. "I must get ready for lunch," he said. "Thank you for the drink." He looked at me. "Perhaps we'll get a chance to speak before the ship brings us to shore."

"Where's that place you were again?" asked Monica Wheetly, after Solly Meyers left. "Buchenwhat? Mr Meyers seemed to know it quite well. Do you think he once lived there?"

"Maybe some of his family," I said.

Ray had been staring at me pretty hard for a while. "You didn't tell me you were there," he said.

"You didn't ask," I replied.

"I'm asking now," he said. "Were you there when it was liberated?"

"A few days after," I said. "I was part of the medical team that they called for when they cut through the barbed wire and saw what started to come out."

"And what didn't, I suppose," said Ray.

"What didn't come out was piled in mounds about twenty feet high."

"Mounds of what?" asked Monica Wheetly. "I do wish you two would tell me what you're being so cryptic about!"

"We're talking about Hell, Miss Wheetly," I said. "The mounds were all the bones that were taken from its fires."

Chapter 25

Ray had ordered sandwiches brought to his room. He and the Wheetly kid had fallen into a literary discussion over liverwurst on rye. Unlike Solly Meyers, I sort of liked Goldblat's chopped-up stuff. It was the stale air from Ray's overheated pipe that didn't do much for my appetite. So I excused myself and went below to hunt up a more conducive meal.

The restaurant was nearly empty when I arrived. The early lunchers had already left. Even Rinexus had filled his pit and gone to roam on Steel Island like a satiated buffalo.

Solly Meyers wasn't there, either. Maybe he was still getting ready for his meal. Maybe he had eaten his cottage cheese and left. Maybe he had gone back to his cabin and fell asleep forgetting about food. Maybe something else. Who knows?

The table was empty except for Roger Lane. He was on his second course. He looked up as I sat down. "Seems like we're the only ones who want to eat today," he said.

"It has to do with changing time," I replied. "We keep putting our watches forward when we reach another zone. But our stomachs are still back in New York."

"It's worse by plane," he said. "At least on ship you have some time to adjust. When you travel by air you've arrived almost before you started. Except you find it's day instead of night. Or the reverse. How do you prefer travelling, Dr Marlow?"

"I prefer anything that gives me time to drink," I said. "If a mule had a bar and water wings, I'd go that way I guess."

The waiter came by and I ordered the hot dogs and sauerkraut. Roger Lane glanced at me over his steak tartare and said, "You enjoy the simple things, I see."

"I don't like to fuss about food," I said. "And I expect it not to fuss about me."

"Well," he said, "as long as you don't have to eat your words."

"I eat my words morning, noon and night," I said. "By the way, how's your wife."

"She's a little off," he said.

"Too bad," I replied. "Would you like me to look in on her?"

He hesitated a moment with his fork to mouth routine and said, "No, I don't think that would be necessary, Dr Marlow. I'm sure she'll be all right. It's kind of you to offer, though."

"Well, let me know if anyone in your room needs help," I said.

He tried to smile. It came more as a frown. "Of course," he said.

My hot dog arrived. I sliced it up and stuffed the pieces in my hatch. Then I wiped my face.

"You seem hungry today, Dr Marlow," he said.

"Famished," I said. "I don't know why."

"Maybe you're going through a biological change," he suggested.

"That could be," I said. "I once read a book about a man who metamorphosed into a cockroach. But cockroaches don't eat very much, do they, Mr Lane?"

He seemed amused. "Do you know Kafka, Dr Marlow? Not many Americans do, you know. It's too bad. He might have been writing just for them."

"Aren't you American?" I asked him. "I know your wife is English but I thought you were from the USA."

"I was once," he said. "Not any more."

The waiter came by again and I ordered a refill for my plate. He gave me a funny look. "The same thing again, sir?" he asked.

"When you hit on something good, why change? Isn't that what they say in Hollywood these days?"

Lane ordered coffee and something from their tray of pies. "Any luck on your quest?" he asked as he spooned some sugar into his cup.

"What quest is that? Are we still speaking of my metamorphosis?"

"I meant your investigation into what happened to Gloria Morgan - the missing movie star." He looked down at his plate and cut a piece of pie in half. "It seems like it happened so long

163

ago that people barely remember her name."

"Gloria Morgan once told me that fame doesn't last. Something about a 'fleeting moment' I think she said."

"That's what it means to be a star," he said. "The brighter you burn, the faster you burn out. They also say that in Hollywood."

"How long were you in Hollywood, Mr Lane? I don't think you ever told us what you were doing there?"

"I was doing almost everything there was to do," he said. He looked down at his pie again. "Would you like the other half? I don't think I can eat all of this. And I really hate to waste food."

"Take it back to your room," I said. "Someone there seems to have a healthy appetite."

He looked at me like he was studying my face. "It's not what you think, Marlow," he said. "I can assure you of that."

"What do I think?" I asked. "It's a rare day at sea when I can think at all."

He finished his coffee and then he said, "Can I buy you a drink? Or are you not a drinking man?"

"I have an occasional shot," I admitted. "Between my beer and rum. I won't say 'no'."

"As long as you can say 'no'" he replied with a little smile in his eyes.

"Oh, I can say 'no', all right. It's just that at this particular time in my life I prefer to say 'yes'."

I finished up my hot dog and sauerkraut, let out a satisfied burp that wasn't too loud, but loud enough, and pushed back my chair. Then the two of us went up to the Veranda Lounge.

The bartender recognised me. I don't know how. "The usual, Dr Marlow?" he asked.

"Play it again, Sam," I replied.

"Do you know where that line comes from?" asked Roger Lane.

"That was Humphry Bogart in 'Casablanca', wasn't it?" the bartender said.

"Everybody thinks it was," said Lane. "But Bogart never really said it."

"I could have sworn he did," said the bartender. "I've seen

164

that movie seven times."

"And you probably heard that line even more," said Lane. "You think it's there, because it sounds like it should be there. It's all a figment of your mind."

"Does that mean I shouldn't bother filling your glass, Mr Lane?" the bartender replied.

"Bartenders are the world's repository of stale humor," said Lane, taking his Cointreau and following me up the three little stairs that I had often trod before.

"That's why most of them look like they've been hung out on a clothes line to dry overnight," I said, finding a quiet table and sitting down. "I should have been a bartender, maybe."

"You're a curious man, Marlow," he said, sitting down across from me. "You always seem to be making fun of yourself."

"Something I learned when I was in the Army," I said, taking a drink of my drink. "Shoot first. Then clean up the mess."

"As long as you don't go around shooting yourself in the foot," said Roger Lane.

"The very first thing they teach you in medical school," I said, "is always heed your own advice."

"Too bad most physicians don't remember that," said Lane.

"If they did, they'd be as bad off as their patients."

Roger Lane let his face relax. He looked almost human now. He lifted up his glass. "Cheers, Marlow," he said.

"Here's mud in your eye," I said back.

He took a drink of his clear sickly-looking stuff and said, "Did you know her very well?"

"Who are we talking about now?" I asked. "My ex-mother-in-law?"

"I meant Gloria Morgan. You said she talked to you about 'fleeting moments' and fame."

"It was a brief affair," I said. "Not much over twenty seconds. How about you, Lane? Did you know her?"

"Oh, I saw her around. No matter what anyone tells you, Marlow, Hollywood's really a pretty small town."

"I suppose it is," I said. "It's just that she didn't seem to recognise you the day she came over to our table."

He shrugged and took another sip at his drink. "Perhaps I'm not the recognisable sort."

"I guess your wife isn't either," I said.

"Oh, my wife didn't know many of those people," he said. "She kept pretty far apart."

"I don't blame her," I said, "If people like Rinexus are any sample of what you find when rocks are tuned over in LA."

"Believe it or not, Rinexus isn't the worst face Hollywood has on offer."

"I guess so," I said. "Isn't Hollywood where they made Frankenstein?"

"They also made some decent films there - once upon a time," he said.

"I remember Tom Mix," I said, allowing a little nostalgia to spill in. "And Charlie Chaplin wasn't bad."

"He left Hollywood after 'Monsieur Verdeux'," said Roger Lane. "Like many others, he won't return."

"We saw a bunch of Hollywood movies when we were in the Army," I said. "They showed them to us so we could forget about the war. Some of them weren't bad - the ones made in the thirties anyway. Probably when people like Ray were working there."

"People like Chandler were there when Hollywood was still alive," he said. "Back then it was an exciting place to be." He looked over at the bartender who was coming with our drinks. "Could I change that for a whiskey?" he asked, snubbing the refill of Cointreau. Maybe the guy wasn't so bad after all, I thought.

"Ray didn't like it much, to hear him talk," I said. "He referred to it as 'The Swamp'."

"An appropriate name for LA," said Lane. "But I think Chandler wanted something that Hollywood couldn't give."

"That's what Rinexus said," I reminded him.

"I haven't much love for Rinexus, either," said Lane, "but he understands what Hollywood is all about a little better than your friend Chandler. And there's someone else on board this ship who understands it even better than him."

"You mean yourself?" I asked.

"Besides myself," he said, with undue modesty.

"You want me to guess, is that it? How about the bartender?"

"I was thinking of the Ambassador," he said. "I once read something he was quoted to have said. It was about the commercial benefits opened up by pictures. He claimed that America produced over 80% of the films distributed worldwide compared to only 20% of the global wheat. He said the motion picture industry could open up limitless markets - that it could be the perfect medium for displaying American products to foreign consumers."

"Sounds like he was a better businessman than Solly Meyers gave him credit for," I said.

"The Ambassador understood the power of films," said Lane. "He was intrigued by the manipulation of people and events."

"So were some other folk, if what the papers said was correct. In fact, some of them it seems were downright UnAmerican."

Roger Lane rubbed his mouth as if he were wondering how to answer that. "It's hard to think that people could be branded UnAmerican by a congressional committee," he said. "America is a place, not a way of thought. We're supposed to have freedom of ideas and speech. At least that's what the history books taught us when we were kids."

"Well, that might be right," I said, "but I still wouldn't want anyone climbing into bed with me dressed up like Stalin."

"How about Tom Paine?" he said. "He was an Englishman, you know."

I took another drink and shrugged my nose. "I'm not political," I said. "Those arguments bore me to tears."

"Some of the people who were kicked out of Hollywood weren't political either, Marlow. They just had the bad luck to have been named."

"Some of them were," I said. "If it walks like a duck and it has a quack..."

"Why not call it a duck? Is that what you were going to say?"

"Something like that. Yeah," I replied.

"The problem was that some of them were artists, too."

"You're not referring to yourself, I don't suppose," said I.

"I was referring more to people like Brecht," he replied. "He was called before the congressional investigating committee, too. He testified and the next day he left for Europe vowing never to return."

"Brecht?" I said. "Never heard of the man. Should I have?"

"Well, for someone who's read Kafka..." Lane began.

"You mean this guy Brecht wrote in German, too?"

"All the time."

"Then he was UnAmerican," I said.

Lane was beginning to look distressed. His cheeks were getting red and his temperature was starting to rise. I could see a gasket being blown if I didn't cool things off. The guy had a low boiling point. I didn't realise just how low until I started turning up the heat.

He pulled a copy of the Times from his pocket and shook it in my face. "I read in the paper right before we left that the Justice department now has 303 organisations on its subversive list!" He opened up the paper. "You want to hear what some of these UnAmerican groups are? Listen to this - 'The Massachusetts Committee for the Bill of Rights, Everybody's Committee to Outlaw War, the Idaho Pension Union, The Committee to Abolish Discrimination in Maryland, the Pittsburgh Art Club, the Trade Union Committee for Common Sense...'"

He looked at me over the top of his newspaper. "And this list is used by all Federal Agencies to screen people who are seeking employment, Marlow. It's also used by every large corporation in the USA."

"Look," I said, "I don't like the crap that Hoover and McCarthy are stirring up any more than you. But most Americans don't support that nonsense, Lane. Most people know its being done by a bunch of half educated politicians trying to manipulate a few votes so they can get elected again to do what they've always done - namely, feather their own nest."

"That's where you're wrong, Marlow," said Lane. "There's an ideological war going on right now in America. It's going on in Europe, too. And its just as dirty as the hot one we just fought. The only difference is that this time not many people are dying

- not by bombs at any rate. But there are thousands of victims who are suffering none the less."

"Do you count yourself as one of the victims in that war?" I asked Lane.

"Maybe I do," he said. "Maybe we all are."

I shook my head. "Anyone who lets themselves be a prisoner of ideas is a fool. I might be drunk," I said, "but I'm not nuts. Not yet at any rate."

Lane smiled with his mouth, not with his eyes. "You're a real American hero, Marlow."

"I'm my own man, Lane," I said. "I make my own mistakes. That's enough for me to handle. I can't be responsible for the human race. I found that out the hard way."

"No one in America can be responsible for anyone anymore," said Lane, finishing up his drink. "And that's why I'm leaving that God forsaken place!"

"Listen," I said, "I don't know where you've lived before, but I think you'll find it ain't much different here, there or anywhere else."

"You're a cynic, Marlow," he said, looking straight at me. "Isn't there anything you believe in?"

I lifted up my glass. "I only believe in things that come in liquid form," I said.

"Oh, that's just fine!" said Lane. "You could run for president on that platform! 'All power to the liquids!'"

I took a long and satisfying drink. "Say, that's not a bad slogan!"

Chapter 26

"I thought I'd find you here!" She plopped herself down on a chair without waiting for an invitation.

"Hello, Miss Wheetly," said Roger Lane. "Can I order you a drink?"

She looked at me and I caught the gleam of mischief in her eyes. "Thank you, Mr Lane," she said. "I'll have a martini, if you please."

"With or without the olive?" he asked, as he signalled to the bartender.

"Better tell him to hold the gingerale as well," I said. "That guy down there fits people with a drink. I'm afraid she's already been typecast."

She took off her specs and batted her eyes at Roger Lane. "I'll have the olive, thanks."

"How's Ray?" I said as Lane was calling for her drink. "Still searching through his books on criminals and crime?"

"He's taking his afternoon nap, Dr Marlow," she said in a huffy sort of way. "He wanted to be left alone." Then she turned to Roger Lane and said in a voice that was oozingly sweet, "I do hope you're wife is better."

"She is, thank you," he said. "I don't think she'll mind it when we dock."

The bartender brought over her martini and she took the long stemmed glass, thanked him and then twirled the martini stick. "Ray told me about Buchenwald," she said, gazing down into its depths. "Now I understand why Solly Meyers looked that way."

"Was Solly Meyers in Buchenwald?" asked Roger Lane.

"No," said Monica Wheetly, taking the olive off the stick and popping it into her mouth. "He was," she said pointing the plastic olive holder my way.

"I don't understand," Roger Lane said to me looking pretty confused, "what were you doing there?"

"He was part of a medical team that was brought in after it

was freed," said Monica Wheetly.

"I was just reading about Buchenwald in the Times," said Lane. "It seems that 50,000 former inmates and their families came back to celebrate the 10th anniversary of its liberation."

"Fifty thousand more were there," I said, "if you want to count the ashes. They weren't celebrating, I don't suspect."

Roger Lane pointed to his paper. "There was a report by a British parliamentary committee that visited the camp shortly after it was taken over by US troops on April 11, 1945. The report said that the surviving inmates were in such terrible condition they were dying at the rate of 35 a day."

"Look," I said, "I'm just about to take that newspaper of yours, wad it up and stuff it down your gullet!"

"He has a lovely disposition, doesn't he?" said Monica Wheetly taking a hesitant drink of her martini and then making a very sour face.

"Your disposition is pretty rotten," said Roger Lane, giving me a cow-eyed look that I could have done without. "But I think I understand how you feel. I know it must be tough for you to talk about. On the other hand, these are things the world should hear. It's only ten years away and people have already forgotten that it happened."

"Solly Meyers hadn't," said Monica Wheetly. "But he's Jewish, isn't he? So I don't suppose he would."

"There's a lot of others besides Jews who died there," I said. "Anyone who was classified as an inferior race - Poles, Gypsies, Russians"

"And anyone whose politics were suspect, Marlow." He looked hard into my eyes. "Communists of any race were thrown into those ovens, as well."

"Not too many, I wouldn't think," I said, gratefully taking the drink the bartender handed me. "It was relatively easy to deny your politics. It's not so easy to say you're not a Gypsy or a Jew."

"I knew some Jews at college," said Monica Wheetly. "Some of them were my best friends. They were rather overly-sensitive people, I think. Ray says the same thing. He says he was disturbed by several letters he received from Jewish readers who

171

criticised a couple of his characters they thought were written as stereotypes..."

"Were they?" I asked.

She took another sip of her martini, making less of a face this time, and then said, "Yes, I expect they were. But most of his characters are stereotypes - especially the women. The difference is that his stereotypes come alive. And he does have a few sympathetic Jewish characters. There's that lovely doctor in High Window for example."

"That was written in the 40's, I bet," said Roger Lane. "Lots of writers who were basically anti-Semites changed their tune about then. Take Orwell, for example. If you look at *Down and Out in Paris and London*, Jews are portrayed as slimy, money-grubbing beasts. Then, when you read his later work, especially his essays, you understand how Hitler made intelligent men come to terms with their prejudices in a very forceful way."

"You wouldn't be Jewish, yourself, would you, Mr Lane?" I asked.

He fumbled with his glass and then said, "Partly, yes..."

"That's funny," said Monica Wheetly, "I wouldn't have taken you for a Jew. Lane's not a Jewish name."

"I'm Jewish on my mother's side," he said, looking down at the table.

"Now Solly Meyers," said Monica Wheetly, finishing her drink and licking the remains from her glass, "he's a real Jew. You can tell that right away." She looked at me. "Do you think I could have another drink, Dr Marlow?"

"Are you asking for professional advice?" I said. "Or is that what they call in college a 'rhetorical question'?"

She lifted up her empty glass. "Oh, Mr Bartender! Yoo, hoo!"

"Mr Meyers is much more than a Jew," said Roger Lane.

"More than a Jew? What is he then?" asked Monica Wheetly who had gotten the bartender's attention and now was wanting to concentrate on the conversation again.

"He's a Zionist," said Roger Lane.

"Isn't that the same thing?" she asked, in her own sweet little way.

"No. A Jew is someone born of Jewish ancestry. A Zionist is someone who puts the nation of Israel above everything else. Someone who thinks therein lies the true Kingdom of Heaven. A sort of super-nationalist who believes that God resides in Jerusalem."

"Maybe they just want someplace where they can live in peace," I suggested.

"Peace?" Roger Lane let out a laugh. He picked up his newspaper again and showed us the front page. "Israel is a nation founded upon conflict. It's a country doomed to be in an eternal state of war. No nation based so much on hatred can ever find peace."

"But Mr Lane," said Monica Wheetly, "it seems to me that Israel was formed precisely because there was no peace. Hitler murdered millions of Jews - or so I'm told. Why shouldn't they have their own state?"

"Because the very notion of an ethnic state is an aberration in our world. That's what Hitler wanted, don't you see? Zionists, like other groups of zealots, see themselves as a chosen race. They don't mind sending their children to die fighting their Semitic brothers."

"Maybe their Semitic brothers don't mind fighting them," I said. "Every nation struggles to exist. Every nation tries to make their founders into saints. Israel's no different. How many nations are really built on brotherhood and justice?" I said.

"America?" said Monica Wheetly, running an unsteady finger around the rim of her glass.

"Ask any Indian," I said.

"I don't disagree with what you're saying," replied Roger Lane, "I just wanted to point out that Judaism and Zionism aren't the same thing. Israel won't save the Jews," he said.

"What will save any of us?" I asked.

"I don't know," said Roger Lane, looking down at the table once again. "I thought I did a few years ago. I'm not so certain anymore. I just know that the fate of the Jews is linked up with the fate of the rest of the human race. Zionists refuse to recognise that notion anymore. They consider themselves too special."

"I think you're the one who's making them so special," I said. "I don't see them as being any different than the rest of us. All governments are basically corrupt. All politicians, whether they're Jews, Irish or from the Outer Hebrides, aren't fit to clean the kitchen sink."

Monica Wheetly was stirring her martini with her finger now. "That poor, sweet, little man..." she said with a sigh.

"Who are you talking about?" I asked her. "Ray or your father?"

Her eyes were beginning to get that special glaze I knew so well. "I was talking about Mr Meyers," she said. And downing the rest of her drink she looked up and wiggled the wet finger she had just used to stir. "Oh, bartender!" she sang.

"That poor, sweet, little man is probably an Israeli spy," said Roger Lane, in an offhanded way.

Monica Wheetly looked upset. "For heaven's sake!" she pouted. "Why would you ever say that?" She chewed on olive number three and then suddenly giggled. "Oh, my goodness! Everything's starting to go round!"

"I keep my eyes and ears open, too," said Roger Lane. "I read the report of Nasser's speech in the daily newsletter the ship puts out. Egypt's purchase of Czech weapons will divide the Arab states..."

"You don't have to be an Israeli spy to know that," I said.

Roger Lane leaned toward me and narrowed up his eyes. "I saw Solly Meyers nosing around the Argentine's room last night," he said.

"I was nosing around there, too," I said, "and I've never been to Israel in my life."

"Do you know that Argentina has the largest number of Jews in the Western hemisphere outside the United States?" he said.

"No," I replied. "What of it?"

Roger Lane stuck his finger so close to my face I thought it would go right up my nose. "Think about it, Marlow. It wouldn't hurt the Zionist cause if the Generals dumped Peron and brought in a military dictatorship."

I shrugged my shoulders. "So they trade one dictator for

another," I said. "What does that prove?"

"Peron might have his faults," said Lane, "but he's also done some good things there."

"I'm sure that Stalin did some good things for Russia, too," I said, "like opening up lots of labor camps."

Roger Lane shook his head. "You're hopeless, Marlow. Forget I brought the subject up."

Monica Wheetly finished off her third martini and said, "Oh, what are we being so serious for?" And then she giggled again. "Let's be gay! What you two are talking about is so boring! I mean, who cares?" She put her elbow on the table and put her chin in her hand and leaned toward Roger Lane and said, "Do you know any jokes? Tell me a joke!"

Lane gave her a tired smile. "OK," he said. "I won't tell you a joke, I'll show you a trick instead."

She leaned further forward till I thought she'd fall flat on her face. "All right, show me a trick. Then maybe I'll get old glum-face Marlow to tell me a joke."

Lane took a coin out of his pocket and tossed it in the air. Then he reached out and caught it in his right hand, clenched his fists and held both his right and left hands out.

"Which hand is it in?" he asked.

"The right one!" she said. "I'm not that drunk!"

He opened his right hand. It was empty.

"Open the other one!" she ordered.

He opened his left hand. It was empty, too.

Monica Wheetly looked like she couldn't believe her eyes. "Where did it go?" she asked.

Roger Lane got up. He stood there for a minute. Then he winked and said, "It disappeared!"

"I don't believe in magic," said Monica Wheetly, looking soppily over at Roger Lane as he walked away. "Do you, Marlow?"

I could see that she was half way to the ceiling now. "I'm a doctor, remember?"

"You said once you killed someone. I bet it was Santa Claus!" she said.

"No," I said, "it was an old man who was barely skin and bones. He had been a famous violinist once."

She stared at me. Her eyes were like frosted cupcakes kept out on the window sill too long. "Why'd you kill him, Marlow?"

I shrugged. "His wife was dead. So was his daughter. So was everyone else he knew and loved. He asked me to help him die. So I did."

"That was nice of you," she said, looking down into her empty long-stemmed glass. "You answer all requests, big and small, with the same charm, wit and grace, don't you?"

"You're drunk," I said.

"And you're a bastard," she replied, staring back into my eyes.

"Maybe I am," I said, standing up. "Let me help you back to your room."

I can manage for myself," she said, trying to stand up and then falling back into her chair. She started to giggle again. "Maybe I'll just stay here till the ship gets in." Then suddenly she put a hand over her mouth. "Oh, oh. I think I need a bathroom!"

I put my hand underneath her arm and gave her a lift. I got her up and then she folded in on herself again. I lifted her once more. She put her head on my shoulder, like she was a floppy rag doll, and whispered, "Oh, Marlow, you're so strong!"

"Not strong enough, Toots," I said, knowing the chances of me dragging her down to her room without damaging the merchandise was pretty small.

Just then Solly Meyers came into the lounge. He saw us standing there, like two marathon dancers too tired to dance and afraid to let go.

"Can I be of assistance?" he asked, coming over.

"Grab the other arm," I said.

He put her arm around his shoulder and we began to walk her to the door.

"Tell me, Mr Meyers," she giggled. "Are you an Israeli spy?"

"Oy, vay!" he said. "First you accuse me of being a gangster and now an Israeli spy. What next? Maybe a thief who smuggles drugs in bagels and sells the holes to orphans, besides!"

Chapter 27

Solly Meyers helped me get Monica Wheetly to her cabin door. Then he left. He didn't want to be accused of doing something else, he said.

I got her inside by myself and let her collapse onto her bed. Her hair fell across her face like tassels from a golden window shade. Her legs draped over the side of the mattress as if they were stuffed with straw. I took off her shoes and lifted her legs back on the bed, wondering how her feet could be so small.

She brushed the hair out of her eyes with a sweep of her hand and said, "Marlow..." And then she began to laugh. It flowed from her lips like water bubbling from a stream, only this stream was more like the River Styx as far as I was concerned. And once you pass those shores you don't return. I tried it once. I know.

"Get to sleep," I said, "you'll feel better in an hour or so."

She grabbed my hand, her fingers wrapped around it like fiery snakes. She wasn't laughing any more. Her face was flushed. She closed her eyes and puckered up her lips. "Kiss me, Marlow," she said.

"Are you sure you want me?" I asked. "Or is this part of your graduation act?"

She opened up her eyes and stared at me again. "I'm not a little girl, you know."

"You're not a big one, either," I said.

Her hair had fallen back over one of her eyes. Her blouse was opened at the top. Her skirt was in disarray. Her lipstick was smeared across her face. She'd never have passed muster like that, but she looked a hell of a lot better than the prim and proper girl who had started on this trip.

"I'm bigger than you think, Marlow," she said. She kept staring in my eyes. Her hand was still gripped tightly around mine.

Maybe I did feel something. I don't know. Maybe it was the drink. Anyway, I pulled my hand away. It was like pulling out a plug. Tears came from her eyes.

"Listen," I said, "if this was ten years ago you wouldn't have had to go this far to get me in your bed. But I'm no good for you. You might not believe me, but it's true."

She took my hand again. Hers was soft and warm this time, not like a claw. "I'm not asking you for anything," she said. "I just want you to be kind."

"The world's a hard place," I said, "it sort of chops away at you. Kindness is one of the first things to go."

"You're always excusing yourself, Marlow," she said, "but you don't have to be that way. Love exists, if you let yourself believe..." She gave my hand a gentle tug.

I stood my ground. "Love exists for girls like you," I said. "Not for men like me. I've seen too much."

"And I haven't seen enough? Is that what you're trying to say?"

I shook my head. "There's no reason to visit Hell," I said. "You don't learn anything from the experience except that hate is a stronger emotion than love."

"If I believed that," she said, "I wouldn't want to live."

She closed her eyes and I pulled my hand away again. "You have it in a nutshell then," I said.

*****

I left her sound asleep. I shut the door to her cabin and walked on down the hall. When I reached the corridor that led to my room, I saw someone standing by my door. His back was turned, but I didn't have to see his face to know who he was.

I walked over and said, "You want something or are you just waiting for the Shopper's Special bus?"

He turned around like a bull dog taken unaware by a scroungy alley cat. He pointed a stubby finger like a snub-nosed gun and said, "The Ambassador wants to see you, chum!"

"Sorry," I said, pushing myself past, "I ran out of publicity snaps. Ask him to try my agent. He lives just a few doors down."

The gorilla grabbed my arm and gave it a nasty twist. "You don't want to happen to you what happened to that broad!"

The pain shot through me like hot wire connected to 3000 volts. I wanted to say that if the broad had a broken arm it was no wonder she couldn't swim. But it's hard to be that witty when a simple-minded simian decides to make you his banana split.

"Now be good and save yourself the bother of two months in cement," he said easing up a bit.

"Is that a moral imperative?" I said. "Or are you asking me to waltz?"

"I'm telling you to shut up, bright guy, and follow me," he said, giving me a shove.

"Where the hell did you learn how to dance?" I said, allowing myself to be manoeuvred toward the stairs.

On the way up we met the kid with the pill box hat. He was loaded down with another heavy tray.

"Lion feeding time?" I asked in passing.

"Yes, sir," he smiled. And then I guess he noticed there was something peculiar in the way I was going up the stairs because he said, "Is there something wrong, Dr Marlow?"

"Nothing a can of Lock-Ease couldn't fix," I said.

The gorilla gave me another twist and pushed me harder.

"Well, see you later, Dr Marlow," said the kid, going down the other way.

We reached the next level and the gorilla shoved again. "You shouldn't have done that," he growled.

"Done what?" I asked. "Allow myself to be born?"

"Said that to the kid." He shoved me onwards down the hall. "I told you to shut up!"

"I was never very good at following commands from gofers," I said. "Especially when they haven't enough brains to dig a hole to piss in."

He pushed me to a door and then let go. He pointed the snub-nosed finger in my face again and said, "Don't move!" Then he gave the door a wicked knock. If it had been my head, part of me would have been inside by then.

179

The door was opened by another monkey-man. The gorilla pushed me through the hole he hadn't dug.

It was like being flung into the eye of a storm where all is peace and calm. There was Ray sitting in one of the easy chairs, a drink in his hand. The Ambassador was facing him on the other side. He was drinking, too. And both of them were laughing.

Ray and the Ambassador stood up when they saw me dancing through the open door. "Marlow!" said Ray. "Glad you could come!"

"We called your room," said the Ambassador. "You weren't there so we sent Dougal here to find you."

Dougal smiled like a hyena who had just been given his daily ration of raw meat.

"What can I get you to drink?" asked the Ambassador.

"Hemlock will be fine," I said, rubbing my arm to try to get the blood flowing again.

"Get him the same thing you got for me," said Ray. "What is it again?"

"Glenlivet," said the Ambassador, nodding to him man.

"It's single malt whisky," said Ray. "You've got to try it!"

"I'll stick to Jack," I said.

"Jack Daniels?" said the one who fixed the drinks.

"Yeah," I said, looking back at Ray. "I'm a loyal kind of fella."

"How do you like it, Dr Marlow?" asked the Ambassador's body guard.

"Straight. No water. No ice. No twist of arm. Just as nature meant. Pure essence of corn - left to sit, untampered until it ferments and transmorgrifies."

"The Ambassador wants to set things right," said Ray, as the gofer brought me over my drink. "He says he wants to clear the air before the ship arrives."

"Fine by me," I said. I looked over at the Ambassador's baboon. "Because as far as I'm concerned the air in here has a peculiar odor."

The Ambassador gave me a stare and narrowed up his eyes. "I've got a campaign to run when I get home. Dr Marlow. I can't have any trace of scandal following me back. You and Mr Chandler have been investigating the disappearance of Miss Morgan for reasons of your own. Why you're interested in pursuing this even after the Captain has issued his report is well beyond my understanding. But I want to be completely open and above board. You see, even the slightest insinuation, the smallest innuendo, can be blown up out of all proportion by the press when it relates to people like myself. I think you can understand that."

"I understand that's the position politicians put themselves in," I said, taking a drink of my Jack. "You talked of clearing the air before, or at least Ray did. Well, as a doctor I can tell you that people can only smell one odor at a time. And that, to me, is what politics is all about. Replacing one smell with another. That way people are always one stink behind."

"Marlow can be rather disarming, don't you agree?" said Ray looking over at the Ambassador.

"I don't mind frankness," said the Ambassador. "That's why I'm willing to put my cards on the table." Then he looked at me. "Mr Marlow is what we call a disbeliever. Well sometimes I'm a disbeliever, too. But I still go to Church because it performs a needed function. Politics performs a function, as well, Dr Marlow."

"I guess if politics didn't work you'd be digging ditches right now instead of being an Ambassador for the United States. Is that why Gloria Morgan is resting at the bottom of the sea?" I asked. "So politics can work?"

The Ambassador glared at me and said, "Gloria Morgan was a former friend of mine. It was purely coincidental that she and I were travelling on this ship. I happen to know that she was suffering from both psychological and economic stress. This isn't the first time she tried to take her life, Dr Marlow. It's only the first time she succeeded in doing so."

"Gloria Morgan said that she had formed a company to make films," said Ray.

The Ambassador looked back at him and said, "Yes, Mr Chandler, that is correct. She wanted the freedom to pursue her art outside the control of the studio system. The problem is that she was a very poor business woman."

"Most artists are," said Ray. "But you helped her out, didn't you?"

"I put the services of my corporation at her call, if that's what you mean," he said.

"Whose company was it then," I asked. "Yours or hers?"

"It was her company," said the Ambassador. "She contracted with my corporation to service it, that's all."

"By servicing, I suppose you mean accounting, legal work, and so on, am I right?" asked Ray.

"Yes, that's correct," said the Ambassador.

"Sounds like a cosy little relationship," I said. "How come you were being so kind?"

"As I told you, Dr Marlow. Miss Morgan and I were friends. I was a supporter of her career. I was interested in films and I wanted to help her out."

"And you thought it might give you a leg up in the industry - isn't that it?"

"I won't deny that I was interested in the industry as well," he said.

"But your corporation didn't provide those services for nothing, did they Mr Ambassador?" asked Ray.

"No one works for nothing," said the Ambassador. "But her company was given special rates."

"So special that she went broke after making a successful film," I said.

He glared at me again. "You can have a successful film and still go broke, Dr Marlow. It happens all the time. Even in your line of work, I suspect. You can perform successful surgery and still not get paid."

"Of course," said Ray, trying to cool the situation down. "What was it John Houston said?" He looked up at the ceiling as if trying to recall a line. "'There's more to it than pink Cadillacs and leopard skin seat covers. It's a jungle - a closed-in, tight, frantically inbred and competitive jungle. And the rulers of that jungle are predatory, fascinating and tough. But the very top rulers of that jungle aren't in Hollywood, they're in New York, smiling like hungry lions and watching from afar.' That's not an exact quote," he said, "but it's close enough."

"John Houston knows the industry very well," said the Ambassador.

"Was Gloria Morgan insured?" asked Ray, with what I thought was a twinkle in his eye.

"I don't know," said the Ambassador, starting to look annoyed. "I suppose she was. Isn't everybody?"

"I meant her company," said Ray. "Isn't it common for a company to insure their star so they can recoup their losses in case a film can't be made?"

The Ambassador's face hardened as he turned to his man and snapped, "Find out about that O'Connor! Send a wire to Hogan! Make it fast! I want all that information by tonight!" He turned back to Ray with fire in his eyes. "I don't know what you're insinuating, Chandler," he said. "As far as I know, Gloria Morgan didn't have any films in progress. And, even if she did, no one would have anything to gain by her death."

"Did she have any children?" I asked.

He shook his head.

"How about a mother or a maiden aunt?"

"Gloria Morgan was an orphan," said the Ambassador. "As far as I know she had no one to leave anything to at all."

"Except to you," I said. Then I sat back and watched Vesuvius erupt.

"What the hell would I have to gain, Marlow? I'm a wealthy man! You think I'm going to dump an old broad like her overboard for a few lousy bucks?"

"I'm not an authority on greed," I said. "I just know it works in mysterious ways."

The Ambassador suddenly stood up. "Gentlemen," he said, "I've been trying to play straight with you. But like the press, you can always convict someone if you try hard enough!" And with that he strode into the adjoining room and slammed the door behind.

*****

"That Ambassador's a real nice guy," I said to Ray as we walked back down the hall. "He has a gentle touch."

Ray was ruminating on something. He turned to me and said, "He's a bastard! He's lower than a snake that eats its eggs!"

"You don't like him much, I guess," I said. "Is that why you're trying so hard to string him up?"

"Gloria once told me a story about him," he said, continuing to walk at his usual hefty pace. "She said soon after he took over her business concerns, that pious man invited her to be a guest at his house. He introduced her to his wife and kids. They had dinner. They said their prayers. And then she was shown to her room and she went to sleep. In the middle of the night she woke up to find him standing by her bed. Before she could say a word he was ontop of her, like a stallion sowing some midnight oats. It took a few minutes, she said, and then he left. And that was that."

"Was rape in the contract?" I asked.

"It was implied. At least it was to him. He owned her, Marlow. He owned her body, he believed. And even when he left her, he never gave her up. When people like him own things they never give them up. They might not want them anymore, but they never give them away."

"That's no reason to think he killed her, Ray."

He looked a little tired and a little sad. "He might not have thrown her in the deep, Marlow," he said. "Not him, personally, anyway. But he killed her. Maybe not all of her. But I'm certain he killed some of her, just like winter kills the buds of May.

184

Chapter 28

By the time we reached his cabin, Ray's mood had darkened like a lantern nearing the finish of its wick. I walked him inside - he had said something about a quick drink. Instead, he lay down on his bed and moaned. "I need something more..." he said.

"Something more than what?" I asked, pouring myself a quickie. If he wasn't going to offer, I'd just make myself at home.

"Something more than what we've got!" he snapped.

"What we've got," I said, "as far as I can see, is nothing much."

"Then you can't see very far, Marlow!" He closed his eyes. "I have to keep it simple," he mumbled, more to himself than to me. "When I get too complicated, I get unhappy. And when I get unhappy, my luck runs out."

"The only problem is that you're not God," I said. "I know sometimes you'd like to be."

He opened up his eyes again. I don't think he heard what I had to say. He was too interested in his thoughts. "We need to find out more about the pharmacist. He's the missing link." His lips were dry, caked with layers of dead skin that was starting to peel off. His face was pale, the color of chalk when you clean a blackboard and it settles on your hands.

"Marlow," he said, "fix me a drink."

"I noticed you'd fallen off your wagon, Ray," I said.

"No snide remarks from you, Marlow. That's not what I need right now. Besides, alcohol isn't a depressant for me. It's an elixir. It helps me think. The only problem is my tolerance is low..."

"That's a problem for us all," I said, pouring him a stiff shot of Old Forester and then admiring the smoky shade inside the glass.

I brought it to him and he took it from me with a slightly trembling hand. "I'll tell you a story," he said. He glanced up at me. There was a wry look on his face. "Don't worry," he said, "I'll keep it short."

"I didn't say a word," I replied. I sat down in the easy chair. I don't mind being amused. One thing at least, Ray's stories were better than TV.

"It was during the war," he began, "I was working for Paramount then. The studio was in big trouble. A number of its contract stars were being drafted into the Army and that meant box office revenues were going down. Then Paramount got word that their biggest star of all was joining up. The place broke into pandemonium. I thought all those men with long initials after their names were going to jump from their office windows. They would have, too, if their offices were more than two flights up.

"Anyway, one day I was lunching with John Houseman. He was an old boy who was doing production work back then. Houseman told me that the studio was desperate to come up with a script for Alan Ladd - he was their big box office star who was about to desert - something that could go into production within a month. I happened to mention a book that I was writing that wasn't working out and that I was seriously thinking of turning into a screenplay.

"After lunch, Houseman came over to my place - we were living in a bungalow a little west of Fairfax then - and he read a good part of the manuscript. Forty-eight hours later, Paramount had purchased the rights for a goodly sum and I set to work on a screenplay for Alan Ladd that Houseman was to produce.

"Three weeks later I delivered the first half of the script. I didn't have any problem with that at all since most of the dialogue and descriptive scenes had already been written. Houseman and George Marshall, the fellow who was going to direct the thing, immediately set up a shooting schedule. Everybody at Paramount was ready to kiss my feet. They had never seen a project like this come together so fast! There was only one problem..." Ray stopped and stared at me.

"They forgot to load the cameras with film?" I asked.

"Worse," he said. "I didn't have an ending."

"Seems like a common problem with you, Ray," I said.

He ignored my comment and went on. "I was hard at work on it the day that Roosevelt dropped dead. A few days later, I got a call from the head of Paramount himself. He told me that the future of the studio would be threatened if the balance of my film script was delayed. However, he said, if it was delivered on time the studio would be so grateful that it would hand me over a bonus check for five grand on receipt of the final page."

"That must have spurred you on," I said.

He looked at me as if I were some laundry nine days old. "Marlow," he said, "sometimes you appall me! The bonus was nothing but a bribe! To accept it for work that had been already contracted would have been a humiliation. It would have injured my pride!" He took a drink and then looked at me again, a little humbler this time. "Besides," he said, "it shattered my confidence. It made it seem that they weren't absolutely sure I could finish it."

It sounded silly, but I knew what that break of trust could mean. Confidence is one of those strange commodities that can't be bought or sold. "What did you do?" I asked.

"There was only one thing to do," said Ray. "I went to see Houseman. I told him what had happened and informed him that there was no alternative but to withdraw from the project."

"He must have liked that," I said.

"Houseman was a public school boy like me, Marlow. He understood my feelings right away. He told me to sleep on it and if I still felt the same in the morning, then he'd abide by my wishes."

"So you slept on it." I finished what was in my glass and poured myself another.

"Yes. And that night I came up with a plan which I presented to Houseman the next day. What I proposed was to finish the screen play at home while I was drunk."

"While you were drunk? And he agreed?" I knew those Hollywood bozos were dumb, but that guy must have been both dumb and desperate.

"Of course he agreed! I told you, he was an old boy! I

explained to him that alcohol gave me the energy and self-assurance that I couldn't achieve in any other way. He understood perfectly. He asked me what I would need and I presented him with a list of my requirements."

"Which were?"

"Two Cadillac limousines to stand by outside the house with drivers available for fetching the doctor, taking script pages to and from the studio, driving the maid to market - things like that. Also, a team of six secretaries to be in constant attendance and readiness and available at all times, day and night, for dictation, typing and other possible emergencies. And, finally, a direct line open at all times from my house to the studio."

I stared at him like a guy watching a thief swipe a tray of jewels from the hands of a pawnbroker. "They really accepted those demands?" I asked.

"Requirements, Marlow, not demands. Of course they accepted them! They didn't have a goddamn choice, did they? Not if they wanted the picture finished on time."

"And you did it drunk?"

"I drank just enough to reach that magnificent state of euphoria - no less, no more. Then I topped it up every hour or so, just to keep maintained. I turned on some classical music and fell asleep whenever I damn well felt the need. When I woke up, I took a drink and started working again."

"How long did that go on?" I asked.

"A fortnight," he said.

"I don't believe it," I replied. "You can't stay drunk that long and still lift a pen, let alone create. All your energy would be exhausted within a week."

His eyes lit up as he let me have that silly grin. "But I had a secret, Marlow! I had a doctor come in every four hours to give me an injection!"

"An injection of what? Morphine?"

"A mixture of high potency vitamins and other things." He pointed to a closet. "I have some in my bag."

I stared at him. "Maybe I can be pretty stupid sometimes, Ray, but I think I can guess why you're giving me this load of cock and bull."

"It's not cock and bull, Marlow. Every word of it is true. For me, it's the only way."

"Tell me," I said, "how did the screenplay turn out? It probably doesn't make much difference, I just like endings."

"Oh, that! I finished it bang on time. You want to know the last line that I wrote?"

"Not particularly," I said.

"The last line of the film, Marlow. What everyone heard just before they left the cinema..."

"All right. I give up."

"'Did somebody say something about a drink of bourbon?'"

"Great," I said. "Can't wait to see the film."

"It's called 'The Blue Daliah'," he said. "The only one of my screenplays to be nominated for an academy award."

"I always wondered how those things were written," I said. "Thanks for putting me in the know."

He looked at me, more seriously this time. "Well, will you help?"

"You're saying you want to solve the mystery of the missing movie star while you're drunk and you want me to give you those booster shots?"

He nodded his head. "And to do a little leg work for me. Not much. The ship will dock the morning after next. Then you'll be free."

"I told you if this ever got too serious then I'm through," I said.

"I understand," said Ray. "Will you help me out?"

"Who are you asking? The doctor or the dick?"

"I'm asking you," he said. "And I'm asking you as a friend."

*****

I don't like to leave things hanging. I guess I'm neurotic that way. There was about thirty-six hours left at sea. That's not much. What could happen in that brief spot of time? Famous last words, you could say.

I collected an armload of Old Forester from the bar and brought them back to Ray. He measured out a quantity and then lay back down with a restful smile on his face.

"I want you to do something for me now," he said.

"Your shoes need shining?" I asked.

"I want you to search through Carter's room."

Maybe I don't hear too well, either. That sometimes happens when your brain begins to sour. "You want me to break into the room of the dead pharmacist?" I asked.

"We need to know what he was up to," said Ray.

"But what would I be looking for? The guy didn't seem the type to keep a diary. Anyway, breaking and entry isn't my style."

"I'm not asking you to break in," he said.

"Funny," I said, "it sounded like you were."

"Bribe one of the stewards to lend you the key," he suggested. "That way you don't have to break anything."

"Well, how am I supposed to get down there?" I asked him. "Passengers aren't allowed into the crew's quarters in case you haven't heard."

"Marlow," he said, "did I create you with a brain?"

"You're starting to play God again," I said.

"Listen," he said, trying to get on my good side again (I should have warned him - I don't have a good side), "you're almost crew. You claim to work in the surgery. You're a real doctor. You just want to know what's going on."

"Who does? Me or you?"

He threw up his hands. "What does it matter? That's your story if anyone wants to know." Then he smiled and said, "Have another drink. Calm yourself down. It's easier than you think, Marlow."

I had given up trying to figure him out. But I was still curious. That much was left of me, anyway. "Ray," I said, "what do you really want from this?"

He took another measured drink and said, "A story. Just a decent story that works well."

"I meant what do you want from the pharmacist."

"I told you," he said. "The pharmacist is the missing link."

"The missing link to what?"

"If the Ambassador didn't pull the trigger, he handed someone the gun. And the pharmacist provided it for him."

"Wait a second," I said, "are you starting to believe your own baloney? I know you were moaning on about that extra dose theory of yours. But it just doesn't fit. First of all you'd need someone to dose her up."

"How about a doctor?" he asked.

"Which one did you have in mind?" I said. "I presume you don't mean me. Anyway, your movie star was seen walking on her own accord, remember?"

"Who saw her?" asked Ray.

"Mr Mendez, the Argentine," I replied.

"Well, that's the doctor I had in mind. He has the skill. He wants his loan pretty bad. And the Ambassador can fix it - for a price."

"But what's the motive?" I asked. "I mean for the Ambassador to put it on the line like that. Even supposing he got the Argentine to bump her off, it's still a pretty big risk. And as Solly Meyers said himself, gangsters aren't keen to gamble all their precious money."

"The motives are as old as the hills," said Ray. "Lust, possession, greed and betrayal. The Ambassador needs the support of the Church if he wants to launch his son's campaign. Gloria Morgan wanted to pay him back. She might not have been big box office anymore, but the lady had a photogenic face. She could still command the media. And she could have blown his plans sky high."

I shook my head. "You're pushing it, Ray. I think you know it, too. Why not buy her off, if that's his game?"

Ray smiled, patiently, like I was a kid first learning his sums. "There are some things money can't buy, Marlow. I think you know that. Revenge is a motive by itself. One of the strongest ones there is."

I poured myself another drink and studied his face. He looked so damn cock sure! "There are just too many loose ends for it to make any sense," I said.

"There are some loose ends," he agreed. "But there are always loose ends. Nothing that's real is ever really neat." Then he pointed to his nose. "You have to follow the scent, Marlow. I've only got my intuition left. But I've pulled it off before. We just need more evidence."

"What am I looking for?" I said, letting my voice hang in a noose of my own making.

"Receipts, bank books, notes. Maybe the guy drew pictures in his sleep. Who knows what you'll find down there. You said he lost big in a poker game. Find out where all that money came from!"

Chapter 29

I went back to my cabin and fixed myself a drink. Ray's story had intrigued me, I won't deny that. But what kind of story was it? An unhappy actress who'd throw her career away to gain revenge? A big time politician who couldn't separate his lust for power and his lust for lust? An Argentine patriot who'd kill an ageing movie star to gain credits for Peron?

I looked at my glass, gave it a little tap and watched the amber fluid ripple in that tiny, enclosed sea. I drank to forget, to numb my mind. Ray drank to create, or so he said. It unlocked something in his head and set it free. For me the closet remained bolted.

Then there was that other story he had told - the one about the young American who had fallen in love with an Englishman aboard ship. He had taken arsenic to spice up his life. It gave him a glow. Enough to raise two families. Maybe his wife gave him a little bit more - the "added dose" that had interested Ray. And that was the irony, I guess - the elixir that gave him power over life became the poison that took it all away, like an orgy in a cemetery with a gorgeous dame who then pushes you into a fresh dug grave. But, as Ray said, maybe he deserved it.

So how about the ageing movie star who needed her barbiturates to sleep? Barbiturates are hypnotics. They alter your mental state. She wanted to transform herself from a shackled film queen to an actress wandering through the mysteries of art. And yet, if Ray had it correct, this led her over the side of the ship into the same primeval sea that millions of years before some slimy amphibian crawled out of.

I took another drink and lay down on my bed. I don't want this to get too serious, I said to myself. What the hell does it mean to me?

But you can't stop yourself from thinking, sometimes. So I

thought. Why would an Argentine nationalist dope Gloria Morgan up? Is that what happens when you go to your local bank? You want a loan - go bump off a movie star. Maybe that's just one of the requirements. On the other hand, what do I know? I've been wrong so many times I'm no longer keeping score.

Then again, how far would the Ambassador go to protect his career. Maybe the question should be how far he'd go to protect his son's career. Maybe you go a little further with that then you went before. Maybe you throw all bad news overboard. Maybe the ocean floor is littered with ageing movie stars. Who knows? I've never been down there.

I rubbed my forehead. When I start thinking like that it gives me the feeling that an elephant is grazing on my bald patch. Then I know it's time for another drink. Make this one a double, Sam, I said to myself.

There was a knock at the door. "Come in!" I shouted. "It's not locked!"

The cabin door opened up. It was the kid with the pill box hat. "Sorry to disturb you, Dr Marlow," he said, "I just wanted to remind you that we'll be docking the morning after next. You can contact the Purser about your landing forms or, if you wish, you can give your passport to me and I'll take care of it."

"Thanks kid," I said, "I'll deal with it myself."

"Very well, Dr Marlow," he said, backing himself out.

"Wait a second," I said. I took out my wallet, reached inside and got a fifty dollar bill. I handed it to him.

His eyes looked like a plugged-in Christmas tree at night. "Thank you, Dr Marlow!" he said.

"Don't thank me," I said. "Thank the man in 131."

"Did he tell you to give this to me?" the kid asked.

"Yeah," I said. "In a way."

He looked at me suspiciously. "I'm not that kind of boy, Dr Marlow," he said.

"What kind of boy is that?" I asked.

"The kind who does certain things," he replied.

"The fifty bills are yours," I said. "If you want to be my guide, that's fine. If you don't, that's fine as well."

"Your guide to what? I'm not from London town..."

"I meant the ship. I'd like to visit someplace."

The smile was back on his face. "Certainly, Dr Marlow. That's not a problem at all. I'd be happy to show you around."

"I'd like to visit the pharmacist's room," I said.

Now his face darkened up again. "The pharmacist is dead, Dr Marlow. There was a fight..."

"I know," I said.

"But why would you want to visit him then?" He looked at me like I'm sure he'd looked at other crazy Americans before.

"Let's just call it morbid curiosity, OK?"

He fingered the fifty bucks and I could see his mind was pumping fast.

"Remember," I said. "There's no obligation. You can keep the dough whatever you decide."

"I suppose that if you were following me and I happened to walk past the pharmacist's cabin and happened to stop to light a fag - I suppose there's no harm in that."

"I don't suppose there is," I said. "The only problem is I'd need a key."

"A key?" His eyes grew large again. "A key for what, Dr Marlow?"

"How am I supposed to get in without a key?" I said. "You wouldn't want me to break the door down."

"But why would you want to go in, sir?" I guess he was really starting to wonder about me.

"Because I want to get inside to look around."

He scratched his pill box hat and said, "I do have a mate who gets into rooms with a screwdriver, sometimes," he said.

"A screwdriver?" I said. "What does he do, take the door off the hinges?"

"No, sir, there's a little screw you turn that releases a catch. If the door's not locked from the inside, you can get in."

"Can you show me how it's done on this one?" I asked him, pointing to the cabin entrance.

He fingered the fifty bucks again and sighed. "I suppose I

can, sir," he said.

*****

The pressure in a ship is greater the further down you go. That's a law of physics. And I don't like breaking laws of nature, no matter what Ray says.

I followed the kid along a series of corridors, stooping through the narrow bulkheads. Things weren't quite as plush down here. The steel had an echo unbaffled by plush carpets.

After a while the kid stopped dead in his tracks and took out a smoke. There wasn't anyone around, but I suppose he felt obliged to keep to his plans even though all he had to do was point. Then he continued walking again and, in a moment, disappeared through another bulkhead.

I was left alone. The vibration of the ship down here was stronger than above. I was still some distance from the engine room, but you could feel the throbbing of the mammoth pistons that sent this Goliath punching through the waves. I knew I couldn't be a sailor then. The sound would drive me batty. And if it was this bad here, several decks above, I wondered about the poor suckers who worked below. A few years down there and your brain would turn to jello.

I took out the little screwdriver the kid had leant me and felt around for the release gizmo he had shown me before. It wasn't as easy as he made it seem. Maybe I was out of practice. I once could split a single strand of hair with the corner of my surgeon's knife. Maybe it was all that booze. Sometimes it gives you the shakes. I stopped and wiped the dampness from my hand.

Was there a noise inside the room? Was there a God? Could I still split a hair? Where do split hairs go when they've been cropped? There are many questions like that which cross your mind when you're doing something dumb. I listened at the door. There was the continuing rumble from the engines down below. If you could hear a mouse with all that background noise, then you've got better ears than I have, Marlow, I said to myself.

So what the hell? What could they do to me that I haven't

already done to myself? I put the screwdriver back in and gave it a nasty turn. I heard a click and then I turned the latch. The door swung open. I walked inside and closed the door behind.

It's dark down there, fifty feet below the water line, unless you turn on the lights. However, in order to turn them on you have to find the switch. That's another rule of nature. Nature won't break her rules no matter how hard you wish.

I felt along the wall until I came to something soft and warm and pliable. I thought it might have been a face. In the instant that followed, I realised, in fact, it was.

My finger was in its mouth. It bit down hard. I screamed in pain. Then it pushed against my chest. I fell backwards and hit my head on something hard. Whoever it was followed me down, beating with his fists. I could hear him curse. I shouted something back. Then he kicked me in the ribs.

I grabbed his foot and twisted it with all my might. He crumpled to the floor on top of me. I lunged myself into a roll and found myself on top of him. I grabbed his neck and squeezed with all my might. He gasped for air. I pounded his head against the floor.

"God damn it!" he shouted. "I give up!"

In my fury I continued to beat at him and then, suddenly, I stopped. I felt my hands sticky with something oozing from his face.

I felt the panic surging up inside me. It came with overwhelming force. I stood up and took a quick step backward. My heart was pounding as hard as that mighty engine underneath my scuffed-up shoes.

My hands were trembling. They were cold and damp as graveyard stone. There was an awful smell. The smell of death, I thought. I doubled over and let out a retch. It came from my lower depths, deeper than my guts - my soul.

My feet were unsteady as I searched once more for the switch. I felt around the wall until I found it. I turned on the light. There was a man on the ground lying in a pool of blood.

I rubbed my face and then I realised I had covered it with the blood that was on my hands. I went over to the sink and turned on the tap. I looked into the mirror above. There was a face, the most terrible face I had ever seen, smeared with sticky crimson stuff, staring back.

I washed my hands, grabbed a nearby towel and got it sopping wet. I rubbed my face till I couldn't stand the pain. Then I threw it down and wept.

Suddenly I heard a groan. I turned around. The man on the floor had opened up his eyes. His hands were on his face, probing at his wounds.

In a second I was kneeling at his side. I felt the artery in his neck. It was strong. But the blood was still oozing from the contusions in his head.

I quickly got back up and grabbed another towel. I used it to mop up some blood draining from his forehead. I whispered, "Can you hear me? Can you speak?"

"You lousy bastard!" he hissed.

I laughed. "Yes! Go ahead, damn you! Say it again!"

"You lousy bastard!"

I felt his neck. "Does it hurt to move?"

"He stared into my eyes. "What the fuck do you think? Some goddamned doctor you are, Marlow!"

And then suddenly I recognised him. For the first time I was able to put the face together with the man and come up with a name. A name for a living, breathing person. It was Hart. The CMO.

I helped him up to the pharmacist's cot and began to see to his wounds. I used the towel to stop the bleeding. He held it to his head while I rummaged around for some supplies.

It was then that I noticed the room. Even without the blood and puke and knocked over chairs, it still would have been a mess. The drawers of the pharmacist's dresser had been emptied. All the things inside had been dumped. And his closet had been opened, too. Someone had broken through a padlock to get in. On the floor were stacks of plastic bags. I went over to see if there were any bandages and alcohol.

"Get away from there!" Hart shouted. "Haven't you done enough?"

"I have to treat your wounds," I said, ignoring his command and opening a bag. Inside were boxes full of empty capsules with different colors and different marks. I opened another bag. There was a press for making pills and boxes of white starch. Another bag was full of drugs - everything conceivable.

"Nice little storeroom your pharmacist had here," I said. "Was he packing them all up? Or were you?" I turned to glance at Hart.

He was sitting up. His face was white. "Listen, Marlow, this isn't what you think. Help me back to the surgery. We can talk up there."

"What do you want to do with all this stuff?" I asked, pointing to the bags.

He looked hard at me and said, "To be honest, I was going to dump them over the edge." He hesitated a moment and then he said, "They'll have my job if they find out."

"You're in no condition to dump anything, right now," I said, staring back at him. "Let's get you fixed up. Then maybe I can help."

Chapter 30

I pounded my fist against the door. Then I pounded it again. "Open up!" I shouted. "I know you're in there!"

The moth-eaten buzzard didn't reply. But by now I knew exactly what to do. I took out my little screwdriver and began monkeying with the catch. I heard it give way with a metallic click. Then I threw open the door and barged my way in.

The room was filled with music. A Beethoven sonata, I guessed. Ray was lying in his bed. His eyes were fixed on a corner where the ceiling met the wall.

"You old goat!" I shouted, wiping the foam from my lips. "If I still had that deputy's badge you pinned on me I'd throw it in your face!"

He didn't turn. He didn't blink. He didn't budge. He just said, "It doesn't fit together, Marlow. We were on the wrong track."

"You're telling me?" I shouted. "You're lying there in bed telling me I shouldn't have almost killed a guy?"

"What are you talking about, Marlow?" he asked, still not moving his eyes. "Who gave you a gun?"

"No one gave me a gun," I said. "No one gave me a knife. They just directed me to a room where I didn't belong, that's all. Unfortunately, someone else was there at the time!"

"And you almost killed him? You didn't have to do that."

Suddenly there was someone else I could have almost killed.

"I guess not, Ray," I said. "I guess I could have let him almost kill me instead."

"I knew you were tough," said Ray. "I could tell..."

"Tough?" I shouted. "Is that what you call it when you almost beat an innocent man's head into pulp for no reason whatsoever?"

"There aren't any innocent men, Marlow," he said. "It's a

jungle out there. The only question is who's the hungriest tiger."

I stared at him in amazement and then I shook my head. "I've had it," I said. "This isn't a game anymore."

"It never was," said Ray. "But you knew that yourself."

I pointed my finger at him and felt it shake. "I told you once before, if this thing got too serious, then I'm out. Well, it's gotten there, Ray! You're on your own!" I turned abruptly and started toward the door.

"Marlow!" he bellowed. I turned back around. He was sitting up in bed. He glared at me. "What about the pharmacist?"

"He's dead. Remember? That's a permanent condition."

"Did you find out anything about his dealings?" he asked.

"His dealings?" I let out a little laugh. "I knew scum like him during the war. Nickel and dime men who wouldn't mind watching their grandmother die if it meant another quarter in their itchy, little hands."

"He was a pusher?" asked Ray.

"Worse than that," I said. "A pusher sells drugs to people who want them. This guy took 'em away from people who need them."

"What are you talking about, Marlow?" he asked.

"He had a little factory right there in his room. White powder, coloring, empty capsules, a press to squeeze together starch to make a pill. He was making fakes and exchanging them for the real drugs. The only problem is that the placebos he put back in exchange for the real stuff were probably given to people who were really ill."

"And the real stuff was sold in bulk to someone else, is that it?" he asked.

"Name your port of call," I said. "The pharmacist didn't need your Ambassador to line his pockets full of gold."

"It was a red herring anyway," said Ray.

I gritted my teeth. "I don't want to hear about it, OK?" I said opening the door. "Not about your fantasies of crime or smelly fish, regardless of their color!"

*****

It was dark and quiet in my room. Especially with the lights out. I had a drink in my hand that I didn't hurry down the hatch. I toyed with it. I let it savour in my mouth till I felt the anaesthesia take effect. Then I let it slowly trickle down. It had a smoky feel; a flavor of forgetfulness.

I was just about to click my motor into cruise and let it glide when some bozo skinned his knuckles on my door. Then, in the dark, I heard something slide from underneath. I lay there for a minute, wondering whether I should just ignore whatever it was and then, cursing to myself, I turned on the bed side lamp. I looked over toward the door. A white envelope was on the floor beside it.

I got up, walked over, picked it up and tore it open. The letter inside was neatly typed. It said: "In October of last year the presidency of Gloria Morgan's company was changed over into the name of one R. S. Garchick. There is a policy in the sum of five hundred thousand dollars indemnifying the company against the loss of its star for a production scheduled to be filmed in Italy this summer."

I folded up the note and put it in the pocket of my trousers. Then I went back to bed and turned out the lamp.

It wasn't five minutes before another clown, this one of gentler persuasion, came rapping at my brain.

"Dr Marlow?"

I recognised the voice. I wished it would go away.

"Dr Marlow? Are you awake?"

"Dr Marlow isn't here," I called out. "Dr Marlow jumped over the side of the ship and is now swimming toward Morocco."

"Dr Marlow, I really must speak with you!" came the persistent voice from the other side.

I sat up and rubbed my eyes. I turned on the light. I reached for my glass and drained the last precious drops of my drink.

Once, some months back, I actually saw a pink elephant in my bedroom. It was sitting in a chair drinking a cup of lemon tea. It was wearing one of those bowlers that Englishmen wear with their umbrellas when it isn't going to rain. When I rubbed my eyes it tipped its hat and went away. Poof! Just like that!

"Dr Marlow! Please open up the door!"

I rubbed my eyes again. This one was being really stubborn. Tap. Tap. Tap. It sounded like a constipated woodpecker.

"I'm not leaving, Dr Marlow! You better open up the door!"

I groaned and got out of bed. I went to the door and opened it up. Monica Wheetly was standing there. She didn't look happy. But, then again, neither did I.

"You're a bastard!" she said, glaring at me through her cheaters and then blinking her big, blue eyes.

"What else is new?" I said.

"Are you going to let me in?" she asked, pushing past me. "I don't like standing in the hall!"

"Who's asking you to stand?" I said. But by the time I got the words out she was already though the door.

I could see she was in a lather. "He hadn't had a drink in over twenty-four hours! Did you know that?"

"And you think I took a bottle of bourbon and forced it down his throat?"

"You're an awful influence on him!" she shouted.

"Not anymore, babe," I said, climbing back into bed.

She watched as I pulled the covers over my clothes. "Don't you even take off your shoes?" she asked. She looked like she had been stunned by a pellet of bird droppings.

"Why bother?" I said. "I'd only have to put them on again."

"Do you have any idea how horrible you are?" she asked.

"You don't have any right to say that," I replied. "You haven't slept with me yet."

She stamped her foot. "Stop it, Marlow! He's dying!"

"Are you talking about God?" I asked.

"I'm talking about Ray!" she shouted back. "Your friend! Your drinking companion! He's in his room gasping for breath. He won't let me call a real doctor. He only wants you!"

"Why me?" I asked. "Why can't you hold his goddamned hand?"

The tears began to flood her eyes like a busted drain. Her voice was softer. "Please, Marlow. Do it for him. And if you won't do it for him, then do it for me. I'll even sleep with you if you want."

I almost laughed. I rubbed my eyes a third time. But she was still there. "OK," I said. "You win. I have only one request."

"What's that?" she asked.

"That you stay out of my room for the rest of the goddamned trip!"

*****

She was right. Ray was in pretty bad shape. His head was hot. His lips were cracked. His eyes were glazed. He looked a little like I felt. I felt good enough to stick my head into an oven - and not to bake a cake.

"Marlow!" he gasped. "I need my shot!"

"Why didn't you do it for yourself?" I asked. "Diabetics inject themselves every day of their goddamn lives!"

"So do heroin addicts," he said. "But I'm neither. And I can't stand injections. I can't do it for myself."

"You're a phoney and a coward, Ray! Do you know that?"

"Stop badgering the poor man," Monica Wheetly hissed. "Just give him his injection!"

I went over to the suitcase that Ray had pointed out before and opened it up. I took out the hypodermic with a sterilised needle I had found and a hermetically sealed bottle of his vitamin compound. I filled the syringe and then squeezed out a bit of fluid from the top. "You have any alcohol?" I asked.

Ray pointed to his bourbon. "Will this do?"

I splashed some on his arm and gave him his shot. The very act seemed to perk him up. "Now pour me a drink," he said.

"Not on your life!" said Monica Wheetly, grabbing the bottle and pressing it to her breast.

"Don't listen to her, Marlow," he said. "I need a drink."

"He's killing himself, Marlow," she said. "You know that!"

I took out the envelope that had come underneath my door and tossed it to Ray.

He took it in his hands. "What's this?" he asked.

"Figure it out for yourself," I said.

He scanned the note and then looked back at me. "Who sent it to you? The Ambassador?" he asked.

"It was delivered tonight by parties unseen," I said.

"Pour me a drink!" he hollered at Monica Wheetly.

"No!" she said, though a little more meekly this time.

Ray sat up in bed. "If you don't bring me that bourbon by the time I count ten," he said, in the most terrible voice he could muster, "I'm going to burn all that poetry you gave me to read!"

She stared at him unbelievingly. "You wouldn't do that, Ray," she said.

"Oh, no?" He smiled like someone who was about to enjoy doing something very mean. He leaned over, opened the drawer to his bedside cabinet and took out some pages of typescript. Then he took his pipe from the ashtray on the top and began to stuff one of the pages into the bowl. "I'm starting my count, Monica," he said. "One...two...three..."

"Stop it!" she cried. She stomped over and slammed the bottle down on the cabinet by his side. "Here's your evil drink if you want it so bad! I don't care if you kill yourself with it anymore!" She grabbed her papers from his clutch, marched over to the door, opened it, and then stormed out.

"Close the door, will you, Marlow?" he asked.

"Which side of it do you want me to end up on?" I replied.

"Stay a minute," he said. "Please..." He sipped at his drink. He seemed relaxed again.

I went over to where the bottle was and poured myself a glass.

"What time is it?" I asked.

Ray looked at his watch. "It's three," he said.

"In the morning, I suppose," I said.

"Yes," he replied.

I sat down in the easy chair and stared at him. "How did you know you had it wrong?"

"Because of the notes," he said. "The ones that warned us to be on guard. Always distrust someone who points the finger, Marlow. Remember that."

"Maybe the notes were legit," I said. "Maybe someone knew

205

something that we don't."

Ray shook his head. "Then why not be more precise? Why not be direct? No, someone wanted just to cast suspicion," he said.

"So how are you going to end it, Ray?" I asked. "In not too many hours you'll have to leave the ship. You don't want to be carried off in a crate, I guess."

He looked at me. His eyes were clearer now - the drink had seen to that. "I'm only inches away, Marlow," he said.

"From what?" I asked.

"From solving the case!"

I looked down at the ground. Somehow I knew what he was going to say next.

"Marlow, I need your help."

I didn't reply.

"Like you said, it's just a few hours more. I won't ask you to search any rooms. Not alone, at any rate."

I kept staring at the floor.

"Marlow, we might be able to save somebody's life."

"Or take it away from them," I said.

He let out a snort. Maybe he was cleaning his pipe. "Investigation is a risky business. No one ever said it was safe. But nothing in life is safe. You know that. When you start thinking it's safe, that's when it's time to give up."

"That's not the point," I said. "I just don't like sticking my nose into other people's affairs."

"But this is different. This isn't nosiness. It's something else."

"What?" I asked. "What is it if it isn't nosiness?"

He lit his pipe. The fire from the match was reflected in his eyes. "It's the simple art of murder," he declared.

Chapter 31

I got up, brushed my teeth and changed into my least wrinkled trousers and my most unsmelly shirt to celebrate my last full day aboard ship.

It was one of those mornings when the air is fresh and the sun is bright and if you weren't an incurable alcoholic it would have felt good to be alive.

I went out on deck to pump some unstale oxygen through my gills. The first thing I saw was her. I cringed.

"Hello, Dr Marlow," she said, cheerily. "Beautiful day, isn't it? They say we'll be in sight of Ireland this afternoon."

"I wonder what the Irish think about that," I said.

"You mean the Ambassador and his crew? Quite happy, I would imagine..." she started to say.

"No, I meant all those potato farmers who stayed behind when his family came to buy up America," I said correcting her. Then I realised she had on her glowing face. "You look pretty chipper this morning for someone whose life's work was almost smoked up last night."

"Oh, that!" she said. "Ray apologised today. He said sometimes he gets nasty when he's drunk. This morning he told me that my poems were some of the most beautiful he's ever read." Her eyes glistened in the sun. "He promised me he'd stay sober from now on. What do you think of that, Dr Marlow?"

"I think that promises from alcoholics are worth about as much as IOUs from a man whose neck is in a noose and is about to be hung."

Her smiled stayed glued onto her face. "Not even your cynicism can spoil this day for me, Marlow. Ray promised to introduce me to his publisher when we get to shore!"

"Well, I hope you'll be very happy together," I said. "Just one word of advice..."

"What's that?" she said.

"Make sure he keeps his pipe filled with tobacco."

The smile dropped from her face. "I knew I shouldn't have asked," she said.

"By the way, where's the maestro now?"

She pointed a pretty finger toward the promenade deck. "He's taking in some sun. I'm going down to fetch him some tomato juice."

"Tomato juice?" I asked, just to make sure I heard her right.

"Yes, Marlow. Tomato juice. Would you like some?"

I shook my head.

"Suit yourself," she said and she smiled at me again. "Toodle-loo, Marlow," she said wiggling her mitt at me. And with that she went prancing down the deck.

I walked further along and then I saw him, half covered in a blanket, sitting in one of those infernal deck chairs with his feet extended out along its length, puffing on his goddamned pipe. His chair was laid out by the base of one of the ship's funnels, which was itself pouring out steam. I guessed Ray's furnace could easily compete.

"Marlow!" he said, seeing me straggling toward him. "Pull up a seat! The show's just about to begin!"

"Is this the third act or the fourth?" I asked. "I was never much good at keeping score."

"Any good play only has three," he said. "Act four is an epilogue."

"Don't confuse me," I said, "Doctors are taught not to believe in epilogues. It's too much like after-life, and if after-life exists, why would you need us?"

"Good point," he said and he gave his pipe another puff.

I looked out into the shining sea, into the newness of the day. Then I looked back at him again. He seemed so bright and full of energy you'd never have suspected that last night he was near enough to death that he might have heard that guy who toots his horn.

"I saw your pup about a minute ago," I said motioning toward the hind end of the ship. "She was fetching you a bone. She said you were going to introduce her to your publisher."

"And I will," said Ray, looking as close to repentant as I'd ever seen him get. "I was terrible to that poor girl last night. I owe her something for that."

"Can she write?" I asked.

"Anyone can write," said Ray. "It's simply a matter of putting some ink inside a pen and touching it to paper."

"Anyone can operate, too," I said. "Of course some patients might object."

"She's got a modicum of talent," said Ray. "But she's young and she's romantic. I was that way once myself. Either she'll learn or she won't. That's not my affair." Then his eyes twinkled like a lusty Santa Claus. "On the other hand, she's pretty and she's charming, when she wants to be, and I don't particularly like the idea of being in London all alone."

"Fair enough," I said. "Just don't lead her to the precipice to drop off it yourself."

"Forget about her, Marlow," he snapped. And then, leaning toward me, he took his pipe out of his mouth and smiled. "I think we've solved the case."

"Nice day for fishing," I said, still looking toward the gentle sea. "You catch yourself a mermaid?"

"Not yet," said Ray. "Not yet." He tapped his forehead. "I'm still setting up my trap."

"Is there anything I should know?" I asked. I didn't mean to say that. It just came out.

"Rinexus was just up here," said Ray, "sitting where you're sitting now..."

"That's enough to ruin anybody's day," I said.

"I asked him to see what he could find out about an R. S. Garchick in that little book of his..."

"You mean that 'Who's Who' of Hollywood he was talking about?" I said.

Ray nodded. "Suddenly a great big light bulb lit up on top of his head. 'Garchick!' he shouts. 'Of course! That's who he is! I knew I seen that guy before!'"

"So he thinks Garchick is Roger Lane?" I asked, knowing

that's who he meant. I'm no detective, but who else could it have been? "Is he sure?"

"I asked him that myself," said Ray. "He said he only saw Garchick once before - maybe ten or twelve years back, so he can't be absolutely certain. But he says Garchick's picture was plastered all over the press during the Hollywood trials. If it isn't him, he said, then it must be his brother."

"So what do you think, Ray? Maybe Lane is travelling under a phoney name."

"I thought about that," said Ray. "It's not so easy to do. The ship's purser has access to all the passports. His name is 'Lane' all right. I checked."

"Maybe 'Garchick' is the phoney one," I said. "Don't Hollywood people change their names every over week?"

"According to Rinexus," said Ray, "Garchick was indicted by the Congressional committee investigating Communist infiltration into Hollywood. Congressional committees subpoena individuals under their legal names - the same names that are on their passports."

"So maybe Lane isn't Garchick after all," I suggested.

"That's what I began to think, too. Except..." Ray's eyes danced an Irish jig.

"Except what?" I said. Marlow's hooked again. Same old tricks. They work every goddamn time!

"Except I had my friend check the passports for me..."

"That fat guy really gets around," I said.

"I asked him to look at Amanda Lane's..."

"And she's Garchick with long hair? Spare me that at least."

"She doesn't have a maiden name. Or rather she has one and it's Lane."

"Wait a second," I said, holding up my hand like a cowboy trying to steady up his horse. "You're going too fast for me. Her maiden name is 'Lane', you say?"

"That's right, Marlow," he said. "You really do learn fast."

"So what's his name?"

"His name is 'Lane'," Ray replied.

"So they're brother and sister maybe? Is that what you're

trying to say?"

"I think they're married all right," said Ray. "And what I think happened is that Garchick took her name."

"Is that legal?" I asked.

"If you do it through the courts," said Ray. "And I bet he did it after the congressional affair. Garchick married Amanda Lane and disappeared into thin air."

"How does this relate to Gloria Morgan, then?" I asked.

"A half million smackers?" said Ray letting his eyebrows talk. "Some people would do a lot for that, especially if they've been blacklisted from their career."

"Hello, you two!" a cheery voice called out. "Here's your tomato juice, Ray!" she said, handing him the sickly-looking stuff. "Now be a good boy and drink it down! There's lots of Vitamin C in there you know," she said, pointing to its lower depths.

Ray took a drink and made a disapproving face.

"Did you tell him all that we found out?" she asked, sitting down in the vacant chair on the other side of Ray. "I always thought it would be him, you know. You really can't trust a communist."

"That's too facile, my dear," he said, taking another sip of the blood red stuff. "Many intelligent people became Communists - especially the kind of people I should be apt to like and admire. Of course how they could become Communists after the Moscow Treason Trials is absolutely beyond my understanding. It's almost as difficult as trying to understand how a decent man could become a convert to a religious system that played ball with Franco in Spain, and still does, and that never in the history of the world has refused to play ball with any scoundrel who was willing to protect and enrich the Church."

"Did you know any of those guys in Hollywood, Ray?" I asked him.

"You mean the one's who were sent up before the Committee? Sure, I knew some of the writers. Some of them probably were Communists, some of them weren't, some of them didn't know what the hell it was all about. I didn't have much sympathy for them but I had a hell of a lot of contempt for the motion picture moguls who decided to expel them from the industry. A business as big as the motion picture industry ought to be run by men with a few guts and enough moral and intellectual integrity to have said to Mr Thomas, 'Sure, I guess we have Communists in Hollywood. But until Congress legislates something that would cause their present or future membership in the Communist Party to be a crime, we propose to treat them just exactly as we treat anyone else.'"

Ray looked at Monica Wheetly. "You know what would have happened if the producers had the guts to say something like that?"

"What, Ray?" she said. I could see the maestro had his student back again.

"They'd start making decent pictures. Because that takes guts, too. Very much the same kind of guts!"

It was at that moment when Ray was suddenly interrupted by an obscene sounding cry. Actually, it was just a simple statement. But the fact that it came from Rinexus' lips made it sound obscene.

"Hey, Chandler! I got it!"

He came huffing and puffing down the deck waving the book in his hands. By the time he reached us, he was almost completely out of breath.

He had just enough energy to thrust the book into Ray's face. Then he pointed to an item with his pudgy finger and waited until a little excess air had the misfortune to reach his lungs. When it did, he read the listing aloud:

"Born in 1915 in Ohio of Polish ancestry. As a young man moved to New York City. Worked for Brazini Brothers, doing the Vaudville circuit. Subsequently helped produce 'The Living Newspaper Theatre Project' in 1934, sponsored by Hallie Flanagan and the Federal Arts Program. Was assistant director in off-Broadway production of 'Mother Courage' by German playwright, Bertolt Brecht. Went to Hollywood in 1938. Worked in productions with Fritz Lang, Lion Feuchtwanger, Arnold Pressburger and Eric Von Stronheim. Was assistant director under Joseph Losey in production of 'The Boy with

Green Hair'. Called before Congressional committee investigating Communist influence in Hollywood in 1951. Refused to testify."

Rinexus looked triumphantly at Ray. "I told you I had him pegged!"

"Who or what is Brazini Brothers?" asked Ray.

Rinexus shrugged his padded shoulders and said, "Probably some booking agency, I suppose. I never heard of them before."

"Are they listed in the book?"

Rinexus shook his head. "I looked."

"How about the guys with the German sounding names?" I asked.

"The Kraut Club?" said Rinexus. "Hollywood was filled with them in '38 and '39. They were as thick as cockroaches in a Mexican cantina. Most of them were commies, if not every last one."

"I thought they came there to escape Hitler," said Ray.

"The only people who had to leave Germany were Communists and Jews," said Rinexus. "And most Jews are Communists, aren't they?"

"How about this Losey fellow?" I asked.

"Another commie," said Rinexus. "He worked with that Flanagan woman, too. That 'Green Hair' film was just a commie load of crap."

"What happened to him?" I asked.

"He fled to England, I understand. Just like this Garchick fellow's doing now. They think they can work under phoney names. But we find them out eventually and expose them."

"What happens then?" I said. "Assuming they're in Britain?"

"We got influence with the British, too," said Rinexus. "If they want their films distributed in the States, they fall into line."

"So they're all commies," said Ray, pointing to the listing. "Everyone who's mentioned here? Is that what you're saying?"

"Sure," said Rinexus. "Maybe not hard core. Maybe just fellow travellers. But that's almost as bad. The only one who's definitely clean is Stronheim. I don't know how his name got listed there. It must be a mistake. He was around in the silent era - in the twenties."

"Didn't Stronheim once do something with Gloria Morgan?" asked Ray.

"Seems to me he did," said Rinexus, scratching the back of his balding head. "Way back when."

"Who was this Von Stronheim person?" asked Monica Wheetly. "He sounds like a German aristocrat."

"He was quite a character," said Rinexus. "Definitely a little strange..."

"Most of you guys are," I said.

Rinexus didn't seem offended by my remark. As far as I know, he might have taken it as a compliment. "Stronheim was the kind of guy who would make his leading lady take off her underwear in the middle of a scene and toss them to her leading man. Then Stronheim would have him put it to his nose and sniff it as he dollied in for a close up. And this was in 1928!"

"Sounds like your kind of fellow," said Ray.

"He had a lot of saviour-faire," said Rinexus. "Too bad there ain't more around like him."

Ray closed the book and gave it back to him. "Well, thank you, Mr Rinexus," he said. "You've been a great help to me."

"Sure," said Rinexus. "Anything to help a friend." Then he narrowed his eyes and I could almost see the oil oozing from his brow. "By the way, what did you want all that info for?"

Ray opened his eyes in mock surprise. "You mean I didn't tell you? You see, I'm writing a new screenplay. The reason I wanted to find out more about Mr Lane is that I was considering giving it to him. And thanks to you, now, in good conscience, I can!"

Chapter 32

Why did I go with him? Why does rain fall? There is an explanation, I suppose. In the case of rain it has to do with a circular process of evaporation by the sun and condensation as the vapours rise into the atmosphere. You can read all about it in a science book. But, as far as I'm concerned, it all boils down to a sophisticated form of rationalisation. It rains because it rains. And that's about as close to the honest truth as you're ever going to come.

I went with Ray because he said, "It's time to see the Ambassador again." I didn't ask him why. I just shrugged my shoulders and went. So did Monica Wheetly. Lemmings do that too, just before they fall over the cliff.

We marched in ragged file, our army of three, up to his cabin door. Ray did the honours of issuing a knock.

The door was opened by gorilla number one. He looked as welcoming as a terminal cancer report.

"Is the Ambassador available to meet with us?" asked Ray, full of charm and smiles. Too bad the gorilla didn't know him as well as I did by now. He might have barred the door and run away. But where do you run aboard a ship? Maybe he could have taken a cue from Gloria Morgan. She would have told him to either jump out the porthole or take a disappearing pill, I guess. I'd take the pill, myself. That water's awfully cold. And Ireland was still too far to swim.

He had us wait in the waiting room where we had waited twice before. It was the drinking room too, I suppose, because he also brought us drinks. He didn't even bother to ask us anymore. Maybe that's why the Ambassador kept him on his coconut farm. His monkey had a memory for things like that - what flavor coconut you drink. I guess as long as you didn't have to think past fermented vegetable juice, he'd be fine. Maybe every coconut farm should have a chimp like him.

"You're on the wagon, Ray. Remember that," whispered Monica Wheetly as Ray was handed a glass full of Glenlivit.

"It's for social purposes exclusively," said Ray, taking a professional taste. "One can't be impolite."

I was given Jack - no water, no ice. She was back to gingerale.

We sat and looked at each other for a while. When I got tired of staring at Ray's puffy face, I looked down at my feet. Feet are good to look at when you've nothing much to do. They remind you that you can always walk away. Unfortunately, they can't tell you where to go.

I could hear a hubbub coming from the other room. Finally the connecting door swung open and the Ambassador walked out. Actually, he was the second one in line, between gorillas two and three.

He didn't smile. He didn't say hello. What he did say was, "I'm a very busy man, Mr Chandler. What do you want?"

"I won't keep you long, Mr Ambassador," said Ray. "We just need a few more details from you. That's all. Do you know this man, Garchick, who you say is listed as the head of Gloria Morgan's film company?"

The Ambassador made a face. It wasn't a pretty one. "I've never heard of the man before in my life!"

"I suspected that," said Ray. "But how could a change like that be made in documents held by your corporation without your knowledge?"

"The changes weren't done by us," said the Ambassador. "It was done from the outside. Her company used us as its official address, so naturally that's where they were sent by the authorities after the changes were enacted. They were put into a file. Far too many papers go in and out each day for everything to be closely examined."

"Do you know a man named Von Stronheim?" I asked. "I think he was a director or something at one time."

The Ambassador glared at me. "I once hired Von Stronheim to do a film for me. It was to star Miss Morgan..."

"What happened?" I asked. "Was it ever made?"

"No. The man, it turned out, wasn't who he claimed to be."

"You mean he wasn't a director?"

"Certainly he was a director!" the Ambassador snapped. "One of the best in the business! Why else would I have hired him?"

"Why did you fire him then?" I persisted.

The Ambassador squeezed his glass so tight I thought he'd fuse his fingers to the rim. "Because he was an evil man!" he said. "Mr Von Stronheim twisted a beautiful script through his contorted mind till it came out as trash."

"I thought that's what Hollywood was all about," I said.

"Besides," the Ambassador went on, ignoring my remark, "it never would have gotten past the censors."

Ray tried to send a cease and desist message with his eyes. "Getting back to the change in the documents, Mr Ambassador," he said, "what do you think it all means? Why would Gloria Morgan have put someone else in as head of her own company?"

The Ambassador shrugged. "For any number of reasons, Mr Chandler. It's often done for tax purposes or to keep the government off your back. Or perhaps this fellow, Garchick, was willing to invest a substantial sum to make a film. Perhaps becoming company head was one of his demands."

"How about that insurance policy?" asked Ray. "Five hundred thou, you said?"

"That's not much indemnity for a star of Miss Morgan's repute," said the Ambassador. "A picture is distributed on the basis of its projected sales. A name like Gloria Morgan is easily worth a half million in revenue. In fact, it's worth much more. Without a star, most films are worth nothing much at all. So a policy like that is often required by the backers."

"Could a man like Garchick profit from such a policy?" asked Ray. "If, let's say, his star fell overboard?"

"Profit personally you mean?" asked the Ambassador. He shook his head. "No. He couldn't pocket the money and run away. It would have to go for production costs."

"But maybe he'd profit by having money to make the film," I said.

The Ambassador gave me a passing glance of contempt. I

guess, to him, I wasn't worth much more than that. "There are less dangerous ways of raising money to make a film, Dr Marlow."

"I guess that's true if you happen to own a bank," I said. Then I polished off my drink. Even in this stuffy room it didn't taste half bad.

"Now, if you've completed your enquiries, gentlemen - Miss Wheetly - I have many things to do before we dock..."

"One other thing," said Ray. "Did the Captain give you a copy of his report into Miss Morgan's disappearance?"

The Ambassador looked at his gofer. "Get a copy for him, O'Connor!" he said in a voice of command. Then he turned back to Ray and said, "I trust this will be the end!"

"Yes," said Ray. "Just one little thing more. I want to know something about an outfit called Brazini Brothers. It seems Garchick once worked for them in New York. Do you think you could wire your office and get an answer for me before we dock?"

"Did you hear that, O'Connor?" shouted the Ambassador. Then, with almost military precision, he did an about-face and made a stage-right exit.

*****

"I just can't understand how you two could be so rude to an important man like him," she said. We were in Ray's room again. I was pouring myself a drink.

"You want me to fix you one, Ray?" I asked.

"No he does not!" said Monica Wheetly, crossing her eyebrows like a school teacher who had just been asked if her star pupil wanted to be buggered in the bathtub.

Ray, himself, was back on his bed studying the copy of the Captain's report he had been given by the Ambassador's number one monkey-man. "Here's something curious," he said, looking over at me.

I walked up to the bed. "What's that, Ray?" I said.

He pointed to the report. "This one's different than the other one I'd seen."

"Maybe it's an updated version," I suggested.

"It says here that the Lanes were observed throwing something over the side of the ship."

"Was it about five foot four and blonde?" I asked.

"It happened the night before Gloria Morgan had disappeared. When the investigators did their interviews someone said that they had seen them struggling with some canvas sacks they were trying to dump over the rail."

"Were the Lanes questioned about it?" I asked.

"Yes. They claimed it was rubbish. They had seen the messmen throwing refuse overboard so they said that they thought it was all right to do."

"What kind of refuse would they have to throw away?" asked Monica Wheetly.

"That would have been the second day out at sea," said Ray. "What could they accumulate in that short time?"

"Maybe they had a dog or cat," I suggested. "Maybe someone told them they couldn't bring it into England."

Ray let his head down to the pillow underneath. "We're almost there," he said. "I need just a while more to think." Then he said, "Monica, pour me a drink!"

She stared at him. A flabbergasted nurse might look that way if she were asked for heroin by the neighborhood priest. "But Ray, you said..."

"I know what I said!" Ray cut her short. "I thought I had it solved! Now I don't! I just need a little more time!"

"A promise is a promise, Ray!" she argued back.

"If you want to meet my publisher, you'll damn well pour me a drink!" Then he turned his wrath on me. "Marlow! Fix me up my shot!"

"Sure, Ray," I said. "How do you want it? Straight or mixed with a little strychnine?"

*****

I'll leave it to you to figure out if Monica Wheetly poured him his drink or not. I'll just remind you that publishers are very hard to see. At least that's what Monica Wheetly told me. And her father owns a little steel mill.

Personally, I didn't mind shooting him up with his vitamin compound. A doctor likes to keep in shape. Besides, I knew where to stick it so it hurt.

I left him there in charge of his fretting nurse. His Beethoven was turned on, his eyes were beginning to regain their far away gaze, like telescopes looking inward, studying an imaginary soul.

I went down to get something to eat. The stewards were being particularly friendly that afternoon. They were offering caviar on toast. It was the last full day, you see. The last day they play it for all they're worth in hopes of getting a decent tip.

Solly Meyers was there. He was eating cottage cheese. "Fish eggs are what they eat in Russia when they run out of fish," he told me. "Give me a good corned beef sandwich any day. And a half done cucumber pickle."

"The food I like best is what they serve at baseball games," I told him.

"Baseball I don't like," he said. "I'd rather watch a boxing match."

"You might as well go to a bull fight," I replied. "At least there they sometimes throw you a tail or a piece of ear."

"It helps my ulcer to see two men who aren't Jewish beat each other up. I don't know why," he said. "I don't like violence any other way."

"It's not unusual," I said. "If black people are beating up themselves, they can't beat up whites. If Romans throw themselves to lions, they can't throw Christ. If Arabs buy Czechoslovakian guns, then Peron's Jews will swim to Israel and the Ambassador's son will become President of the United States. It's just a matter of simple logic."

Solly Meyers ate his cottage cheese, wiped his mouth and said, "You're too smart to be a doctor. Perhaps you should become a politician."

"The only problem with that," I said, "is then I'd have to shoot myself and there's too many bottles that still depend on me."

"Well, with that I can't help you, my friend," said Solly Meyers. He stood up to go and then he turned and looked at me with his watery eyes and said, "Were you really in Buchenwald?"

"Maybe I was," I said. "Sometimes I can't remember any more."

"There are some things I can't remember any more, too," he said, shaking his greying head. "There are other things I can't forget. But I can't always remember what they are."

*****

After I finished my dinner, such as it was, I went out on deck. It was a balmy evening, as they say in the tourist books. The western sky was turning red. To the east were swirling specks, an off-shade of white, hovering above the water like ghosts of past sea life.

"Seagulls," said a voice from behind. "They're still far away. But it means we're getting close to land."

I turned around. It was Roger Lane. "I suppose that's what you were staring at," he said, pointing out to the birds.

"I was just wondering how far it was to swim," I said.

He came up to the rail and leaned forward just a bit. "It's always further than you think, Marlow," he said.

"Did you say that to Gloria Morgan, too?" I asked.

"Maybe she said that to me," he replied.

"I wonder how good of an actress she really was," I said.

He pointed again toward the seagulls. "Watch them dive for fish," he said. "Did you ever see them catch a single one?"

"I never looked," I said.

"I have. I've watched them for hours. I've never seen a seagull ever catch a fish. They swirl and dive and circle around from morning till night. For what?"

"Maybe they're just acting," I said.

"Maybe we all are," he put in.

"Anyway," I said, "I wouldn't like to be those birds. The ocean is too cold and deep. I wouldn't like to spend my life catching phantom fish."

"Neither would I," he said. "There are too many wonderful things out there to do - once you reach land, that is."

"And they all cost a hell of a lot of money," I replied.

He laughed. "Not all. Money really isn't as important as most Americans think it is. Not if you have a lust for life."

"I never knew a poor man who was lusty," I said. "Hunger kind of breaks your sex drive."

"I'm not talking about one's need to eat, Marlow," he said. "Sure, you've got to have enough to survive. I'm talking about what you need after that. Too many creature comforts are like drugs. They anaesthetise the mind."

"Is that why you're on this ship?" I asked. "To get away from creature comforts?"

"I'm on this ship to get across the ocean. I don't like to swim and my wife doesn't like to fly."

"You didn't have to go first class," I said.

"We needed the room," he said.

"For the two of you or for three?"

"We don't have any children, Marlow," he said, giving me a searching look. "I thought you knew that."

"Did you know a man by the name of Von Stronheim?" I asked.

"Eric Von Stronheim? He was an actor..." he said.

"I thought he was a director."

"He directed a few films, I think. He was what Hollywood likes to refer to as a 'maverick.'"

"Is that a polite word for smut?" I asked.

"Smut?" Lane laughed again. "He might have been toying with psycho-eroticism, but I'd hardly call it smut."

"Is psycho-eroticism a fancy word they use in your neck of the woods for smelling women's underwear?"

He looked at me more seriously now. "Von Stronheim might have been saying something about power relations. Haven't you read Reich?"

"The only Reich I know anything about is the Third," I said. "I saw first hand what they had to say about power relationships."

"Listen, Marlow, I don't know where you're driving, but wherever it is, I think you'll find you've gotten on the wrong road - again. Von Stronheim was a brilliant technician and a man with

some fascinating ideas, but he didn't have the political understanding of a Brecht or the insights into character of a Losey. If
one learned anything from him, it was how to visualise through
the eye of a camera."

"Is that what you learned from him?" I asked.

"I wasn't privy to the man," he said. "I'm talking in theoret-
ical terms."

"Theoretically, I'd watch my step if I were you, Mr Lane," I
said.

"Thanks for the warning, Marlow, but I always step carefully.
I've been down too many slippery roads. You know what I
mean?" he replied, meeting my eyes with his own.

Chapter 33

I was back in my cabin later that evening when I received the call. The telephone rang. I answered. It was her.

"Marlow? Come quickly!"

"Leaky pipes?" I asked. "Or stuffed up drain?"

"No time for smart replies!" she snapped. "He needs you now!"

I fixed myself a drink, sat down in the green chair and stared at the tapestry of trees and birds hanging on the wall. I decided I'd rather be a bird than a fish if it ever came to that. Birds have more air to breathe. They can fly from tree to tree. Some of them can even fly across the ocean. But we're never asked to decide those sort of questions. I mean the really important ones - like if you'd rather be a fish or a bird. If we could decide those kind of things then maybe we'd have some control over our lives. At least, that's the way I felt. Maybe I felt that way because control was quickly slipping out of mine.

I got up, rinsed out my glass at the sink and dried it with one of my used shirts. Then I placed it next to my half finished bottle of Jack. I pointed to it. "Don't go away," I said.

I walked down the corridor connecting the port with the starboard side of the ship and then I hung a left. I saw the kid with the pill box hat coming my way.

"We'll be docking tomorrow, sir," he said. "Is there anything else I can do for you?"

"I'll let you know," I said. Then I reached for my wallet and pulled out another fifty dollar bill. "Meanwhile, you can take this on account."

He looked at me strangely. I guess I would have looked at me strangely, too. "On account of what, Dr Marlow?" he asked.

"On account of I won't be needing it anymore," I said.

He stood there looking at the fifty smackers in his hand and then, looking back at me, he smiled. "Thank you, Dr Marlow!" he said. "I do know a few places in London town, if you'd like to see..."

"Maybe I'll take you up on it, kid," I said. And then I walked along to 313.

I knocked on the door. She opened it. "What took you so long?" she hissed at me.

I walked inside. Ray was sitting up in bed. He looked as light and airy as a drunken cherub. Saliva dribbled from his lips as he said, "Marlow! The case is solved! The lady has been found!"

I went over to the bottle, poured some in a glass and took a drink. Then I looked back at him. "How do you know where she is?" I asked.

"It's simply a matter of not wanting to believe what's staring you in the face," he said. "This isn't the first time it happened. Sometimes you have to go through every possibility before you allow yourself to believe the obvious."

"But how do you know?" I asked again.

"Because nothing else makes sense!" He said with that note of finality I've often used myself when my mind has grown too tired to think anymore.

*****

He was a master of tactics and strategy was Ray. He left nothing much to chance. He had diagrams of the rooms and corridors and "x's" where he wanted us to stand. He went over it several times and then he asked me, "Marlow, have I left anything out?"

"Nothing much," I said. "Just why you want them caught."

His eyes were too drunk to reply coherently. His voice, though was still sharp. "They've committed a crime, Marlow - or they're about to do. And criminals have to pay for their offence. It's the rule of law."

"Rules are made to be broken, Ray. Didn't the Ambassador say that once?"

"Dr Marlow!" Monica Wheetly began, angrily. "Kidnapping is

a terrible thing to do!"

I turned to her. "Has someone been kidnapped? I hope it's not you, Miss Wheetly," I said.

Ray didn't need any defending. He never did. "I've written about criminals and crime since you were a kid, Marlow. I know passions are often justified. But if you let them get away from you, then there isn't any dignity. And dignity's the most important thing of all."

"You know, Ray," I said, "it seems to me that I've heard other incontinent alcoholics make speeches like that, too. Somehow, all that moral outrage loses something as the spit dribbles down their chin."

"I drink only when I need to drink!" he shouted.

"So do I," I said. "And I need to drink all the time. But that's not the point, is it Ray?"

"What is the point, Dr Marlow?" asked Monica Wheetly giving me the evil eye.

"The point," I said, still looking at Ray, "is that you should go to sleep and dream whatever dreams you want. Tomorrow is another day. You'll be off this boat and onto something else - most likely of your own designs. If you want, you can drink England dry. Just don't stick your nose where it doesn't belong."

"It's to late, Marlow," he said, "my nose is already stuck."

"It's never too late, Ray," I replied. "Just pull it back out and wipe it off again."

"It is too late," he insisted. "The plan has already been put into operation. The lady must be saved!"

"Even if she doesn't want to be?" I asked.

"The trap, Dr Marlow, has already been set!" said Monica Wheetly. I looked at her. Her eyes were gleaming. Maybe she was having some fun herself.

"What trap?" I asked.

I hardly got the words out, when there was a knock at the cabin door. Then the Fat Man came in.

*****

They went through it backwards and forwards again, ironing out all the details. In the end, it depended on the kid with the pill box hat.

The Fat Man, Ray's officer friend, scratched his balding head. "I certainly hope you're right, Mr Chandler. I'm putting it on the line, you know. If she isn't in there, the Captain will have my..." He pointed a pudgy finger at his bottom. And then he smiled the way a fat man smiles, making his face into a dimple.

"She's in there all right," said Ray. "Either there or back inside her room."

"We have some men searching her room right now," said the Fat Man. "I'm having them stay inside while we do our business - just to make sure she doesn't sneak back."

"And you have your men stationed in all the corridors?" asked Ray.

"I've placed them all exactly where you said." He took a handkerchief from his pocket and wiped the beads of sweat from his brow. It wasn't hot, but that's what obesity sometimes does to your glands. "I must say, it's terribly exciting working with a man of your repute on something like this, Mr Chandler. I've always loved your mysteries!"

Ray was much too drunk to blush. He was red enough already. "What time has she ordered her meal to be brought in?" he asked.

"At nine o'clock." The Fat Man looked at his watch. "That's just ten minutes from now."

"Fine," said Ray, getting out of bed. "Then let's be on our way."

"Are you sure you're all right, Mr Chandler?" the Fat Man asked, seeing that he was a little unsteady on his legs.

"Never better!" said Ray. He rubbed his hands like a man about to carve a Christmas roast.

The Fat Man held open the door. And as we filed out, he said, "Do you think you'll write this up?"

"Could be," said Ray.

The Fat Man said, "Then maybe I should tell you how to spell my name."

*****

I followed them out of Ray's cabin and then through the narrow corridor to the stairs. I stayed somewhat behind, but I continued at their tail till I reached the deck above. Then I stopped and took out a little notebook that I used to keep addresses and things and tore out a piece of paper on which I scribbled a quick note.

In a moment or two, I saw the kid coming up the stairs, lugging a big tray.

"Hello, Dr Marlow," he said. His face wasn't quite as bright as it usually was.

"How much are they paying you to do this?" I asked him.

"It's my job," he said. He said it without much pleasure. "I'm just supposed to bring the tray. Then I leave. Just like I always do." He stopped and then he said. "You think I shouldn't, Dr Marlow? Is it wrong?"

I took the note and stuck it under the saucer on his tray. "Like you said, kid, it's your job. Just do me a favor, OK?"

"Certainly, Dr Marlow," he said. "Anything you say..."

"Before you leave their cabin, hand Mr Lane this cup of tea."

He looked at me curiously. "Should I ask you why?"

I shook my head.

I watched him go. I watched him knock on the cabin door. I watched it open and I watched him go in. Then I went over to where Ray, Monica Wheetly and the Fat Man were crouched, like hunters stalking an unsuspecting prey.

In a few minutes the kid came out. He came over to where we were crouching. He looked even smaller without his tray.

"Did everything go as planned?" asked Ray.

"Yes, sir," said the kid. "I put the tray on the table where I always do. I laid the setting, put the flowers in the vase..." Then he turned to me. "And I gave Mr Lane his tea, Dr Marlow."

"His tea?" said Ray. "What about his tea?" He stared at me.

"I thought the condemned man deserves a cup of tea," I said.

The Fat Man looked at his watch. "It's time to go," he said.

Ray held out his hand. "A minute or so more," he said. "Give her a chance to enjoy her meal."

We waited a few moments more. Then Ray sprang up, light as a panther who'd been around a while and was subject to a bronchial cough.

Monica Wheetly grabbed his hand. "Are you all right, Ray?" she asked.

"Just a little giddy, my dear," he said.

The Fat Man was already a few steps ahead. He was at the cabin door. He pounded on it with his fist.

"One minute, please," came a voice that was higher than a man's but lower than an opera soprano.

"Mr Lane! This is the ship's officer here. I'm sorry, but I must insist you open up your door!"

Hearing no response, the Fat Man looked at Ray and Ray nodded his head. The Fat Man took out a key and inserted it through the keyhole. He turned it and then shoved. It didn't budge. "Damn!" he said. "They've locked it from the inside!"

"Try again!" Ray commanded. His face was pale. Tiny balls of spittle rolled from his lips.

The Fat Man tried the key again and pushed at the door. No luck.

"Tell them the ship is burning down! Tell them anything! Just get them to open up the door!" Ray hissed.

But the Fat Man didn't need to do all that. For just at that moment the door swung open by itself. Amanda Lane stood before us, a gentle smile upon her lips. "I'm sorry to keep you waiting," she said. "You see, I was in the middle of my lunch."

Ray's face had been transformed by a charming little grin. "We're so sorry to disturb you, Mrs Lane," he said. "May we come in?"

"Of course," said a deeper voice from inside. "Tell them to come in, my dear. One mustn't leave guests standing in the hall."

"Where are my manners!" said Mrs Lane, ushering the four of us through the door. "Please do come in. We're in the midst of packing up, you see, and it's been such a rush. I hardly know where my head is any more."

"I find it's often like that right before the ship comes in," said Ray. As he was saying that his eyes moved quickly round the room.

So there we stood. Monica Wheetly, Ray, the Fat Man, Roger Lane, his wife, Amanda, and myself. And dominating the center of the room, with its enormous bulk, was the magnificent sea chest with the picture of the dragon and the knight, that I had seen being heaved into the cabin my first day aboard this tub.

Ray rubbed his hands together, again, and whispered to me, "I've always wanted to do this, Marlow. I hope you'll forgive me..."

"It's all yours, Ray," I said. "I just hope you feel the same about it in the morning."

Ray cleared his throat. And then, just like one of those parlour-room detectives in the books he so detested, he began:

"Since our second night at sea we've been racking our brains trying to find out what happened to Gloria Morgan. Was it one of those mysterious suicides that can never be explained? Was she pushed overboard, into the murky depths, by some fiend with a twisted mind? Or was she merely a victim of a violent storm - a woman, unsteady on her feet, swept over the rail by a mighty wave?"

He looked at us one by one.

"Ladies and Gentlemen, I submit to you that none of the possibilities I've stated, are, in fact, the case. I submit to you that Gloria Morgan did not take her life, nor was she murdered, nor did she fall into the briny deep. Indeed, Gloria Morgan, for reasons of her own, decided to set up a ruse with her confederates. And, at this very moment, Gloria Morgan is..."

All eyes were upon him now. Ray was really doing swell.

He pointed with as much drama as his shaky finger would allow as he trumpeted, "INSIDE THIS CRATE!"

The room was hushed. For a moment nobody spoke or even moved a muscle.

Then Amanda Lane put her hand over her mouth. "She is?" she gasped. "I wonder how she got there?"

"I'm sorry, Mrs Lane," said the Fat Man, "but your little game has been found out by one of the most brilliant investigative minds of our century."

I suspected Ray would take a bow.

Then the Fat Man looked at Amanda Lane and said, "Would you please open up your sea chest now?"

Amanda Lane glanced over at her husband. "Do we have to, Roger?" she asked.

Roger Lane shrugged and then threw me a quick look. "I'm afraid we must, my dear," he said.

"Oh, very well," she sighed. And she undid the latches and let the door to the enormous chest swing free.

Not a sound was heard. Not even the squeaking of Ray's sinking mouse.

"Let me by!" Ray shouted, pushing me out of the way. He stared into the darkness of the chest. He pushed away the clothes. He probed his hand, once, twice, three times. He tossed things onto the floor.

The Fat Man looked in amazement. "But, Mr Chandler! You said..."

"She's here, damn it!" Ray shouted. "I know she's in this goddamn crate!"

"I can get you a couple of swords to push in from the sides if you want," said Roger Lane.

His wife gave him a dirty look.

"That won't be necessary," said the Fat Man. "I hope, for the sake of my company, that you accept our sincere and heartfelt apologies."

"She's here someplace!" Ray yelled. "Search the other room!"

"Of course," said Roger Lane. "Satisfy yourself." He opened up the door to the adjoining room of his suite.

"Roger!" said his wife.

"No, Amanda, let them look! In fact, I insist they search everywhere. Search in the closets, under the bed, in the shower stall. Look in the drawers. Maybe we put bits and pieces of her in there!"

Ray stomped around like a madman. He did look under the bed and in the shower stall. And, yes, he looked inside the

231

drawers as well.

As Ray marched through the room with Roger Lane at his heels suggesting he open this and search through that, I looked into the chest again. I moved the clothes away and stared into the darkness. Then I saw a glimmer of reflected light. I looked at Amanda Lane who was still nearby. I asked, "May I?"

I pulled out a black sequinned dress, thin of waist and sensuous. It looked like something you might have worn if you had wanted to be noticed by a blind man in the dead of night. "A little small for you, Mrs Lane, don't you think?" I said.

"It's not mine," she said. "It's for my sister."

"That's right," I said. "I'd forgotten. You family's still in England, aren't they?"

She nodded her head. "I'm Irish, actually. But I lived in England as a child."

"And you sister lives in London?"

"She does now," said Amanda Lane. "She hasn't been back there for a while.

"I'm sure you'll be happy to see her again, won't you?" I said.

Chapter 34

Ray had been pretty good about it, I thought. All things considered. He was gracious in his apology and his assurances to make amends.

The Fat Man, though no longer a raving fan, was promised ten free copies of a forthcoming book to compensate for any embarrassment.

And then we walked him to his room, Monica Wheetly and I. He was quieter with us. His movements, strained almost. Like an unoiled engine left to rust.

I asked him if he wanted a drink. He didn't reply. Did he want to hear some Beethoven? Not necessarily. The light had left his eyes. He seemed old. Worse than old, I think. He seemed done in.

I left him in Miss Wheetly's care and I went back to my cabin. Just like Ray, I felt as if I wanted to be alone. Sometimes it's better that way. Sometimes it's worse. But even if it's worse, sometimes it's still better to be alone.

*****

The following morning I got up early, took a shower and shaved the stubble off my face. Then I went down below to pay my respects.

The surgery was quiet. Nobody had time to be sick today, I guess. Hart was there, working on his report. He glanced up as I came in.

"You're not signing on for the return passage, are you Marlow?" he asked.

"Once is enough," I said. "No one needed an operation. I figure I lucked out."

He touched the bandage wrapped around his head. "The

way I see it, Marlow, so did they."

"Maybe you're right," I said. Then I nodded toward the pharmacy. "Everything OK in there?"

"OK?" He gave me a look and then let out a sarcastic laugh. "Can you tell a placebo from the real thing by sight? There's about a thousand drugs in bottles on the shelf. Some may be genuine, some might be just sugar, starch or salt. I can't blame it all on my pharmacist - my ex-pharmacist, I mean - because it's my responsibility. And I can't forget about it and do nothing either. Because then someone will take those phoney drugs and maybe die..."

"So what are you going to do?" I asked.

"You want a job as CMO?" he said. "They'll be taking applications in about a week."

"No thanks," I said. "I'm running away from my own mess."

"Well, I hope you have a lot of money saved," he said. "I've got about a thousand quid myself."

"How long can you live on a thousand?" I asked.

"Maybe a year."

"Well, I got six months then, providing I ration what I drink."

"England will ration it for you, Marlow. Don't worry about that." He let out a sigh and stuck out his hand.

"I could have killed you. Do you realise that?" I said.

"I guess I could have killed you, too. But that's what happens in war. You fire your rifle into the night and someone falls down dead," he replied.

I took his hand and gave it a shake. "Good luck, Hart," I said. "Do me a favor and don't write any books."

He looked at me strangely. "Why not?"

"Ask Ray," I said.

*****

I went for my last meal aboard ship. Most people had already eaten and had gone back to their cabins for a last minute pack. Solly Meyers was still there dallying over a bowl of Cherrios. So was Rinexus, gorging himself with smoked salmon, sausages and

234

an eggy dish. But I would have expected that.

Solly Meyers lifted up his spoon and inspected a soggy Cherrio. "I asked for a simple breakfast and they gave me this," he said with a certain amount of contempt. "A miniature bagel soaked in milk."

"They got bagels in London, pops," said Rinexus. "Go down to Pettycoat Lane. You'll get all of them you want."

"They have bagels everywhere in the world, Mr Rinexus," said Solly Meyers. "Wherever you find a hungry Jew, you'll find a bagel. Even in China, I would guess."

Rinexus turned to me. "I've written a really juicy article about spotting that guy Garchick on the ship," he said. "I'm trying to think of some way to tie it into that missing Morgan dame. What a story that would be, huh?"

"How would you do that?" I asked.

"I don't know," he said. "But I'm working on it. Maybe there's some link in their past. Maybe they worked together on a film. I don't know..."

"Maybe you can accuse him of murdering her," I said.

"Murder?" he looked at me and laughed. "That wimp? He probably wouldn't have the guts. Anyway, why would Moscow make him bump her off unless she was a commie, too, and somehow she went wrong - or right, as far as we're concerned."

"Say! Maybe you hit on something," I suggested.

Rinexus rubbed his chin. "You think so? You think Gloria Morgan might have been a red who finally saw the light?"

"And if she was a red, think of all those secrets she could betray," I said. "She knew the Ambassador pretty well, didn't she?"

He put down his fork. You could almost see the gears begin to crank up in his head. Then, suddenly he ran his hand through the air as if he were scanning the text of an imaginary story. "Beautiful movie star. A secret agent of the Comintern. Set to betray Hollywood. But she falls in love with Ambassador and exposes Garchick's plans. Garchick wants revenge. He follows her aboard the ship with one thing in mind..." He looked at me. "You think maybe it would work?"

"You never know," I said. "Of course, you might be hit with a libel suit."

"Nah. The great thing about Hollywood now is that you can say almost anything about anyone and as long as they can't prove you did it with malicious intent, they can't get a thing."

"But if you wrote an article like the one you just described you would be doing it with malicious intent," said Solly Meyers.

"Yeah, but they don't know that," said Rinexus. "Besides, I wouldn't put anything past a commie like Garchick. Who knows? Maybe a story like that is true!"

"How about Miss Morgan?" I said.

"She's dead. And like they say, dead broads can't tell tales." Rinexus gave me a fishy smile as bits of salmon fell from his teeth.

"Of course, if you did write anything about Mr Garchick, I'd have to tell the authorities how I overheard you plotting with a real Russian spy," I said.

Rinexus stared at me with his trap door open wide . "What are you on about, Marlow?" he asked.

"Just that I happened to see you chumming up with the Ambassador the other day. Then I saw you whispering something into the Argentine's ear. And everyone knows that Peron is a commie, right?"

"What's that got to do with anything?" he said, narrowing his eyes.

"It's just real suspicious that right after you had a little chit-chat with a representative of the US government you'd go and whisper something into a commie orifice."

Rinexus' face expanded like a hot air balloon about to be launched into the sky. "I had my suspicions about you, Marlow, ever since we started this voyage. You're a real sneaky SOB! I wouldn't be at all surprised if you're a Communist!"

"Maybe I am, Rinexus," I said. "And maybe I've been told to set you up. Maybe I have a tiny camera and maybe I took a shot of you whispering to the Argentine."

Rinexus let out a nervous laugh. "You're lying, Marlow! I

got you figured out! You're just trying to throw a scare into me because you're another commie symp!"

"Maybe I am," I said. "Maybe I'm not. You're just going to have to wait and see, aren't you?" I gave him a pleasant smile.

"Crapolla!" he shouted, getting up from the table and throwing his napkin in his plate. "You're ruined my appetite!" He turned and started to leave and then, suddenly, he whirled back around like a fat dervish and pointed at my face. "I'm going to break you, Marlow!" he shouted. "I'm going to see that you never practice medicine anywhere in the civilized world!"

"Does that include Syracuse, New York?" I asked.

Rinexus put a finger to his head, such as it was. "I've got a memory like an elephant, Marlow! And I hold a grudge! I don't forget things like this so fast!" And then he stomped off, bumping into a steward on the way and making the poor guy drop his tray.

"An enemy like that you don't need," said Solly Meyers. "But to tell you the truth, I don't like that man very much either."

"An enemy of an enemy is a friend," I said. "Isn't that what the Arabs say?"

"It's also what the Jews say, too," said Solly Meyers. Then he gave me a searching look. "You don't really have a tiny camera do you?"

"Why?" I asked. "Do you want to borrow it?"

"Perhaps. But I think you were just trying to scare him. It's always amazing to see how fast a bully will scare."

"The medical term is paranoia, Mr Meyers. I'm afraid there's a lot of it going around."

"Anyway," said Solly Meyers getting up, "you should take better care of yourself. A doctor is meant to help other people, but he can't do much unless he takes care of himself."

"I'll remember your kind words of advice, Mr Meyers," I said, "and you remember them yourself."

"But I'm not a doctor," said Solly Meyers.

"Then you're better off," I said.

*****

237

After breakfast I went back to my cabin for a drink and then a rest. I hadn't poured my second shot of whisky yet when there was a knock on my door. I went over and opened it up. It was the kid with the pill-box hat.

"I just thought I'd tell you that we'll be docking in an hour, Dr Marlow. I wanted to give you this." He handed me a slip of paper.

"What is it?" I asked.

"It's the address where I'll be in London town. There's also a number if you want to ring me up."

"Thanks," I said, "maybe I'll do that." I stuffed the paper into my shirt pocket. He watched. I guess he thought that's where I throw all my trash.

"I keep all my important papers up there," I said, patting the pocket of my shirt. "Even my medical degree."

"Really, Dr Marlow?" He let me have a grin.

"I kid you not," I said.

Then he left and I threw what stuff I had into my bag and closed it up. I said goodbye to the birds in the trees, to the green chair, the white telephone and all the empty bottles of Jack. Then I opened the cabin door one last time and walked out onto the deck.

Chapter 35

The deck was lined with passengers watching as the ship came into port. People who I'd seen only once - as we were about to leave New York - suddenly reappeared. They were the confetti and Champaign crowd, I guessed. I wondered what they had been up to the last five days. They looked a little weary. Maybe it was hard work popping all those Champaign corks.

Monica Wheetly was hanging onto the rail. She waved to me. She was smiling like a little kid.

"Look at it, Dr Marlow!" she said pointing toward the city emerging into view. "Isn't it wonderful? Have you ever seen anything quite as magnificent before?"

"Not since anyone tried to sell me the Brooklyn Bridge," I said. "Where's Ray?"

She pointed to the other side. "He's standing over there. He said he wanted to be alone for a while." Then she lowered her voice. "I don't blame him. It was so embarrassing yesterday!"

"Does he have someone meeting him?" I asked her. "Did he say?"

"No one's meeting him. But my daddy's having a car sent round. I told Ray I'd give him a lift. You're welcome to come, too, Dr Marlow," she said.

I gave her a chance to see my fresh brushed teeth. "Thanks," I said, "but I think I'll walk. It was a pleasure knowing you, Miss Wheetly. I'm sure that in a year or two the world will be at your feet."

"I won't say the same thing about you, Dr Marlow," she replied. "If you keep drinking like you do, you'll be living in the gutter before the year is up."

"Then I'll be at the world's feet, Miss Wheetly." And tipping my hat to her, I said, "I think I'll say goodbye to Ray."

I walked over to the old man on the other side of the deck.

His profile seemed calm enough, set against the pale blue sky, the smoke drifting upward toward the hint of clouds like a lazy melody from his eternal pipe.

"Hello, Ray," I said. "I just wanted to say goodbye."

He turned to look at me. There was something in his eyes I had seen once before - a gentle melancholy.

"Hello, Marlow," he said. He pointed with his pipe. "There it is. The greatest city in the world. I've missed it, you know."

"So you've said," I replied. "I hope it works out for you, Ray."

His smile was thin and not very self-assured. "It will, Marlow. You needn't worry on my account."

I nodded. "I guess you won't have any trouble finding someone to give you your vitamin shots."

"No need," he said. He gave his pipe another puff. "I'm on the wagon for good this time."

"Well, I was going to invite you for a drink. Maybe that's not in the cards."

"Oh, we'll meet again, Marlow. I can assure you of that."

"I hope so, Ray," I said. I held out my hand. He looked at it uncomfortably.

"I'm sorry, Marlow..." he started.

"Oh, yeah," I said. "I forgot you don't shake."

He looked away and pointed again with the stem of his pipe. "We're just about to tie up to the dock," he said. "This is the most exciting part!"

"Lots of action down there," I said. The dock was lined with stevedores and cars and people who had someone up on ship to meet. They weren't there for me. Nor, I suppose, for Ray.

As we floated slowly to the pier, the activity increased. The gangway was being readied by strong men with smelly shirts like mine. A shore crew was putting shoulders to the moveable stairs. The air was filled with a mighty whir, the sound of rising cranes. On deck, the stewards were beginning to line up with the cabin baggage, jostling for a position that might help speed their way. And through all this hubbub I could hear someone call Ray's name.

"Oh, Mr Chandler! There you are!"

It was the Ambassador.

"I hope you got my note this morning. It wasn't too late?"

Ray patted the pocket of his tweed. "I have it right here. Many thanks."

"So everything's settled now? No more concerns?"

"None at all," said Ray.

The Ambassador looked relieved. "Well, I hope you enjoy your stay in England then."

"I'm certain that I will. In fact, I'm here for good," said Ray.

"Are you now? Well, I'm still thankful that my ancestors left these isles. But it's nice to return for a visit." The Ambassador tipped his hat and started to walk away.

"Oh, Ambassador!" Ray called.

He turned again. This time he showed some of his old displeasure.

"You were a good friend of Gloria Morgan's. Was that her real name?"

"Did you ever know an actress who used her real name on stage?" he said. "She kept it a secret though she might have told it to me once."

"She was Irish, wasn't she?" asked Ray.

"Of Irish origin. Yes. Her family moved to England, I think." He rubbed his chin. "Her real name was something like 'Street'." He shook his head. "I just can't remember. Is it important?"

"Not in the least," said Ray. "I won't trouble you anymore."

The Ambassador nodded. "Well, good day to you then."

As he left I glanced at Ray. "What's this about a note?"

Ray puffed at his pipe.

The gangway was now in place. The stewards were heading down the incline with their dollies stacked high with passengers' suitcases and trunks.

I recongnised the one nearest us as the giant with the gentle eyes. He had the Lane's enormous chest. It was all he could handle.

"'Scuse me, sir," he said. "I'm trying to get past."

"Hi there, Popeye," I said. "Remember me?"

He turned. "Oh, yes sir!" he let out a fog-horn kind of laugh. "You're the gent who asked me if I ate spinach when I said this 'ere box was getting light!" He shook his head. "You should 'ave told me that today! Now I think it weighs a ton again!"

"Oh, porter!" I heard a voice cry out from behind. "Please be careful with that case!"

I turned and saw Amanda Lane coming over with her husband.

"You'd think she's got the Queen's jewels in 'ere the way she watches over it!" the porter grumbled under his breath.

Roger Lane came up to us. "Well, so long, Mr Chandler," he said with a little grin on his face. "I hope your books turn out better than your real life adventures."

Ray glanced at him, bit down on his pipe and didn't say a word.

Amanda Lane wasn't quite so impolite. "Mr Chandler was only doing as he saw fit, Roger. He was concerned about that poor woman..." She put a finger to her cheek. "You know, I've already forgotten her name!"

"Gloria Street," I think," I said to her.

Roger Lane looked at me. "Cherrio, Marlow. Tit-tut and all that. Keep a look out in the entertainment guide."

"What should I be looking for?" I asked.

He winked. "Maybe something called 'The Snake Pit.'"

Amanda Lane gave her husband a nudge. The porters were beginning their move down the ramp. "Come on!" she said. "It's time to go!"

"Say hello to your sister for me, Mrs Lane," I said to her. "I hope she likes the dress."

"I'm sure she will, Dr Marlow," she said as she moved on.

We stood at the rail, Ray and I, and watched them go. "How about that note?" I said. "Are you going to show it to me?"

He reached into his pocket and handed it over. The note was actually the telex that had been sent back to the Ambassador in answer to Ray's request the other night. What it said was this: "Barzini Brothers was a vaudville booking agency specialising in magic acts. R. S. Garchick was one of their performers. He worked with them for two years - from '34 to '36. His act was known as 'The Lady in the Box'. His partner was a woman called 'Amanda'. Her last name is unknown."

I handed him back the telex and then I watched the Lanes disappear into the crowd. "You're not going to stop them?" I asked.

He didn't say a word. He just took out a match, lit the end of the paper and let it go. It hovered in the air for a minute, like a tiny flaming star, till it carbonised and was again taken by the wind. It drifted down to the waters and then was swept up by the tide. And then it floated, silently out into the endless ocean.

Chapter 36

I left England the day the headlines in the newspapers told about the coup in Argentina and the fall of Peron. A military dictatorship had been set up that kicked the Russian trade delegation out and swore allegiance to the USA. More ships were filling up with refugees again. Bound for Spain this time. And if Lane was right, Israel as well.

In Europe I followed the war I had known in reverse. I travelled to Germany and then through France and then southward down through Italy. I stopped off in Rome and Naples and then continued on to Sicilly. From Palermo, I took a boat to Bizerte on the Tunisian coast and then overland, across the vast highway that runs below the Atlas Mountains, to Algiers.

It was hot in Algiers. You could have toasted muffins on the brim of your cap. But the weather wasn't the only thing that was hot. The French were preparing to fight another war. Against the Arabs this time. And the Europeans were staying in their houses after dark.

I was drinking in a cafe one night. Maybe I had too much. I stumbled back to my cheap room where I was hoping to fall straight into my lumpy bed set mercifully under the propellers of an overhead fan. Halfway back I felt someone give me a shove. The next thing I knew, I was in an alleyway exploring the stars. Someone had massaged my noodle with a lead pipe from behind. When I woke up all my money was gone.

I asked around at the American Embassy and was put in touch with a medical agency in Rabat that needed help controlling a cholera outbreak. I got a ride with a Jewish camel salesman named Selim who was headed for Casablanca in his pre-war Citroen. He left me off just outside Kenitra where he said he had some business to attend. I telephoned the mission from there and they sent a young man in a jeep to pick me up.

I stayed at the mission in Rabat until Suez blew up and the French and British joined together to try and separate Nasser from his Russian guns. The US kept aloof. Maybe the Ambassador had other plans. Maybe Solly Meyers did, too, for all I knew. But I didn't really care. I moved on to Casablanca where I started drinking again.

A month later I suffered my first blackout. When I woke up, I was looking into the deep blue eyes of a beautiful French nurse.

Her name was Monique. I fell for her like one of Selim's camels dropped from the top of the Eiffel Tower. Within a week, I had moved into her apartment to convalesce. She cooked the best cous-cous this side of Nevada.

Monique got me a job with one of the Catholic relief agencies that were trying to pump powdered milk into the thousands of children still starving from the war. It was more than ten years now and some of these kids had still never seen a piece of meat. I spent a year pleading for care packages of food to be sent direct. Somehow the good stuff always ended up on the black market. Even putting in twelve hour days, more kids were dying by the time I left than the day I had gotten there.

I started drinking pretty heavily again. Sometimes I'd black out for a few weeks at a time. I'd find myself in a hospital or maybe in a ditch somewhere. In January, 1958, Monique went back to Paris. She wanted me to come with her, she said.

We had a few drinks the night before she left. Maybe it would be OK, I thought. Maybe I'd dry out. I'd get a job. I'd settle down. Maybe have a family. So I decided that maybe I'd go to Paris with her.

I stopped off at a bar for one last drink before I went back home to pack. Then I blacked out again. By the time I came around her plane had gone. A friend said she had waited for me till the last minute. Maybe she didn't know how lucky she had been.

I left Casablanca a few weeks later on a banana boat bound for Panama. I got a job in the Canal Zone, working at the Walter Reed Center helping to control a new outbreak of malaria. I stopped drinking for a while because the humidity and heat was making me so ill. I stayed there for a year. I lost forty pounds in weight one month alone. One day I looked in the mirror and saw a prisoner from Buchenwald. The next day I decided to go.

There was a young soldier I knew who had been stationed in the Canal Zone and was crazy enough to want to drive back home to Lubbock, Texas, where the poor kid was born. I told him I'd go with him, since he didn't want to drive alone. It took us a week to get to Managua and one week more to reach Guatemala City. The car broke down in Oaxaca, in Southern Mexico. The engine blew. And we didn't have the dough to fix it.

The kid decided to stay in Oaxaca. I took a bus through Guadalajara and Durango. A few days later, filled with tomales, rice and refried beans, I landed in Tijuana on the Mexican border, about twenty miles from San Diego.

I drank so much tequilla in Tijuana that it pickled all the amoebas I had picked up on the road. I was staying in a cheap dive with no name trying to make up my mind whether to cross the border or to turn around and go the other way. By now I had been out of the States about four years. I didn't particularly want to go back again. But there was no where else to go.

I had about fifty bucks to my name when I got onto the bus headed north. A young woman sitting next to me didn't seem to like my smell. When a seat became free at Chula Vista, she got up and moved. It was real nice to be back home.

Chapter 37

The sign outside the station said I was in Esmeralda. It wasn't the prettiest town I ever saw. It wasn't the ugliest, either. But it was the only town I've ever been in that had eucalyptus trees growing through the sidewalk.

Not far from the station was the main shopping street. It wasn't sign posted, but if it was like other small American towns I'd known it would have been called Main Street.

I didn't have any trouble finding a bar. I went inside and ordered a whiskey and then I sat down at a table and had my drink. The place was dark and anonymous like most bars in anonymous towns seem to be. This one was nearly empty as well. The bartender was a bland looking man with a pasty face. He was methodically dipping glasses into disinfectant and then wiping them dry by stuffing in a towel, giving it a twist and then pulling it back out. It was a moronic little assembly line sanitising glasses for sanitised lips and sanitised minds.

I was on my second glass of whiskey when I began to hear a buzzing in my ears. By now I knew what that meant and that I better stop while I was still ahead. I finished my drink and went up to the bar.

"Any decent cheap hotels around here?" I asked.

"Depends on what you mean," said the bartender, dipping another glass into the disinfectant and looking at me suspiciously. "How decent and how cheap?"

"No bugs," I said. "And maybe five bucks. Seven tops."

"This ain't Mexico, mister," he said. "You might find one outside of town."

"You got any names?" I said.

He shrugged and stuffed in his towel, gave it a twist and took it out. "Ask a cabby," he said. "He'll tell you want you want to know and take you there besides."

I walked down the road to the train station. That's where the cabbies usually hang out in towns like this. I passed the municipal building and the police station and then another row of shops. At the end of the row there was a little bookstore called 'A Room of One's Own'. Something in the window caught my eye. I decided to go inside.

A pretty young woman with a light brown pony tail, wearing jeans and a loose fitting blouse was sitting at a cash desk engrossed in a book. She didn't hear me come in. I guessed that because she seemed startled when I cleared my throat.

"Oh, I'm sorry," she said. "I wasn't expecting anyone. Not at this time of day."

"Pretty quiet around here," I said.

She nodded and the pony tail flapped up and down. "We do most of our business on Saturdays and then in the afternoon when the commuter train comes in. To tell the truth, I don't know why we stay open any other time."

"It looks like the kind of place where they roll up the sidewalks at night," I said, motioning outside.

"It used to be really quiet around here," she said. "Now we're starting to get artists from LA moving in. There aren't any poolrooms but we do have some nice restaurants and shops. It's not a bad place to live."

"If you got the money," I said.

She shrugged. "If you don't have money, no place is nice to live, I don't suspect." Then she smiled, real sweet, like a young woman I once knew. "Can I help you find a book?"

"I was interested in the one you've got displayed in the window," I said. "*Playback*, I think it's called."

"Oh, you mean the new Chandler mystery." Then she stopped herself. "It's not new, really. It was published last year, but we still have it on display because he's a local author."

"I thought he was living in England," I said.

"He came back about a year ago," she said. "Something to do with taxes, I think. And the weather, too. I understand he's very ill. Have you read many of his books?"

I shook my head. "No. Which one would you recommend?"

"I like them all," she said. "*Playback* was a bit of a disappointment though. It was originally written as a film script, I believe. But Hollywood didn't want it so he made it into a book." She thought for a moment. "If you want to know the one I like best, it's *The Long Goodbye*. It's more of a novel than a mystery, really, and it does seem to go on and on, but I think it's vintage Chandler. Besides," she said giving me a little wink, "it's been done in mass market paper and you can get it for a dime."

I let out a little chuckle. "How much do you sell it for?" I asked.

"I've got a used one I'll let you have for a nickel," she replied.

"You can't go any lower than that?" I asked.

"If you're short of money, I'll let you borrow it if you want," she said, giving me an understanding smile.

"That's very kind of you," I said, fishing out a nickel from my pocket. "But I think I can see my way clear."

"You sure?" she said, looking at me seriously.

"I'm sure," I said. "After all, you can hardly get a cup of coffee anymore for a nickel. And a good read is worth a lot more than that."

"You won't regret it," she said, going over to a shelf to get the book. "Do you want me to wrap it for you?" she asked, bringing it back.

"That won't be necessary," I said, giving her the nickel and then taking the book and putting it in my pocket. "Tell me something, though. Do you know Mr Chandler? I mean, personally, that is."

"I've met him briefly," she said. "Sometimes his housekeeper orders books for him. I bring them up to his cottage. In fact there's an order I'm bringing over there today." She pointed to a small pile of books sitting on some wrapping paper.

"You might tell him that an old chum from his days at sea dropped by," I said.

She smiled again. "I thought you might be an old friend of his, the way you talked. What name should I say?"

"Marlow," I replied.

She laughed. "Yes, I'm sure he'll remember you, all right!

Where should I say you're staying?"

"That depends," I said. "Can you recommend a cheap motel?"

She thought about it for a minute and then she said, "You might try a motel called Rancho Descansado. It's on the edge of town."

"Rancho Descansado?" I repeated, taking a pen from my pocket and noting the name inside the cover of my book.

"Yes," she said. "I'm sure you'll like it. The name is Spanish for 'relax.'"

*****

I found the taxi stand by the train station. One was waiting there for me. The Mexican driver had his feet hanging out the open door and was reading a newspaper. He seemed surprised when I got in.

"I know," I said, "you don't expect any passengers this time of day."

"I didn't see the train come in," he said, straightening himself up.

"That's because I came by bus," I said. "You know a place called Rancho Descansado?"

"Sure." He turned around and squinted his eyes. "Say, didn't I take you there before?"

"Not in this life," I said.

The cabby shrugged his shoulders. "Maybe you got a brother," he said. Then he started the engine and drove off.

He drove through town and then down the ocean highway. On the left, beyond the rugged canyon, the Pacific had come into view. The road began to narrow as we headed down the slope. At the bottom there was a shallow beach with a gate and a large sign which read, "El Rancho Descansado".

The driver stopped outside the gates. He turned to me and said, "You want to get out here?"

"Why not drive inside?" I asked. "You have trouble backing out?"

"It's just that last time you wanted to get out here."

"Why would I want to do that?"

"You were following some dame. You put dark glasses on and hid behind that bush," he said, pointing to some shrubs. Then he grinned. "You on another case, Mac? Don't worry, I won't tell no one you're around."

I got out of the cab, took out my wallet and gave him a fiver. "Make sure that you don't," I said.

He gave me a salute. "Thanks, pal," he said. And then, in a spray of gravel, he sped down the road again.

I walked across the highway to the motel office. I went inside and leaned my elbow on the reception desk. "You got any rooms?" I asked.

A bright young man with a polka-dot bow tie grinned at me and then turned to the fresh-faced girl working the telephones and said, "Hey, Lucille! Look who's back!"

Lucille swung her head around. She had nice eyes, I thought. "Hello!" she said. "It's good to have you with us again!"

I pointed to her horse tail. "Do all young women around here wear their hair like that?" I asked.

"It's the style nowadays," she said, with a little giggle. Then she came over to the desk, held out her hand and wiggled a finger at me. "Look! Me and Jack got hitched!" She put her arm around the guy with the bow tie and smiled lovingly at him.

"That's great," I said. "I hope you'll be real happy." I took the pen that Jack had placed in front of me and filled out the registration form.

"I'll give you the same room as before, if that's all right," said Jack, handing me the key. He looked down at the registration form. "Say, didn't you spell 'Marlow' differently before?"

"Did I?" I said.

"Maybe not," he shrugged. "How long will you be staying this time, sir?"

"I don't know," I said. "It depends on how fast I catch up with a couple of missing time zones."

*****

It wasn't the Ritz. It wasn't even the cabin on the ship. But it was OK for a cheap motel set back on a deserted beach. The furniture wasn't the kind you'd like to sit on for very long, if you valued your back. But there was an alcove with a three burner stove and a fridge. The three burner stove was a waste, as far as I was concerned. The fridge, however, was another story. I opened the door and took out the ice cube tray. I cracked out some frozen dice and threw them in a glass. Then I got my bottle from my bag. I used to take my whiskey straight. But, lately, my body wasn't taking orders from me anymore.

I sat down in a cushionless chair and sipped my drink. My head felt light already. Maybe it was a lack of food. Maybe it was something else. I'd given up asking questions by now. Too many things had happened that I just couldn't understand. Sometimes you can write them off as freak weather conditions, like a hailstorm in Spain in the middle of July. But too many summer hailstorms in Iberia start to make you think twice. Maybe it's not summer. Maybe it's the start of a new ice age. Or maybe you're not in Spain.

I took another sip of my drink. I was starting to hear voices through the wall. It was a woman's voice, the one I could make out. She sounded troubled.

"...we'd better understand each other. I like Esmeralda. I've been here before and I always wanted to come back. It's nothing but sheer bad luck that you live here and that you were on the train..."

I took my drink over to the bed. There was an old beat-up radio on the side table. I turned it on so that I wouldn't hear the voices anymore. I twisted the dial till I beamed into the classical music station. They were playing Beethoven. A sonata. I took Ray's book out of my pocket and lay down on the bed. I opened it up and began to read.

Chapter 38

It was later that evening when I heard the knock at the door. I had drifted off to sleep after I had finished reading the book. It was dark when I opened my eyes. I felt around for the bedside light and switched it on.

"Dr Marlow?" called out a woman's voice. "Are you there?"

I rubbed my eyes and dragged myself over to the door. I opened it. The moon was high up in the sky. It was bright enough to illuminate the porch. I recognised her at once. She was the young woman from the bookstore. She looked worried.

"I told him you were here," she said. "He's very ill, Dr Marlow. He wants you to come at once."

"I'm not a doctor anymore," I said. "Maybe I never was."

"Please, Dr Marlow," she pleaded. "If you could only see him..."

"OK," I said. I went over to the chair where I had draped my jacket and I put it on. "But there's nothing I can do for him."

She smiled thankfully. "He said it's enough if you just come."

Her Ford coupe was parked in the drive. I got in the passenger side and closed the door as she started up. She lurched into gear and then sped out the driveway and up the narrow road, climbing to the top of the canyon I had recently gone down. Then she turned onto the freeway and headed north, toward LA.

We passed the exit for Pacific Beach and then went a few miles more until we reached the turnoff for La Jolla. She drove through the center of town and then on a little more toward the ocean road till she got to Prospect Street. Then she turned right and pulled up at number 824. She set the brake, took out the keys and handed them to me.

"This is his car, Dr Marlow," she said. "Mine's over there," she said pointing to an older Chevy.

"Why are you giving me the keys?" I asked.

"He thought you might need them," she said. Then she put out her hand. "Goodbye, Dr Marlow. It was nice meeting you."

I took her hand and gave it a little shake. "Aren't you coming in?" I asked.

"No," she said. "He wants to see you alone." Then she got out the driver's door, gave me a wave, walked over to the Chevy across the road, started it up and drove off.

I sat in the Ford a moment more studying the cottage perched on the cliff overlooking the Pacific sea. It was what some might have called "charming", I suppose. The front garden, bathed in the moonlight, would have done an English country house proud with all the rows of flowers and neatly trimmed shrubs.

I got out of the Ford and walked up the narrow path to the front door. I gave a knock and waited. A few moments later it opened. A middle-aged Mexican woman with thick black hair piled high on her head stood in the doorway. She was nervously fingering some beads.

"Come in, señor," she said. "He is waiting for you."

The front door led into a small study. Ray's desk was covered with books and papers. In the typewriter was the beginnings of what I suspected was a new manuscript.

I followed the housekeeper through a short hall into the living room. Just beyond was a glassed-in dinning room with a magnificent view of the sea.

The housekeeper was putting on her coat when I looked back at her. "I must leave, señor. My husband is waiting for me." She pointed to a door off to the side. "Mr Chandler is in there."

I went over to the door and gave it a gentle knock. I heard a voice that I barely recognised. It was weak. But I heard him say, "Come in, Marlow!"

*****

Ray was lying propped up in bed. His face was thin. His eyes were set in hollow tunnels of dark rings. But I saw them light up slightly as I walked in and closed the door.

His voice had a throaty sound. "It's really good of you to come."

"Well, I was in the neighborhood," I said. Then I smiled. "Can I fix you a drink, Ray?"

He tried to smile back at me. It was as if he couldn't work those muscles anymore. He motioned to me with his hand. "Come closer," he said. "Pull up a chair."

I did as he asked. I pulled up a wooden chair and sat down. I looked into his eyes. I had seen eyes like that before.

"I thought you'd stay in England, Ray," I said.

"I wanted to," he said. He spoke his words slowly, as if he had trouble getting them out. "But I couldn't stand the goddamn weather!"

"Yeah, it's pretty bad. But that couldn't have been all..."

"No," he said softly. "You can't go home again, Marlow. Not after so many years. It's just not the same."

"I guess not," I said. Then I winked. "But you must have had some good times!"

"Good times? Sure." He finally worked his face into a smile of sorts. "I was a celebrity, Marlow. For the first time in my life! Something I never was here, I'll tell you that. You know my last book only sold nine thousand copies over here?"

"Nine thousand books stacked on top of each other would probably reach pretty high," I said.

"For a writer of my reputation? That's chicken feed!" Even at death's door, the old guy could still get his dander up over something like that. "It's doing great guns in England, though."

"Well, it sounds to me like you should have stayed," I said.

"Maybe I should have stayed," he said. "I had a lot of friends. Dinner parties almost every night. You know, I almost got married!"

I let out a little chuckle. "You're a sly old fox!" I said. "Was it that Wheetly girl?"

"For God's sake, Marlow! What do you take me for? It was my literary agent, Helga..."

"Yeah, well I really didn't think the two of you would last.

Whatever happened to her, though? Did you introduce her to your publisher?"

"Yes I did," he said. "I'm a man of my word. You ought to know that by now!"

"I do know that, Ray. So what happened to her?"

"She's a famous author now. She sent me her latest book. It's over there someplace," he said, trying to wave his hand at a pile on the table by the window. "It's called *Love's Flowers Bloom* or some nonsense like that," he said with a note of disgust. "It's in its second printing. Sold over fifty thousand copies in hardback alone"

"I guess people like romance," I said.

"People don't know what they like," said Ray. "The reading public today has television minds."

"But you'll be remembered, Ray. She won't."

He looked at me with his hollow eyes. "I wouldn't be so sure of that, Marlow."

"I am. I read *The Long Goodbye*."

"You did?" He seemed surprised.

"There's greatness in it, Ray," I said.

"The critics didn't like it," he said. "They said it wasn't a real mystery. Too much of a novel, they claimed."

"What do the critics know?" I asked.

"Nothing," he said, looking over toward the window and the view of the sea. "They don't know a goddamned thing." Then he looked back at me and said. "We had some good times, Marlow. Didn't we?"

How can you hurt a dying man, I thought? "Sure, Ray. We had some good times."

"I think of her pretty often," he said.

"Who's that?" I asked.

"Her," he said. "The woman with the cornflower eyes."

"All your women had eyes of cornflower blue," I reminded him.

"There's a film you ought to see if you ever get the chance, Marlow."

"I don't go to the movies, much," I said. "But what's the name in case I'm every feeling so bored I don't know what to do."

"It's called 'The Snake Pit,'" he said.

I rubbed my head. "It wouldn't have been made by Roger Lane, would it?"

"Made by a man called R. S. Garchick," he said. "It's about an ageing actress who leaves Hollywood in a crate."

"Who played the staring role?" I asked.

"An unknown Irishwoman," he said. "The critics said they were reminded of Gloria Morgan."

"What do the critics know?" I said.

"Not much," he replied.

"Was it good?" I asked.

"It wasn't bad," said Ray. "Not bad at all."

"I guess you have to run away from Hollywood these days to make films that aren't bad," I said.

"I guess so," said Ray. He fell silent for a while. I thought maybe he was drifting off to sleep. Then suddenly he opened up his eyes. "It's funny, you know. Hollywood made me. And Hollywood took it all away."

"What do you mean?" I asked.

"None of my books sold over five or six thousand copies until Hollywood took them up," he said. "The movie industry gave me something publishers never could."

"What's that, Ray?" I asked.

"Glamour," he said. "Hollywood gave an old codger like me glamour."

"Well, you're a pretty glamorous guy, Ray," I said.

"Don't patronise a dying man!" he warned.

"I'm not patronising you," I said. Maybe I was at that. I thought for a moment and then I said, "You know, there's one thing that's been puzzling me..."

"Just one thing, Marlow? You're pretty fortunate then."

"It's that note Rinexus got at the beginning of the trip. I always wondered why the Lanes would write a note like that."

He didn't reply right away. Then he said, finally, "The Lanes didn't write that note, Marlow. I did."

"But why did you do it, Ray?"

257

"I wrote 'Someone on this ship is going to die' because at that moment I thought someone really was."

"Who?" I asked.

"Me," he replied. "I really thought I was, Marlow. I wanted to - when I pasted the note together, at any rate."

"Why did you give it to Rinexus, then?"

"I didn't give it to Rinexus, Marlow! I gave it to the blasted media! It was my farewell to the world, or it was supposed to be."

"Maybe you wanted someone to save you," I said.

He looked at me and said, "And so you did, Marlow. For a while..."

"How about the second note? The one to the Ambassador."

"I wrote that too. The first one set off a chain of events beyond my control. But once things were set in motion, I wanted the Ambassador to sweat!"

"For what? He wasn't guilty, Ray."

"Of course he was guilty, Marlow! Guilty as hell!"

I thought about it for a while and then I figured he was right. I got up from my chair and walked over to the window. I looked out at the ocean, at the endless sea, bathed in the special light of the moon.

"Fix yourself a drink, Marlow," he said. "There's whiskey on the table. You can get me one, as well."

"I'm trying to cut down," I said. "Strange things are starting to happen to me, Ray."

"Do me a favour," he said. "There's something I want to ask of you."

I didn't like the sound of that. So I thought maybe I better fix myself a drink. I fixed one for him, too.

I brought it over and he struggled to make himself sit a little higher in the bed. He took his drink in skeleton-like fingers and raised it to his lips. I drank mine straight down and felt it immediately go to my head.

"I want to die, Marlow," he said. "I don't want to live anymore."

I considered his words and then I said, "I passed your study when I came in, Ray. I saw the beginnings of a manuscript in your typewriter."

He shook his head. "The page is blank, Marlow. There's nothing there. I'm dry."

"I suppose all writers go through that sometime. It probably comes back..."

"Not for me," he said. "Not anymore." He stopped for a minute and took another drink. "I've written all that I have in me to write. I went to London to reap my rewards. For a while I was a star. I had beautiful and intelligent women around me. I went to parties - even though I can't stand small talk. I did all that. And then I realised something"

"What?" I asked. "It all sounds pretty good to me."

"I realised that I'm nothing without her."

"Without who?" I asked.

"Without my Cissy," he said. "Without my girl with cornflower eyes. Before I met her, I was nothing, Marlow. I wrote soppy poetry and strung tennis rackets for a living. It was only after I met her that I really started to write. She was a pianist, Marlow. She was an artist, too. She knew how much it meant. She understood the sacrifice."

"I guess she did," I said.

"I dedicated my life to her, Marlow. After she died, I wanted to end it all. Instead, I went to England. I tried playing around but it wasn't any good. I slipped further into my solace, into my drink. After *The Long Goodbye*, I never really wrote anything of substance again."

I looked at him. His old eyes were growing red. Even now, I couldn't stand to hear him moan.

"What do you want me to do?" I asked.

"You know what I want," he said.

"Why don't you do it yourself, Ray? I'm not your hired gun anymore. I retired, remember?"

"I can't," he said.

"Why not?"

"I'm scared."

"You're not going to be any less scared if I do it, Ray."

"I will if I'm asleep," he said. "I've taken Seconal. I'll be drifting off any moment now that I've had my drink. What you need is in the drawer in the bedside cabinet. It's all ready for you, Marlow."

"I don't want to do it, Ray," I said. "When you go to sleep I'm just going to walk away."

"No you won't," he said. "You're a knight and I'm in trouble. I know you won't let me down. Fix yourself another drink. I promise you, I won't keep you long."

I poured some whiskey in my empty glass and drank it down. True to his word, in a few minutes Ray was fast asleep. I sat down by his side and gazed at him. And sitting there, staring into his emaciated face, so pallorous, so white, I was reminded of another man, a violinist I had known, who had also wanted to die and whose face had haunted my life ever since.

I finished my drink and stood up to go. The thin lips moved once more. "Please, Marlow. I'm begging you..."

I shut my eyes. I could hear the buzzing in my ears and I could feel the cold sweat on my brow. I shivered. I felt my heart pounding as I opened up the drawer and took it out. I held the syringe up to the light and squeezed a few droplets. Then I knelt down at his side. I rolled up the sleeve of his pyjama shirt and felt for a vein. I patted it gently to pump it up.

It slid in so nice, so easily, I was almost proud. I squeezed in the fluid and then I pulled the needle out. I rolled his sleeve back down and covered the old man up. Then I put the syringe back in the drawer.

I waited for a moment until I was sure he was fast asleep. Then I went and opened the door. Before I left I turned around and said, "It really was a long goodbye, wasn't it, Ray?" Then I walked out of the bedroom, closing the door behind.

*****

I got into the Ford, started up the engine and drove down to the beach. I parked by an access road and then got out. I walked along the sand till I came to a rocky cliff. I climbed up on a jagged boulder and looked out to the ocean. I felt the cool spray of the sea as the waves hit against the rocks.

I sat there for a long time thinking. I sat there until it got light. Then I went back to the Ford and started it up.

I drove along the ocean highway and then through the city of La Jolla and onto the freeway again. I drove past Pacific Beach and got off at the exit for Esmeralda.

I drove into town and parked the Ford near the train station. I walked back to the bookshop where I had gone the day before and dropped the car keys into the mail slot. Then I strolled across the street to the municipal building. I walked up to a door, opened it and went in.

A man in uniform was sitting behind a desk. His hat was pushed back on his head. He was chewing a toothpick as he whittled on a piece of wood. He looked up at me as I walked in.

"Can I do something for you, son?" he said.

"You the sheriff?" I asked him.

"Could be. Jim Patton's the name." He pointed to a chair. "Take the weight off and sit down. Watcha got on your mind?"

"I killed a man," I said.

He studied my face and then he put down the piece of wood and pulled his tooth pick out of his mouth. "What's your name, son?" he asked.

"Marlowe," I replied. "You spell that with an 'e' on the end."

He took a pen and jotted that down.

"First name?" he asked, looking back up at me.

"Philip." I said. "You spell that with a 'P.'"

www.ingramcontent.com/pod-product-compliance
Lightning Source LLC
Chambersburg PA
CBHW031217020726
47499CB00002B/626